A Piece of the Silence

A Piece of the Silence

A Murder Mystery

Jack Livingston

St. Martin's Press, New York

To Gladys Blackwell

Copyright © 1982 by Jack Livingston
For information, write: St. Martin's Press,
175 Fifth Avenue, New York, N.Y. 10010
Manufactured in the United States of America

Library of Congress Cataloging in Publication Data

Livingston, Jack.
  A piece of the silence.

  I. Title.
PS3562.I937P5   813'.54   81-21536
ISBN 0-312-61065-3   AACR2

10 9 8 7 6 5 4 3 2

A Piece of the Silence

Chapter I

She was in the pool when I got there, basking, it seemed, and as naked as a carp. I felt the light shock that any man feels intruding on a naked lady, although it was her behind that turned to me as she floated face down in the water. I faded back into the house through the sliding glass doors, grateful for the chance to disappear without being seen. When I peeked back to see if she had noticed, however, some bubbles appeared around her hips and she began to sink into the emerald light, her red hair fanning out in the water.

I ran down, jumped in, and grabbed her around the waist, tugging her down to the shallow end, where I heaved her up onto the poolside. Her green eyes glimmered out from behind half-closed lids. It seemed to be one of those lucky arrivals, when something can still be done, but after I flipped her over and began to work the water out of her, I saw that I was very wrong indeed. There was only a tiny trickle coming out of her nose and mouth. I went by the numbers for twenty minutes,

1

just to be safe. I've done it before—pumping a corpse. The lady was irrevocably dead. She had been dead when she hit the water.

I squatted back on my heels and began to listen to my machinery. My cigarettes were wet, and I went into the house to see if there were any around. There were something called Virginia Slims. I lighted one and began to tramp soggily through the house to see what I could see. Upstairs, downstairs, in my lady's chamber. Ten rooms—thick carpeting, expensive, heavy, cliché-ridden furniture. In the kid's room cheap, light, cliché-ridden furniture. The machinery was loud and angry.

It wasn't until I got back to the pool and saw her again, stretched out leisurely on the tiles in death's still sunbath, that I began to think. She wasn't supposed to be there at all. She was supposed to be at the studio. The maid was supposed to be on her day off—the kid out stealing hubcaps. I put my soaking suit coat over her and went off to roust the next-door neighbors, but not before taking a discreet look at her arms. Seven punctures—seven. Odd number.

The next-door house was another sheet off the mimeograph. Eighty-five thousand when built, not too long ago, now maybe running two hundred and fifty thousand—three? They had one of those crummy signs—*The Bennets*—out in front that always made me think that the family within was a bunch of paper dolls that hadn't yet been punched out of their perforations. "Ms. Bennet?" I asked when the woman answered the door. It obviously wasn't the maid.

How wary they are! The eyes frightened—taking in my wet clothes—the lips barely framing the word, "Yes?"

I took a deep breath and wrote it in my head. "The lady next door has had an accident in her swimming pool. Will you please call the police and tell them to come to 155 Quince Drive? Tell them that I will meet them there. My name is Joe Binney."

That's the trouble with writing it in your head. It comes

out flat, I suppose, unconvincing. She took a good grip on the door and gave me a stare that had no doubt wilted grocery clerks all over Long Island. The nonsensuous mouth said, "May I ask what is the matter with using the telephone next door yourself?"

I said, "I am completely deaf, ma'am, and am unable to use a telephone properly because I cannot hear the tone or the responses. Please do not be alarmed. This is not a trick. I will leave your porch now, but I urge you to call the police and relay my message." The old machinery clanked and groaned.

She was more than wary. Her enunciation was gorgeous. I could read her like a book. "If you're deaf, as you say, may I ask how you can hear what I'm saying? Do you take me for an idiot?"

"I read lips, ma'am. I really do. Please do as I ask. I won't trouble you any further."

I backed off the stoop, coming as close to a kowtow as I dared without seeming to mock her. She had nowhere to go but to the telephone. I returned to the backyard.

The syringe and the glassine envelope I found right away, near the spring of the diving board. The bikini took a little longer. It was upstairs, in my lady's chamber, kicked under the bed—still soaking wet.

That's what they pay me for, sir. When you see a naked lady in a swimming pool with the pure-white outline of a bikini on a deeply tanned hide, you're aware that she doesn't habitually swim or sunbathe in the nude—not even in her own backyard. She hadn't taken that bikini off by herself and kicked it under a bed in this immaculate house. The little cabana behind the pool stood with its door bolted shut. There were no signs that it had been used. By the time I had worked out the scenario, the police had arrived.

3

Chapter II

Deafness always spooks the cops. Oh, they try to be nice, but you can see that they're suspicious and upset. They often count on impressing people, and it's hard to impress a guy who's reading your lips. Shouting does nothing for you. Turning purple might help a little. Finally they get frustrated and hostile.

Lieutenant Probcziewski (the lip-formed name came out *pro-chef-skee)* spoke very carefully to me. "Let's hear it again why you don't think she drowned."

"When I rolled her over there didn't seem to be much water coming out of her stomach or her lungs, just a slight trickle. I could be wrong, of course, but I've seen a number of drowned people, and they usually cough up more than that."

"Where did you see drowned people?"

"When I was in underwater demolition in the Navy."

"That where you lost your hearing?"

I nodded, and he asked me a few more pointed questions about my hearing, most of which I was able to answer readily. Then we let the unwelcome subject go and went back to matters instantly at hand.

"Give it to me again why you're here," said Probcziewski.

"Mr. Penton, the husband of the deceased, wanted to install a very good burglar-alarm system in the house. Rather than try to evaluate the systems himself, he asked me to come over and look at the house and make my recommendations."

"Where'd he get your name?"

"I did some credit checking for him and some investigation on prospective employees. He knew he could trust me."

"He did, eh?" Probcziewski's eyes were a light, fanatical blue. I found it easier to watch his mouth. He watched my eyes. My eyes are a nice spaniel brown. "He could trust you so much that he'd give you the key to his house?"

"Only temporarily. After all, I do have a license."

"Yeah, yeah, yeah." The blue fanatics roved elsewhere. "He didn't expect his wife to be home at the time, right?"

"His wife had an appointment to listen to an audition at the record company."

"Why pick a day when there's nobody here?"

"He didn't want anybody to get scared or worried."

You could freeze hot coffee right in the thermos with those eyes. "We'll work back to that one later," he said.

The doctor and the sergeant converged on Probcziewski simultaneously. The doctor opened his mouth to say something but then gestured at the sergeant's hand. "There's your answer," said the doctor. The syringe, on a handkerchief with the empty glassine envelope, glittered in the sergeant's palm. "O.D. A late user. We might find tracks someplace else, but I counted seven on her arm."

"Skin pop?" asked Probcziewski.

"Mainlining," said the doctor. "Right off the bat. No wonder she O.D.'d."

The lieutenant watched the covered figure disappear through the sliding doors. "When can we get a report?" he asked the doctor.

"We'll put everything on it," he answered, and followed the little procession into the house and out the front.

Probcziewski looked at the syringe as if he were trying to shatter it in the sergeant's hand. "No rusty spoon under somebody's stairway for this chick, huh?" he said. "Nothing but the very best—the best shit, everything. The best kind of house, good food, good liquor, part of a business, something to do. A live one, hey? A dead one."

5

He looked at me. "Did you ever see her before today?"

"No. My business was strictly with Mr. Penton. He didn't even want his wife to know I'd been retained."

Probcziewski glanced at his watch—a Rolex, no less. "Penton ought to be here pretty soon, but before he arrives, how about it? What's he like? Nice guy? A prick?"

"Nice guy," I said. "Look, lieutenant, the guy's my client. What could I tell you that you could use?"

"Like that, eh?" The blue ice laid a sheet on me. "I tell you what, Binney. I'd stop being cute if I were you. And I wouldn't bleed too much about the client relationship. Unless you're half-witted you must know that this setup stinks. She was supposed to be sitting out here at the pool stark naked, mainlining, right? We find the syringe and the envelope right here, where we're supposed to. But there's no tourniquet. Not a piece of string. Nothing. Now cut out the crap."

"You check my story with Mr. Penton," I said, "and you'll find that I'm telling the truth. As far as what I can guess is concerned, it's not my place to tell you your business."

"It's not your place to withhold evidence, either," said the lieutenant.

The machinery was roaring in my ears, and I cursed the Goddamned wet bikini I had seen under the bed. There was no way they'd know I'd found it. With Probcziewski's sharp eyes boring into me, I didn't want to know anything about it, any part of it.

Penton came onto the patio accompanied by a policeman. He was very quiet and very white. Somehow, his clothes didn't go with the layout, and I could see him slipping into old slacks, etc., when he came home of an evening. Looking at him, I couldn't see those clothes in a business office either—or the haircut that verged on the modishly long. It was a good time to be silent, and I used the time to put him all together. He surprised me. In the back booth of the restaurant, where we'd made our arrangement, he had looked normal. But here, adding up the tie, the haircut, the suit, which again verged on

6

the mod without quite making it, the manicure, the sunlamp tan, through which his shock was glowing—put in consecutive letters, it all spelled *jerk*. I was suddenly ashamed of having anything to do with him. However, he was my client.

Probcziewski, too, I could see, was measuring Penton for the fall. I realized that Penton was offensive to people like the lieutenant and me because he belonged nowhere in God's world but a nightclub. No—not even a country club.

Penton said, "Where is Iris? What have you done with her?"

I couldn't see what the lieutenant told him, but, no doubt, it was straight off the druggist's shelf. Penton relaxed slightly, and began to take hold of himself. I shifted around so that I could see them both. For all I knew, it was going to be mongoose and cobra. "Would you like a drink?" Penton asked. I brightened instantly, but the lieutenant scowled.

"Do you really need one?" he asked Penton.

"Yes," replied Penton with school-yard defiance. I sang out, "Make mine bourbon on the rocks, please."

When Penton had gone toward the house, Probcziewski said to me, "How old do you make him?"

"A little over thirty-five."

"And her?"

"Pushing forty."

"Any kids?"

"One—hers—by an earlier marriage."

"Where's the kid now?"

"I don't know. You'll have to ask Penton."

Probcziewski said, "Tell me about this record company she was mixed up with."

"As far as I know, it's just another label doing rock—far-out acid rock—punk—anything they can wax. It's the Groupe label."

"How deep was she in?"

"Very deep. Controlling interest, as I understand it."

"Making money, was it?"

7

"Breaking even, anyway."

He waved a heavy arm to indicate the surroundings. "The money for all this crock—he bring it in?"

"You'll have to ask Mr. Penton about that," I replied primly.

"Client relationship, eh?"

"Not necessarily," I said. "I only know just so much about them."

"Well, you seem to know a hell of a lot for a guy sent down to check out the windows for a buzzer system."

"I have to know *something* about my clients before taking them on."

He smiled at me—a fearsome sight. "You're a real doll," he said.

"But not the Chatty model." His smile vanished and was replaced by a scowl even more fearsome, demonstrating his gamut of A to A. Fortunately, it wasn't me he was scowling at. It was Penton, who even at this moment was nudging me in the elbow to put the drink in my hand.

"Thank you," I said. I really meant it. I dived in gratefully, and we all sat down on the lawn chairs.

Probcziewski said to him, "How long has Mrs. Penton been using heroin, Mr. Penton?"

Penton had thought this one over before he had even come out of the house with the drinks, the son of a bitch. He held the oversized glass in both hands between his knees and stared meltingly at his shoe tops. His expression would have embarrassed an undertaker. I knew what was coming, and I restrained myself from standing up and kicking him right in his white, capped teeth.

"For quite a while, I'm afraid. I'm sure Mr. Binney has explained it to you."

There it went, like a manhole cover at Forty-second and Broadway, thirty feet in the air.

The good lieutenant didn't even look at me. "Yes, of course," he replied. "But I'd like to hear it from you, too, just to check things out."

Penton's mouth tightened with petulance—it being perfectly all right that he had just double-crossed me, but not that I might have sold *him* out, which, indeed, I had not. He didn't dare look at me under the long rifle of Probcziewski's eyes. Penton said, "Well, that's why I had Mr. Binney come down to the house—to see if he could find the cache of drugs I knew she must be keeping here."

"What would that solve?" Probcziewski asked rudely.

"I was going to confront her with it and force her to look for help," he said. I was about to stand up and act out my fantasy, but the lieutenant pushed me back with an oaken arm.

"What kind of help is that?" Probcziewski's expression was pleasant, for him.

"Psychiatric help, of course. It was very obvious that she was sick."

"Were you going to say something?" the lieutenant asked me.

I gripped the arm of the Molla chair—scant comfort. "No," I said. "Nothing important."

"What about it, then?" the lieutenant said. "Did you find the cache?"

"No," I answered.

"Well, well," said Probcziewski. "Maybe we can be a little more efficient than that. Mr. Penton, would you like to accompany me for a quick look around?"

"I don't see that it matters now," said Penton.

"Well, we ought to satisfy our suspicions, anyway."

I got up.

"Not you," said Probcziewski. "You wait here."

And so I remained very much alone in the Molla chair by the poolside with my machinery. I stared at the pool surface, which stared pacifically back, antiseptic and uninformative. My eye kept wandering to the diving-board spring—point A— and my interior eye to the bikini under the bed—point B. I let my mind search for C, and while it ruminated on the angle, the pool, the sky, and the whole world were suddenly blotted out by a pink fuzzy face surrounded by hair. The mouth was extended into a yell.

"Are you deaf?" the mouth yelled silently.

I scrambled backward, pushing the light chair under me, and stood up. I put my hand out to keep the face at arm's length. "Yes," I said. "I'm deaf."

The pink face with its blond promise of beard was overwhelmed by the dirty-brown shoulder-length hair, but it managed a sneering exclamation point above the unbuttoned Army blouse. The jeans were not even faded. They had never been washed. The feet were bare and abused by city streets.

"You must be Larry," I said, trying not to make it sound like a rebuke.

"So who are you?"

"My name is Joe Binney. Your father asked me to come over."

The gray-green eyes, of which I had seen only a hint in his mother, became dark and remote. The mouth pursed. "So where is he?"

"In the house somewhere."

"On a Thursday? Is something wrong?"

"Maybe you'd better sit down." I pushed a chair forward with my foot, but he wasn't having any. I had the feeling right then that everything I was going to say would be superfluous—redundant. The gray-green eyes had opened wide and were staring far beyond me into a room full of time.

"Something's happened," he said.

"There's been an accident." There is no right way to say these things, although there are many wrong ways. "Your mother had an accident in the pool."

The eyes withdrew again—not just from me but from the world. "Was it bad?"

"Your mother is dead," I told him.

He sat very quickly in the chair, the Army blouse ballooning out around his chest. He wore nothing under it, and his expanding rib cage told the world how much muscle he had. He did not appear to be saying anything. The rib cage

10

worked like a bellows. Now, however, it seemed that he had been asking me something while his face was turned away, because his head jerked up angrily and he said, "I asked you how it happened."

"I don't know what you're saying unless I can read your lips," I told him. "I really am deaf. If you want to talk to me, you'll have to look at me." His expression did not change. "Apparently, your mother drowned in the pool."

"Never," he said. "She was like an Olympic swimmer."

"She may have fainted," I suggested, "or hit her head. Good swimmers drown. I've seen it happen."

"Not her," said Larry. "Not in her own pool. Besides, she wasn't even supposed to be here."

"She might not have felt well and just stayed home," I offered. "She might have thought a dip in the pool would make her feel better, and gotten sick in the water. Did she say anything to you this morning before you left?"

"I wasn't here this morning," he answered. "I haven't been here for about three days." He turned his head away from me then. I saw the big shoulders begin to shake and bob inside the blouse.

I was aware of their coming out of the house before the kid was. I caught them in the corner of my eye while he was sunk deep in his tears. They weren't carrying anything—not even the bikini. Probcziewski raised his eyebrows at me and I nodded toward the boy. Penton stood absolutely stock-still, as if afraid of wrinkling his suit.

"Do you want to come along with us?" Probcziewski asked the boy. The kid stood up mechanically. I looked at Penton.

"Did you find what you were looking for?" I asked him. Oh, my! If looks could kill! It upset him every bit as much as I had meant it to. Penton gave me a murderous stare and shook his head.

The question roused Larry. "What was he looking for?" he asked.

Probcziewski gave it to him. "Mr. Penton thought that

11

your mother was taking dope. We were looking for the stash."

If it had connected, it might have taken Penton's head clean off. But the kid's stiff-armed swing at his stepfather whistled on by and I caught the boy by his elbow, pulling the loose sleeve of the blouse on back. "Easy, there. Easy," I told him. I could feel the shuddering right through the raw heavy bones. I held on to him, staring at his elbow, until the tension subsided, and then I let him go.

He was his mother's own, the young man was, a sterling lad, a white-haired boy—with a habit as long as his arm.

Chapter III

I tried to put it all behind me on the long drive through the broiling expressway back to town—the big white house, the lawn, the emerald-sparkling pool. While the temperature needle on the dashboard climbed toward apoplexy, my brain gauge registered a sizzling indignation at Penton's betrayal.

So I wrote a letter. Oh, not in pen and ink. Even the lapses of the Long Island Expressway aren't quite that long. It was to be the kind of letter that would never see paper—my usual—to be composed and filed away in one more wrinkle of my memory.

Penton had made me vulnerable with blowing our story, and I am quite vulnerable enough, thank you, without any help from my clients. The tale about the burglar alarms for his house had been perfectly adequate. Even the exact truth was nowise contrary to law. But he had put me in the middle of a lie, and the law doesn't like being lied to, not even with little white lies. He had put me on the wrong side of Probcziewski, a very large area that no sensible person would want to explore.

I had verged on that country the minute Probcziewski learned I was deaf. The expression on his face was familiar enough to me, caught halfway between a sneer and disbelief. He'd said, "They gave you P.I. papers? I don't believe it." It may be that his voice was softer than his expression, but I am in no position to judge. Then he'd said, "How in hell did anybody like you get into this racket?"

And that will be the subject of this letter, sir, *in re* how anybody like Joe Binney got into this racket. A car far ahead of me is doing an interesting imitation of a Stanley Steamer in distress. I wait as the tormented motorist and his passenger clamber out, raise the hood, and watch the traffic crawl around them.

I had told Probcziewski, "Just drifted, I guess."

"Drifted!"

I had shrugged. It is my stock reply. What the hell do they expect? *Well, sir, throughout my childhood I tossed restlessly in my narrow cot with hot-eyed plans to become a private investigator?* Balls.

I began, sir, as an humble bookkeeper. Better, I suppose, but far too long in the telling, what with the dead lady only recently carried away, and a busy Probcziewski straining the back of his sports coat with impatience.

I began as a near idiot, stumbling around the corridors of the Philadelphia Naval Hospital. Well, that was the truest beginning, and it would do to start my unmailable letter.

Dear Lieutenant Probcziewski:

It all began when—well, what the hell—when they shipped me back to Philly. I had only recently learned to walk again. All the balance mechanisms of my ears had gone out of whack along with my hearing. The medical crew had waited until I was an established upright citizen and regained the balance in my inner ear before they told me. Then they'd introduced me to the fact that I was permanently deaf (they did this in a carefully written letter), lacking even the rudimentary apparatus for hearing anything.

The trouble was that I did hear things—a grinding and moaning that they explained away as "subjective noise"— noise that I would be aware of forever—but the *only* noise, my personal machinery.

Today they call it depression, and they've got whole cabinets full of medicine to treat it with. But in those days, sir, there was nothing to treat it with except a kind word, which I couldn't hear, and an occasional kick in the ass to straighten you up. I didn't need pills to sleep, as so many of the other patients did. I escaped into sleep. They prodded me to keep me awake, to face reality.

My reality became another kind of unreality in the hospital library. Books became more real than the world around me. Why? Because I could *hear* the human voice in books. If sound had been blasted out of my life forever, the memory of sound had not. The people in books were the real people in this world, rather than the silent white-coated figures that glided around me or the men in blue bathrobes like myself who staggered or wheeled silently down the halls.

I hadn't ever really read before, sir. Oh, I was flogged through *Silas Marner* by Mrs. Pierson, with her octagonal-framed glasses, in high school (where my education ended, as did that of my family and my friends). And when I popped through graduation with diploma in hand, I thought that I was done with books forever. But in the hospital I returned to them, looking for the reassurance of the human voice in the clanking silences of my skull.

I read endlessly, slowly, sensuously, measuring out each word of narrative like a cough drop on my tongue, acting out all the parts, rolling and plunging through Conrad, Melville, and McFee, tasting the bitter dialogue of Chandler and McGivern, galloping through the West in the saddle of Max Brand, and floating through the twilight sleep of Proust's end-of-century France, a stranger place to me than the surface of the moon.

14

And what would Mrs. Pierson have thought, staring through her octagonal-rimmed glasses at the sight of me reading Proust? She would have drilled me in the word *eclectic* (the operative word, incidentally, in the McGuffey series, by which this whole country learned to read, when it could read). Also, she would have threatened me with a painful dismemberment for moving my lips while I read.

Yes, sir. Laugh as you well might. I was a lip mover. The print was not symbols on a page, but audible words to me, and I formed them with my lips as I went along. A slow reader? Oh, yes, sir, very. I still am. I've stopped moving my lips these days so as not to convulse the passengers on the subway with merriment. But to this day the words I read are audible, drowning out the noise of my machinery.

And perhaps, just perhaps, now, sir, the savoring and smacking of each word with my lips made me just a bit more receptive to the introduction of lipreading when my moment came.

For they had finally gotten sick of my moping and mooning around the hospital, and handed me a packet of literature that contained the future of my verbal communication. I read the stuff as if looking at it through a telescope, word by word, and with a tiny spiral of dread in every word. The whole packet spelled destiny. This is your destiny, now; now you are going to be different from everyone else around you. Now you are going to be a lip-reader.

I kept putting the thing aside, but they wouldn't let me alone. They asked questions (all this was done by notes passed back and forth). They demanded answers. They were pulling me kicking and screaming (silently, white faced) back into the real world, back into the real reality. They took away my library privileges, a blow that almost killed me. And when I finally confronted them to learn my future, it was with a face set in hatred.

If I hadn't been receptive to the technique, I probably never would have learned, because I was full of natural resistance and apprehension. I didn't want to learn to lip-read.

I wanted to hear again. I wanted to hear familiar, down-home, everyday American English, sir, such as you hear from the slouching waitress at the lunch counter. Lipreading spelled permanency. Lipreading meant that they had given up any hope of fixing my ears. So you can see, sir, that my major battle was not so much to learn as to accept. I was never very good at accepting things. I'm still not.

About ten lengths in front of me there has been, apparently, some kind of mild contact between two cars. The drivers, impeccable in gray business costume, have gotten out of their cars and begun an amicable civilized discourse. Hold on, now. Now they're swinging at each other in an approximation of mortal combat. Ah, finally each of them has realized that he couldn't break a light bulb with his Sunday punch. They have subsided and slunk back to their cars. The traffic is lurching forward.

When they had practically nailed me to a seat in the hospital, I was forced to learn that there were not one but two schools of lipreading, the Jena and the Nitchie. The Jena is the purist concept, which depends almost entirely on reading of the lips alone. The Nitchie system diffuses attention to expression, gesture, context—any clue that can aid in understanding. The difference may seem slight to you, but philosophical differences are involved that have caused many a quarrel.

They started me off on Nitchie, I suppose because they wanted to get me functioning as soon as possible, and to hell with purity. Out of a kind of desperation, a fund of rage of which I still have quite a large amount, I began to learn to lipread—attack it. I devoted my every waking hour to the technique. I stared at the speaking-hearing population of that innocent hospital until they fled my scrutiny. I got into three fights for eavesdropping. The fact is that I plunged into lipreading the same way I had plunged into the library—to keep myself from thinking about me. But I learned it all: how to handle the tricky vowels, how to handle the puritanical,

16

tight-lipped, tight-assed citizens who seem to attach a prize to every word they utter (and let's not kid around here—some of them defeated me absolutely; some of them defeat me absolutely to this day; with some I have to communicate by note). My mentors were delighted with my progress but dismayed by my attitude. I was getting into at least one fight a week. It didn't matter whether I won or lost. One time I lost so badly that I was doing my lipreading through two very black eyes.

Now what? No, please. A gigantic semi has managed to straddle two lanes, where it has expired. The air is blue with smog and no doubt with curses, too. No doubt the atmosphere is thick with the braying of automobile horns. Deafness can have its rewards. A trickle of traffic has begun in the last remaining lane.

But here, Lieutenant Probcziewski, we come to the crucial question, don't we? *What does it mean when I tell you that I learned to lip-read very well?* Can I be trusted? If I recount a conversation that I've had, do I know what I'm talking about? Am I a reliable witness? Can I ever be truly believed? These are serious questions. Indeed, my livelihood depends on them.

All right, straight off, the best you can do with lipreading is to comprehend about fifty percent of the actual verbiage.

Jesus Christ! You mean you only understand half of what's being said to you?

That's not what I told you, lieutenant. Please pay attention. What I told you is that I am dead certain of fifty percent of the words I lip-read. The rest is fill-in. That sounds terrible, doesn't it? It isn't, really.

The fact is that, audibly, you don't do much better, if as well. Can you really give a good account of all the waves of conversation that wash over you as you go about your business? Of course not. Most of the time your ears are just a fishing net through which the seawater of ordinary conversation flows without much notice, until, suddenly, there is the mackerel of significance flopping around inside it. That's when real comprehension takes over.

Lipreading does better than that because nothing washes over *us*. It always takes effort, attention, concentration. Conversation is never really idle. We cling to meaning, and because concentration is required, the memory is engaged more quickly and more deeply. And also, lieutenant, we listen to each word twice in our heads, examine each phrase twice, sifting it for meaning, context, nuance.

Ah, but I can see your big map wrinkling with suspicion, and I can see you asking, *How do I know that you know what you think you know when you recognize only half the words?* Well, the answer to that is the theory of context and predictability, otherwise known as Binney's Unassailable Theory of the Toilet on the Moon.

If you ask the time-worn, all-too-human question of the waiter, policeman, caddy, or other functionary, "Where's the toilet around here?" and he replies, in whatever language, "The toilet, sir, is on the moon," you are aware, both intellectually and viscerally, that you have hit a clinker. It defies predictability and context. Sweat beading your forehead, you pursue this point until you have a predictable answer in context, or until your functionary is carted off in the crocheted station wagon.

We lip-readers, sir, know very definitely that the toilet is not on the moon. When words are out of context, we check and check again. If they are really incomprehensible, we ask the party to write them down. Those of us who are good at it, and I am very good, manage to get things pretty straight.

Pretty straight! you say. *And you think that's good enough?* Well, yes, sir, I do. In the courtroom I have watched witnesses disagree wildly among themselves over conversations they *thought* they had comprehended, and these witnesses, sir, do not exclude trained policemen, or even trained psychiatrists. It is an unlovely fact that each of us goes through life with his own version of events, and when required to relate those events, we color the tale with the tinct of our own comprehension. Each of us constructs his individual world through the interpretation of his senses. None of those worlds is truly like another. None is a duplicate. I am not really all that different from most of your witnesses, sir. My enforced concentration makes me better than most.

I cannot really believe what I see ahead of me in traffic. A portly businessman has climbed out of his Lincoln and has engaged the driver of the semi in a violent dispute. The driver has raised both hands above his head as if to drive the portly businessman through the boiling pavement. Can this be? Certainly the businessman did not expect it. His eyes have popped. He has scurried back to his Lincoln, very luckily unscathed.

Predictability—unpredictability. My first jolting experience with it came at the behest of Mrs. Armistead, the extraordinarily patient therapist at the hospital. I got a note from her requiring my presence one morning in her office for counseling. I presented my surly self at the little table she used there and watched her warily as she looked at me through her gold-rimmed glasses. She smiled sweetly. "Joe," she said to me with perfect framing of the lips, "you're getting to be a terrible pain in the ass."

Chapter IV

I am following the trickle around the stranded semi. The beached driver is sitting in the cab far above us, glowering down. Would someone else like to quarrel with him? I think not. Finally, I have passed the big shiny grill, and I zoom away in the traffic that always rockets out of a bottleneck. I proceed in full flight until I reach the outer edges of the immense pileup at the tollbooths that guard the entrance to the Midtown Tunnel. Here I subside and sulk.

Well, sir, had I read her correctly? I was getting used to repeating everything in my head before accepting it, and I repeated to myself—*You're getting to be a terrible pain in the ass,* and put it in the context of that soft forgiving face. The next words she framed dispelled any doubt. "You have to grow up, Joe, and you have to do it now, or you'll never be a real man at all."

It would be nice to say that I remember every word of the session that followed—which was one of your famous "turning points"—but I don't. I don't remember because I perceived the entire session through a red haze of absolute rage. *Be a real man?* How in the hell did she think I'd gotten here? Wasn't that being a real man? Apparently not. She had further qualifications. Terrifying qualifications.

She said something like "This isn't a home, Joe. It's a hospital. You're going to have to be discharged, and you're going to have to earn a living in the world." She went on to talk about college and other educational opportunities—she had bales of brochures—and I interrupted her. *"I ain't going to anybody's school!"* I guess it burst out of me. Words were still stiff in my mouth because I couldn't hear them and was never quite sure of what I had put up in the air. *"I ain't going to be anybody's class freak!"* My fists were bunched on the table. My face burned.

Her expression changed without changing. Not a muscle in her face had moved, but something had expired behind her eyes. Later, much later, I realized that I had failed the most important test in my life.

She reached for a different stack of brochures. There was training for this and training for that, and finally I jabbed one with my forefinger, a correspondence course for—bookkeeping! Why? Why in God's name did I pick it? Was it simply the friendly appearance of the word—*book*—the only friendly word I knew, and *to keep*? To keep and hold books? Yes, yes, my nutty subconscious, running around like a rat in an outhouse, must have jumped at the only friendly opening it saw.

So they packed me up with the beginning lessons of my correspondence course and sent me home to Boston to study. Home! It was the last place I wanted to go. My mother had died while I was in high school. My older brother had decided to make a career of the Army (we'd had one brief, crazy, joyous reunion in Korea, where he still was posted) and my sister had married a lawyer from Topeka, Kansas, which is where she was living. Home was an empty frame house with my father rattling around inside it. I don't mean really empty, of course; the furniture, the dishes, pots, and pans were all there, but my mother wasn't there to give them life. My father trudged off to the docks every morning to work, as he had for the past thirty years, and came home with his usual load on. His attitude toward me was a mixture of fright, defiance, and contempt. He was enraged that I'd let myself get wounded—crippled, in fact. He and his cronies on the docks had an abiding hatred of anything that was "different." I was now different. After one disastrous evening in the corner saloon, where we'd all tried to be "just like old times," he had dropped all pretense of communication. The evening had ended in a wild free-for-all with my father not really knowing which side he was on. I had become a stranger, and an undesirable one at that.

I stayed in my room and plied my correspondence course. I finished it up in record time, said farewell to the ugly little house for, I hoped, ever, and returned to Philly for another sample of Mrs. Armistead's patience.

I have come into view of the tollgates, and the spires of Manhattan across the river beckon mockingly. This is the moment of truth for drivers on this highway. Does one have in

21

one's sweat-soaked pants pocket the silver change that will let one through the inviting EXACT CHANGE lanes? Or must one begin to inch his vehicle crabwise from lane to lane in the hope of reaching the side gate mandatory for trucks, buses, and changeless undesirables? A tortuous search produces two dimes. I begin to inch my vehicle crabwise from lane to fist-waving lane.

I would be happy to relate, sir, that Mrs. Armistead greeted me like a long-lost etcetera when I returned. But such was not the case. There was no shortage of maimed veterans needing counseling. Mrs. Armistead, although she held on to the smile, had little enough time for me—out of sight, out of mind being the operative philosophy of the moment. She was miffed that I did not plan to set up in Boston and "enjoy the emotional support of my family and my childhood roots." In all the time we had spent in counseling, I think that was the only time I laughed. The smile got lost. What about Phila-delphia? Did I want to live in Philadelphia? No. I did not want to live in Philadelphia, the only city in the world that built a subway with an entrance but no exit.

Where then? A hint of real asperity. In my Navy travels, I had passed through New York and spent a couple of goggling, enjoyable days there. Coming back down to Philly by train, this time, I had passed through New York again. It had revived memories of blessed anonymity. Yes. I thought that if, perhaps, I could take my new-found skills to New York, I could start my new life there cut off from the past completely.

Was I wrong? In retrospect it seems not, although at first I thought I was. Mrs. Armistead had plumbed the depths of the job placement services and had fixed a bookkeeping position for me with a company that had openings for veteran on-the-job trainees supported by your friendly U.S. Govern-ment, sir.

It didn't really work out. I worked along, all right, performed my bookkeeping tasks and learned the wrinkles not covered in the correspondence course, but it was wrong, all wrong. Just as I hadn't wanted to be the class freak, neither did I want to be the company freak. I had conceived of bookkeeping as a solitary task, where I would be required to speak to no one, to absorb only a few brief instructions and then sit in a dim corner, secluded and protected from the world.

But that was not to be. I found myself platooned with a lot of other bookkeepers posting away for a big hardware outfit—this was in the days before computerized billing, you know—with my head down over my desk in an attempt to be invisible. The people who worked alongside me were very decent people, but many of them were little girls just out of high school who had taken a commercial course and launched themselves upon life from this musty section of the world. I felt so huge, so rough, so out of place with them that my pursuit of invisibility seemed hopeless. Eventually I felt that my flesh was growing through the fabric of the suit I was required to wear.

I quit after three months—no hard feelings, etc. I holed up in the room I had rented on Fifteenth Street just east of Seventh Avenue, cooked my meals on the gas ring provided therein, exhausted the resources of the lending library on the corner, and began the same process on the local liquor store.

I almost threw away the little envelope along with the junk mail, which was the only mail I got besides my disability check. One of the little girls in the platoon had looked up my address. "Dear Joe," the pink note said. "Been wondering how you're getting along. I'm going to be in your neighborhood next Thursday, the fourteenth, at three in the afternoon (dentist's appointment!). Why not meet me at De Marcy's drugstore for a coke? Lorraine."

Well, now, De Marcy's was the drugstore that held the lifeline of my lending library, and the building that rose above it threatened the world with a multitude of dentists. The trouble was that I couldn't identify Lorraine among the girls in the office. Nonetheless, I made up my mind to be there, went out, and did my laundry.

So she was *that* girl, the heavyset, dark-complected,

sweet-faced girl with the large mole on her jawline. We had a terrible time at the soda fountain because the novocaine hadn't quite worn off and her lips were stiff. When it did begin to wear off, she grimaced with pain, and I announced, "What you need is something to drink." She looked dubious, but surrendered.

A very good and very cold martini did the trick for her. We were in a nice bar I had noticed but never entered during my perambulations. She asked me why I had quit and I told her. She understood. "That doesn't mean you can't work, though," she said. "I know what you want. You want to work alone, free-lance, right?"

My eyes widened, and I played back what she had said to me. She'd opened up another world. She continued, "There are a lot of little businesses, and professional people who have their books done once a month or once a week, depending. They have free-lance bookkeepers come in and do them. Would you like that?"

"Where do I find 'em?"

"There's an agency that sends you out. Wait, I've got the address." She took out a little silver pencil, consulted a small black book, rummaged for a scrap of paper in her purse, and handed me my magic passport.

I was still staring at the slip of magic when she tapped me on the shoulder and excused herself for a few minutes. I stood as she left the booth and then sat down to plan and scheme. I had raised my head only to stare speculatively at the ceiling about five minutes later when I noticed that she had been stopped on her way back to the booth. A big raw-boned guy in a gray flannel lounge suit at the bar had put his arm out to impede her progress. I couldn't see what he was saying to her, but whatever it was, it shocked her so that tears sprang to her eyes. Her gentle face was rigid with dismay and revulsion.

I moved up and took her arm, asking her to step over here, dear. I looked up at the big tan fellow, giving him my best "dummy" smile. His returning smile contained a sneer

24

full of viciousness. It's too bad that he didn't go down when I hit him. If he had had room to stretch out on his back along the front of the bar, why that would have been the end of it, and we could have all gone home happy. But he got tangled up in a barstool, and then propped up against the bar, and then up against the wall so that he could not drop, while I industriously worked away at him like any lumberjack.

They had pulled me away and calmed me down before I turned around to reassure Lorraine. But now her face was even more rigid, frozen with fright and horror. "Get me a taxi" was all she would say. "Please, please get me a taxi." Woodenly, I flagged one down and handed her into it. It was the last I ever saw of Lorraine. But I still had my magic slip of paper.

Would you believe that I am at this very moment entering the tollbooth—the changemaking tollbooth with a live human being in it who makes change? But why is he glaring at me? Aha! The bill I have offered him is a twenty. He begins to harangue me, but I tap my ear and shake my head to signify my deafness. Maliciously, he hands me a packet of singles with the tacit implication that there are nineteen of them, plus a quarter change. Unhappily, I observe the sign COUNT YOUR CHANGE as I grind past the raised barricade. Before me lies the white-tiled tube that leads under the river to Manhattan. It is jammed with vehicles of all descriptions.

Chapter V

And you will be happy to know, lieutenant, that The Man in the Gray Flannel Suit recovered with no apparent harm. I saw him six months later in the same bar and noted that even his suit had recovered. We avoided each other.

More to the point, the magic slip had worked for me. I was entrained on the free-lance bookkeeping dodge, which suited me very well, although I would have starved to death if the proceeds had not been supplemented by my disability pay. I was content to trudge from one dingy office to another, pick up the books and the bills, both payable and receivable, the canceled checks, the check stubs, the payrolls to match to my withholding chart, and put all these into a coherent whole. I pursued it for a year throughout Manhattan, the Bronx (before the Bronx began its tumultuous collapse), the forested precincts of Queens, and even parts of Brooklyn.

The bulk of my work, however, remained in and around the garment district, where I learned to lip-read a Yiddish accent, and not without a struggle. A dear favorite of mine there was Mr. Finkelman, who, because he had his books done up on a Friday afternoon, had me in as a *Shabbas goy*— the posting, toting up, and payroll often going far beyond sundown. His little firm, which sold volumes of buttons and buckles, was called Finkelman and Sons, but alas there were no longer any sons. Two of them had been killed in World War II and the remaining son in Korea. He made do, now, with a son-in-law, Herbert Markewitch, whose name shall live in infamy.

It was far, far beyond sundown on one late November Friday evening that I finished up the books and looked at Mr. Finkelman curiously, wondering whether I should speak. Finally I nerved myself, as much on the basis of his seamed and kindly face as my own courage. "My goodness, Mr. Finkelman," I said, "you certainly have taken on a load, haven't you?"

"A load?" he inquired. "So a load of what?"

"A load of brass buckles. You must have a shipload of them."

"Brass buckles? A shipload? What nonsense is this?"

26

I showed him the canceled checks—forty-five thousand dollars' worth—made out to the Ben Toy Brass Buckle Company and signed by—what rang out of Mr. Finkelman's lips was not a name but an epithet, one that I had become familiar with over the past year. He framed it from white, trembling lips and put it in the air for all to see:

"*Goniff!* My own son-in-law. My Mirabelle's husband!"

I thought he was going to faint. I put my arm out to help him and he seized hold of it as if he were drowning. "Where is Mr. Markewitch now?" I asked him. "He can probably straighten this whole thing out."

But no. Herbert had been gone for the entire week on a buying trip, and a hasty phone call to Mirabelle by Mr. Finkelman produced the dismaying news that Herbert had not followed his inevitable custom of calling home every evening for a heartening word with the wife and kiddies. Nor had Mirabelle been able to reach him at any of the scheduled hotels.

From where I'm sitting here in the tube beneath the river, the blue haze of exhaust that shimmers under the fluorescent lights has a peculiarly deadly look. Yet even when traffic is stalled here, as it is now, I can feel fairly patient and serene. I know that at the end of this tube lies Manhattan. It is a straight shot into the bustle of the big city, and from there a sharp left turn into the pathway home.

And not to put too poetic a face upon it, lieutenant, I was at that moment at Finkelman and Sons entering a tunnel that would lead me to the answer to your question. I guided Mr. Finkelman back to his office and asked him, "Do you think we ought to take a look at his desk?"

The interior of the desk produced nothing but a few bent paper clips and other junk that had piled up over the years. On top of the desk was one of those huge scratch pads meant to hold the jottings of a week. The jottings were all prices and bids of grosses and lots. But I had read enough detective stories to know that sometimes impressions are left on notepaper, and I looked for these. Near the bottom of the big pad there was the dim impression—unfamiliar words for this business—*Shank and Mole*.

"Mr. Finkelman," I asked him as gently as I could, "do the words *Shank and Mole* mean anything to you?"

"Shank and Mole!" cried Mr. Finkelman. "What kind of filthy language is that?"

I certainly didn't know. I'd thought that they might have something to do with the button and buckle business. It had seemed logical at the moment.

I looked more closely at the dim impression and realized that there was something wrong with the *a* in *Shank*. The more I stared at it, the more I became convinced that it wasn't an *a* at all. It was a *u*. A very loose association began to knit itself together.

I looked at the trembling, distraught face of Mr. Finkelman and took the plunge. "Mr. Finkelman," I said, "if you want to locate Mr. Markewitch, I just might be able to help, although I can't make any promises."

He snapped up in his chair. "You can find him, the rat?"

"I can't promise. I might be all wet. It's a long shot, but it's the only thing I can see that we've got to go on. I think he's not in New York, but he might not be all that far away, either."

"You will go to him? Bring him back?"

"Mr. Finkelman," I said, "I probably don't have any right to interfere or make wild guesses like this. I could be very wrong. But if you want me to, I'll try."

"You need expenses, money?"

I thought it over. "A hundred dollars would cover every possible expense that I can think of, and it shouldn't cost nearly that."

Mr. Finkelman had a draw to the wallet that Wyatt Earp could have envied. He handed me five twenties. "I'll give you an itemized account when I get back," I told him. "It shouldn't cost nearly this much."

And finally, he smiled. It was a slow, sad little smile. "An itemized account," he repeated. "Every dime, every nickel, every penny—all balanced out even, square." He touched my shoulder. "You are a good man, Joe Binney."

I had him dig out a recent photograph of Herbert Markewitch. It had been taken the previous year at the company picnic. He was in bathing trunks, better set up than one might think of a button salesman. He was certainly hirsute, and he sported a thick black mustache that acted as a counterweight to his beetling eyebrows. On top, however, he was as bald as an onion. Mr. Finkelman did not quite understand why I should want the photograph. "But you know what he looks like," he complained. The next morning, Saturday, I took the snapshot to a photography shop I was doing the books for. They promised to have the job done for me when they opened on Monday morning.

Do all roads lead to Philly? The classy word for all this is *fortuity*. The street language is *shithouse luck*. Shunk and Mole is a street corner in South Philadelphia, not terribly far from the hospital in which I had languished. Usually, my walks from the hospital grounds didn't take me beyond Marconi Plaza, where I would sit and stare. But sometimes, animated by wanderlust, I would stroll down to the docks along Oregon Avenue and meander along the waterfront. When I wandered in the other direction, I would stroll along Shunk Avenue, which intersected with Mole Street.

There was nothing to fix them in my mind. They comprised a small neighborhood intersection of which I could remember no distinction, and they had not changed on that November afternoon after I got off the municipal bus I had taken from the train station and strolled the few blocks to their corners. For a few alarming moments I was convinced that I was pissing away Mr. Finkelman's hard-earned, much-contested money. There was, however, a tiny ice-cream parlor, with only a few tables, on one corner of Shunk and Mole. I pondered going in to make an inquiry, but the atmosphere was so intimate, so neighborly, that I was sure any inquiry would be quickly passed on to the object. Neither did I see any hope of loitering about for a glimpse of Mr. Markewitch. Both streets were very narrow, old-fashioned streets, and the wall-to-wall row houses with their peering front windows suggested that any stranger hanging around would be noted and braced, particularly when the children came home from school.

I circled away from the corner and repaired to other blocks, where I showed the photographs in candy stores, saloons, grocery stores, and even a few gas stations. *Have you seen this man? Do you know this fella?*

I had been legging it westward, but now I reversed my field and headed back toward Broad Street, the main artery. I began to walk north on Broad, there being more establishments there to check. It was a stock Italian restaurant on Broad, with the obligatory red-and-white-checked tablecloths, that yielded up the gold. It being the hiatus between lunch and dinner, Giorgio's was somnolent and empty except for the blue-haired cashier who was checking the register. I showed her the blowup of the mustachioed face of Mr. Markewitch. "Do you happen to know this fellow? Recognize him?" She squinted at the portrait, looked dubious, and shook her head.

"There's something," she said, "but . . ."

"How about this?" And I showed her the retouched portrait with the mustache airbrushed out and a toupee painted in over the gleaming dome.

"That's Mr. Fordyce." She beamed. "He has a standing reservation for dinner with his wife one day a week."

"And that day is . . .?"

"Monday. Always Monday."

It was a shiny black new Chrysler he handed her out of half a block down from the restaurant. Darkness had dropped, and I recognized him only when they passed under the streetlight. I had taken up my post in a store doorway at a bus stop, hanging back each time the municipal bus went by. Emerging from the depths of the entrance, I took a good look

30

at the lady. She conformed to another word I had learned to lip-read in the garment district. She was, indubitably, a *shiksa.* From where I stood, she appeared to be a very nice, blond, genteel creature. The fur on her shoulders was unidentifiable to my unexperienced eye.

I watched them go in and calculated the time they would spend over a cocktail, reading the menu, and ordering. I flagged down a taxi and asked the driver to wait in front of the restaurant.

I went directly to their table, where they had just finished their cocktails and were holding hands. I avoided using his name. "Sir," I said, "Mr. Finkelman is in a cab just outside the restaurant and would like to have a word with you." The pale band of flesh beneath Herbert's shorn mustache turned the color of Greenland ice.

He and I exited peacefully while the young lady stared passively into space. At the curb, outside, he peered into the darkness of the cab. I nudged him aside and opened the door. "Get in," I commanded. There was one spasmodic crucial period of his body's stiffening in rebellion—and then he got in. I sat next to him.

"It's too dark in here for me to read what you're saying," I told him, "so just listen. Give the driver enough money to cover the bill and to see the lady home. You stay here with me. You're going to be next to me like a Band-Aid until we meet Mr. Finkelman." I watched him hand the driver some bills and say a few words to him. The driver nodded.

Message accomplished, the driver returned and headed up Broad to the train station. I paid the driver there and got a receipt. "We have got just enough time for you to call Mr. Finkelman and tell him we'll meet him in the office," I told Markewitch. I steered him to a phone booth and handed him a fistful of change. After he had made his ashen call, I collected what was left of the change and took him down to the train, where we sat together. We might have walked to the office from Penn Station in New York, but I took a cab for safety's sake. The lights were on and shone through the big front window of Finkelman and Sons. Mr. Finkelman opened the door, and I looked at him inquiringly. "Do you need me anymore?" He shook his head—no. I waved farewell and faded back into the street. The two men looked at each other, both stunned.

Markewitch and I had had only the briefest of conversations on the train. I had nudged him to get his attention. "Why Shunk and Mole?" I had asked him. His face had collapsed.

"We didn't want to be seen," he said. "She knew about this little ice-cream parlor from when she visited relatives as a tiny kid. Who would know her there now? Who would know about the ice-cream parlor? Who would know about Giorgio's? Who would know Shunk and Mole?"

Who indeed?

I agree, lieutenant, that it wasn't much of a collar, not even for a tyro. But Mr. Finkelman elevated me to the status of Sherlock Holmes and Batman combined. The next afternoon I gave him back what was left of the hundred dollars—a little over sixty dollars—along with an itemized account. He examined it carefully and counted the money. "If everything's O.K.," I told him, "I guess I'll be going."

"Just like that, eh?" said Mr. Finkelman. "For thirty-six dollars and change you work a miracle, and then you say, 'I guess I'll be going'?" He reached into the labyrinth of his suit coat and took out an envelope. "This is for you," he said. There were five one-hundred-dollar bills in it. "You are blushing," observed Mr. Finkelman.

And that, lieutenant, was possibly the last blush that young Joe Binney ever blushed. Mr. Finkelman joyously spread my fame. (I never asked what happened to Markewitch, the blond lady, or the Chrysler. Somehow, I never wanted to know.) And so tasks more complicated than bookkeeping came my way. Finally, I fell afoul of an N.Y.P.D. lieutenant detective who advised me severely and stringently that if I didn't want to join a gravel factory I had better get a license to practice my nefarious pursuits. So I sat for the P.I. ticket, and there were complications, but I got it. During the making of all this, of course, I forgot how to blush.

There is, by God, a light at the end of the tunnel. The traffic has speeded up and cars are zipping off to their Manhattan destinies. With a quick left turn on Second Avenue, I am entrained in the route to my happy home.

And now, as I wing down Second Avenue, I must consider your final demanding question: *Tell me, Binney; honest to Christ, can you think of a worse handicap for a man to have out in the street?*

I have thought it over very carefully, sir.

How about stupidity?

Chapter VI

Penton came into my office the next morning. "My secretary is making out the bill," I told him. "You can pick it up on the way out."

"Don't be like that," Penton said. It is one of the statements I hate most in all the world.

"I don't see where there's anything else I can do for you now," I said. "The whole project is immaterial. What's more, I don't think there's anything more I want to do for you. I don't like being shot down in front of the police."

He lounged against the chipped brown paint of the doorway. "I apologize for that." It wasn't so much an apology as a gift. "I was scared and I was upset. I thought I'd better tell the police the truth."

"But you didn't tell them the truth," I objected. "All you did was blow the cover story that we agreed on and substitute another lie."

"A half lie."

"But why not the truth? Why didn't you tell him I'd gone there to get evidence for a divorce? It makes more sense. He didn't believe you anyway with all that routine about getting a psychiatrist."

He came up to the desk and dropped into the chair next to it. "You're a merciless bastard," he said. "Can't you put yourself in my shoes? I came in to find that Iris was dead. Do you think I wanted to talk about getting a divorce just then? Or even admit it to myself? And there was more to it than I'd told you, too. I mean, I hoped I could get a divorce uncontested if you found dope in the house, but I have a pretty good idea that Iris was going out with some guy, too. I didn't want to start that kind of thing with her—looking through keyholes and getting dirty pictures. But I wanted out. All that doesn't mean that I didn't still love her."

"Really," I said.

"If I hated her I would have set up a divorce for adultery, and that would be that."

I leaned back and twiddled my thumbs. "Well, well," I said. "You've got boxes inside of boxes."

He smiled as if this had been a compliment. It was the kind of rueful, heavy-lidded smile that is supposed to make girls wet themselves with protective passion. Its effect on a man is the inspiration to hit him right between the eyes.

"I need you now more than ever," Penton said. "I was hoping that you wouldn't desert me. I promise that I'll stick to the rules from here on in. I swear it."

Like any other businessman's, my convictions are instantly for sale. I sat up in my chair and asked him, "What's the proposition?"

"Iris had more equity in Groupe than what shows up on

paper," said Penton. "She was bringing a band along that ought to make it big with their next record. It would mean real money for her boy."

I must have looked startled, or puzzled. Sometimes you can't be sure that what you read is what the man really said.

He dismissed the vast and vaporous sum with his hand. "I don't need the money," he said. "But her boy has got it coming to him, and he ought to get any money that develops out of her work."

I gave his face a pretty narrow examination. "After the kid tried to bomb you," I said, "I got the idea that perhaps you and he were not on the best of terms."

He was very good at dismissing things. "What can you expect of a boy in that situation? I got cast as the wicked stepfather. What the hell. I accepted it. I played the role without doing anybody any injury, I think. He was shocked when he saw that his mother was dead, and he took a swing at the nearest likely target. There's no mystery there."

"But there's a mystery in this stuff about the equity," I answered. "What am I supposed to do about it?"

"Wet your finger and put it up in the air," said Penton. "If I start asking questions down at the Groupe studio, they'll clam up and I'll find out exactly nothing. I'd like you to go down there on some pretext and find out what kind of an agreement she had. Hopefully, there's a piece of paper somewhere. If it's verbal and there's a witness, I can still rip a chunk of money out of them in court."

"For the boy," I said. He was as unguarded as a gibbon hanging from its favorite branch.

"Yes, of course," he said, giving free lessons in instant recovery.

He gave me a few details. The name of the outfit was the K.C. Sourballs. The studio was off Eighth Avenue in the Fifties. He left then, trailing clouds of Caswell and Massey. Something lovely had just passed by. Promise him anything, I mused, but give him a kick in the ass.

I called my secretary, Edna, into the office. I number

among the legion of high-living New York businessmen who have never been laid by their secretaries. Edna is twenty-four years old and what the columnist E. V. Durling used to call a green-eyed honey blonde. The mere fact that I can recall E.V. Durling puts me out of the league and settles me deep in the dirty-old-man category. She is also what he called a long-stemmed American beauty, and sometimes I get dizzy thinking about those long white legs.

I sat her in the big wood chair in front of my desk, where I could drink in the scenic grandeur. "Edna," I said, "take notes, because I'm going to ask questions after class."

She poised her pencil agreeably. "Millard Penton," I began, "contracted with this agency to locate evidence in his home that would facilitate a divorce from his wife, Iris Penton. He said that he was convinced that she was taking drugs, although he could not specify what kind, except that it was hard. His logic was that if a cache was discovered he could hold it over her and force her into an agreeable divorce settlement.

"His original request was that this agency, if it failed to discover a cache, should deposit a quantity of drugs in the household so that he, personally, could discover it and use it as an evidential threat against his wife. This agency declined to participate in a clearly illegal maneuver."

Edna interrupted—something I love because she always shifts her legs when she is troubled. "This is pretty hard-skulled stuff," said Edna. "Why all the square corners?"

"I may have to have it by heart," I told her, "if some wiseacre attorney has me up on the stand after all this explodes.

"This agency did agree to search for a drug cache in the home of Mr. and Mrs. Penton, but that is all it agreed to.

"Details of the discovery of Mrs. Penton's body have been filed with the police under the care of Lieutenant Probcziewski."

"Spelling," said Edna.

I spelled it for her and resumed: "A search of the house

by the police lieutenant failed to reveal any cache of drugs. However, when Mrs. Penton's son, Lawrence, entered, the boy became emotionally upset and a scuffle ensued. In restraining the boy, this agency noted that he had numerous needle tracks on his arm, which may be the result of a heroin addiction.

"Since Mrs. Penton revealed upon cursory examination seven needle tracks in her arm, all of which appeared to be very recent, the claim that she was an habitual user of heroin is unsupported, unless further examination reveals other sites of insertion. The alternative is that she was an habitual user of cocaine. Autopsy examination of nasal and nasopharyngeal tissue—"

"Spelling," said Edna.

I spelled out *nasopharyngeal,* commented on how pretty her kneecaps were, and continued. I happen to be a kneecap man—kneecaps are richly innervated, I think, anyway —"will indicate whether Mrs. Penton was habituated to cocaine."

"Think she was?" Edna asked me.

"No.

"In the event that she was not addicted to any hard drugs," I dictated, "we are left with the assumption that Mr. Penton hoped to discover the drug cache of her son and to use the threat of involving her son in a drug arrest to exact his terms for divorce."

"Bastard," said Edna.

"Subsequent conversations with Mr. Penton," I said, "indicate that he entertained a strong suspicion that his wife was having an affair. He expressed the desire to avoid the unsavory practices that revealing this side of her character would entail.

"Following his wife's death, Mr. Penton retained this agency to investigate her interests in the Groupe Record Company."

"The next morning, in fact," said Edna. "Why don't you put that in?"

If they weren't richly innervated, why would they hurt so

much when you bang them? "Have you ever accidentally banged yourself on the kneecap?" I asked Edna.

"What's that got to do with it?"

"Answer the question."

"Yes."

"The result?"

"It hurt like hell."

I smiled a good old seraphic smile. One of these days I would begin by ever so absentmindedly stroking her kneecap. What girl could possibly object to having her kneecap stroked? Irreversible excitation would occur, and before you could say antidisestablishmentarianism, she would become a throbbing vassal to my desires.

"What's kneecaps got to do with Mrs. Penton?" demanded Edna.

"It's a theory I'm working on," I lied. "I'll let you know when I have something substantial."

"I'll bet."

"That's all for the record," I announced. "Put the notebook away, but type it up later and file it. Now, my girl, I want you to apply your pretty head to a problem. How in hell is a deaf man going to find a pretext for asking questions in a recording studio?"

While she considered the question, I considered her. I thought of all the poetry I could recite to her—*If you can keep your head when all about you*—stuff like that, but I didn't know how it would sound. No—poetry was no good. And I also knew that whatever golden phrases I summoned up in my head, it would all add up to just one thing—coming out in a croak—

"Howsaboutit, baby?"

No. It was hopeless.

I decided to devote my weekend to a less difficult problem: finding a logical reason for a deaf man to visit a recording studio.

Chapter VII

Edna's kneecaps were terribly important. They circled in front of me, the size of Rolls-Royce headlights, whirling in concentric circles and shining into my brain. Interspersed with them was another globe, a beautiful white face with brilliant eyes. The lips were parted wide as if in a cry, and long black hair streamed out behind it as a comet's tail. The unbearable circles slowed and grew closer, merging at last into one single blinding light. My machinery roared like an inferno.

Something dark exploded against my mouth, and my head slammed back against a wall. The light divided and began to whirl in separate circles again. I felt sick. I was beginning to swallow blood, which meant that I would vomit soon.

Speaking made me gag. I said, "Turn the light off. I can't hear anything. I'm deaf. Turn the light off so I can see what you're saying."

Somebody turned the floodlight toward the ceiling, and the room was suddenly shot with distorted shadows. There were three men in front of me; I didn't know any of them.

The center was a well-dressed man, a gleaming opal on his hairy finger. The nails were lacquered; opal links gleamed at his cuffs. The suit was good, gray-blue, chalk stripe, double-breasted. Above it was a strong, dark face with Latin America written on every hair of its mustache. He bent over me and his lips writhed in elaboration.

"Do you understand what I'm saying?"

I nodded, and the ring arced up to chip one of my front teeth. The back of my head hit the wall again, and the lights went into their dance. I puked on his shoes.

It had quite an effect on him, apparently. He began hopping around the room, waving his arms in the air and stamping his shoes on the floor in the burlesque of a flamenco. It was probably funny, but I wasn't laughing. The two apes were petrified.

Ape Left was blond, and Ape Right was dark. Aside from that I couldn't make much distinction. Both were dressed in work clothes and had the look of longshoremen or truckers who work off the docks. They were staring at their hopping chief with their mouths open, and I could see their pink tongues and bad stumpy teeth. After they tired of watching him prance around, they turned to stare at me. There was something like awe in their faces.

Our local emissary of the Pan American Goodwill Policy pointed at Ape Left and barked out something at him. Ape Left—all right, I'll call him Leftie—shambled back into the deep reaches of the room. As I watched him roll out of the light, I began to get some idea of the size and shape of the place. It was a loft. The walls were cinder block, and the room was so long that the light died before I could see the end of it. There didn't seem to be anything in the room except us, a small bare table with two chairs behind the floodlamp, and the chair I sat in. On the table was an object that looked like an old-fashioned coffee grinder, but as my eyes adjusted, I recognized it for an army field telephone. I wondered stupidly what it was there for—no telephone service up here, probably.

Leftie emerged from the darkness carrying an old towel. Mr. Latin America was staring at me, his eyes glittering and his chest heaving—from passion or exercise, I know not which. Without looking at Leftie, he put his shoe up on the chair next to the table. Leftie, with solemn diligence, bent over the shoe and began to clean it, working the towel into the crease between the sole and the last. Good boy, Leftie.

40

Something the well-dressed man spat out animated Rightie, who took a small double-edged switchblade out of his pants pocket and ambled over toward me. He pressed the flat blade against my cheek, and I concentrated.

I didn't know if it would work, but it was all I had. My hands were manacled behind me to the chair. The chain of the leg irons was twined around a rung of the chair, so that my feet were pulled back and put me off balance. I concentrated on my blood and all my blood vessels. I saw my heart and tried to slow it down—it had been racing and gasping. I saw the whole network of my vessels and I tried to squeeze them shut so no blood could get out. I concentrated on keeping all the blood in my body because I didn't want to bleed to death when he started cutting—not if I could help it.

It was a very good little knife. It went through my leather belt as if it were butter. It whisked the tie out from under my collar, and I hardly felt it. It went through the seams of my suit coat that fell off me in the same pattern the tailor had stitched it together with. I was denuded of my shirt. My pants were cut along the seams and lifted off me. My shorts went in just two swift slashes. Not a drop of blood had been spilled. The knife had not touched my skin.

I was shaking uncontrollably, and my heart, which I had lost sight of early, was racing helplessly. The man with the opals pulled a chair up in front of me and took my jaw in his hand. "Do you understand what I am saying?" he repeated.

"Yes," I answered. The hell with the blood. I was trying to hold myself together, to keep myself in me. They were very bright. They had, slit by slit, unmanned me. I tried to focus on this and build my rage.

"What were you looking for in the studio?"

"I was trying to find out how much it would cost for my son . . ."

He cuffed me very gently alongside the jaw, almost a fatherly gesture. "I am going to talk to you," he said. "Experience teaches us that we should not deprive the

41

interrogatee of hope, but I am not going to bribe you with hope. You have no hope. You have nothing, not even your clothes, not even your manhood. Even your information is not important. It is nothing."

"You're doing this just for laughs?"

"Partly—also partly for research, and again partly for the information. Now, your story at the studio was that your son wanted to make a record with his electric guitar and that you wanted to talk to someone about how much it would cost and so forth. Is that right?"

"It's the truth," I said, aggrieved.

He laughed. He had splendid teeth. "You do not have a son, Mr. Binney, at least not a legitimate one that you have ever seen. There's an important opportunity missed, because now we can all be sure that you're never going to have one. You came to the studio for some other kind of information, and now you're going to tell us what it is."

"Give me a cigarette."

He put a gold-tipped black Sobranie between my lips and lighted it with a gold-encased flame from Cartier's. "We have all stumbled into the wrong bag," I said. "Let me talk. You'll get all the information I've got. You could have bought it for the price of a drink, instead of going through all this mumbo jumbo."

His black eyes narrowed. He wasn't liking it. The simian component stirred uneasily. "As you know, I'm a private investigator. I was retained by Millard Penton to look over his deceased wife's holdings at Groupe records to make sure that the estate would include everything he was entitled to. The reason for my cover was just that I wanted to look around without anyone being on guard. That's all, and that's all there is."

"What kind of assets did Mr. Penton think she might have?"

"There were some new performers she developed and was bringing along, a band called the K.C. Sourballs . . ."

42

"Apparently you take me for an idiot, Mr. Binney."

"No," I protested. "That is the truth, the whole truth. Look, I don't owe Penton a Goddamned thing. You've made a mistake . . ."

"You've made a mistake, Mr. Binney, not me. A very serious error. Tell me, have you ever used a telephone?"

The relief broke out on me in a cascade of perspiration. I even smiled around the gold tip of the cigarette that had got stuck to the blood on my lip. "If you're thinking about anything you heard on a tap, forget it," I said. "I couldn't have been involved. I don't use the phone. I'm deaf." And I almost added, *thank God.*

"You misunderstand," he said. "It's a little joke I make. But I had forgotten that you're deaf, you carry it off so well. The joke goes: 'Do you ever use the telephone?' The proper answer is 'Yes.' Well, then I say, 'Perhaps you won't mind if the telephone uses you.' What do you think of that?"

The corners of his mouth went back and his eyes crinkled. He was laughing heartily. I was not.

"We are going to get a much better story out of you with the aid of this field telephone—an ingenious method of communication, don't you think? We have only to turn the crank, and instantly there is communication."

"I don't know anything!" I shrieked as loud as I knew how. We might as well all have been deaf.

How much memory of what one said is the memory of one's own voice? I remember what my voice used to sound like, before the wound, but now I do not, and so I cannot hear myself as I must have sounded shrieking, babbling, pleading, praying. Perhaps it is just as well. The apes forced me back in the chair and attached one wire between my legs and another to a nipple. Leftie turned the crank at signals from the well-dressed man, who watched me with great intensity. I thought that my spine would fracture itself through spasm after spasm. All bodily functions opened up, including the last reaction of the hanged. I choked on my own sobs. Time was a free fall.

43

It stopped at last. When my eyes could finally focus on his face, his eyes were very bright and his breath was coming very rapidly, although he had not exerted himself that I knew of. He took me by the hair and held my head back. "You have nothing more you wish to say before we begin again?" He was sober, puzzled.

"I don't know anything more."

He dropped my head and gestured to Rightie, who jerked the wires off me.

"I'm sure you must be in great pain," he said. "But we are going to do something about that." He reached into his breast pocket and removed two ampules, which he held under my face.

"One of these ampules is pentobarbital," he said. "We are going to give you an injection. It will stop the pain, and it will be the last sensation you will ever feel. It is to keep you quiet and inert. The second ampule is a rather crude suspension of strychnine. It is just to make sure you stay dead. You will be removed from here and thrown in a suitable place, naked as you are. Perhaps the rats will find you interesting."

I was trying to tear the chair apart when the needle went into my shoulder. After a while things dimmed, and I felt the manacles being loosened. I was on the edge of blackness. It was not the last sensation, however. Just before I dropped off, I felt the second needle go in.

Chapter VIII

Sometimes I wonder if dead men dream.

I have two visions of myself: one, drifting in the mouth of

the Yalu toward the Yellow Sea off Sinuiju, my mask filled with blood, my wet suit imitating flotsam; and the second, myself, as if seen in the wrong end of a telescope at the bottom of a freight elevator shaft, naked and filthy, and the curious rats coming out.

You cannot see yourself when you are dead, and, of course, I know the trick from childhood. You are told, and in the telling it all takes image and you become the teller, and you see yourself—sometimes dead.

In the Yellow Sea, it was a fisherman who found me. In the shaft, a janitor. That's all right. He was supposed to find me. Only I was supposed to be dead.

The first thing I saw when I awoke was this gleaming washtub next to me. I was connected to it by a tube in my forearm, and there was blood running through the tube. My blood.

The doctor looked like a pirate—an old pirate. He had a patch over one eye, and his white hair stuck out over the black elastic. The lens of the glass on his other eye was as thick as a Polish ham. He was laughing and shaking his head.

"You can see me all right, hey, sonny?" he asked.

I nodded my head in agreement and felt as if I had been clubbed.

"Don't move around any," he said. "It'll hurt like hell."

I tried to smile.

"I suppose you think you're pretty Goddamned smart," he said. "How'd you get all that crap in your system?"

"Some people stuck me with needles," I said.

"Stupid bastards," said the doctor. "Morons."

I was very glad that he hadn't been a friend of Mr. Latin America.

"That thing you're hooked up to is an artificial kidney," he said. "Hemodialysis. Takes all the crap out of your bloodstream. Pretty good." He gave the tub a rap with his knuckles. "It's all done with cellophane. What do you think of that?"

I tried to smile again.

45

"I'll bet you thought you were a goner, hey?" he asked me.

I remembered not to nod. "Yes," I said.

"They shot you full of barbital, right?"

"Yes."

"And then they hit you with a whole barrel of strychnine, right?"

"Right."

"How do you know that?"

"They told me what they were doing, just to make sure I'd enjoy it."

"Stupid bastards, morons." His face was grave and the good eye flashed behind the lens. He called them a lot of other things that don't need recording and wouldn't add anything to the literature of medicine.

"It's a shame you didn't know about it while it was happening," he said. "You could have been a lot more comfortable."

"Know what?"

"Strychnine and pentobarbital are antidotes for each other. They balance each other out. Not too many people know that."

I started to cry. The doctor came over with a tissue and blotted my eyes.

"You're a good man," he said. "I can tell. You've been through a lot, but you're going to be all right. There's something I've got to tell you, though."

"What?"

"Better than having you find out accidentally. You're going to have a pretty bad scar. The rats gnawed away on your cheek some. We did the best we could."

I became aware of the bandage on the right side of my face. He didn't have to tell me any more, and he didn't.

"I wasn't winning any beauty contests anyway," I said.

"Don't get depressed," said the doctor. "I won't put up with that kind of crap. You get depressed around here, and I'll kick your ass out in the street."

46

"I'll be good," I promised. "Let me stick around for a while."

"Okay." He paused, as if in deep thought. "What's your name, anyway?"

"Joe Binney."

"Good."

"What's good about it?"

"I don't have an amnesia case on my hands. That's what's good about it."

"Were you asking just for diagnosis, or didn't you know, really?"

"Well, your name isn't tattooed on your butt, and you were as naked as a jaybird when they brought you in."

"Does anybody know I'm here?"

"The police know that somebody was brought in, of course. The ambulance brought you here."

I was trying to make my head work, but nothing came of it.

"How come your ears got blown out that way?" said the pirate.

"Korea," I told him. "Underwater demolition. I put a charge on the shaft of a North Korean gunboat, but the charge went off before I did."

"Lucky you're alive," the pirate observed.

"Lucky Joe Binney."

"You got any noise?"

"Machinery."

"Whole factory full?"

"Yes—the Ford plant."

"Nothing can be done about that."

"Congratulations on being the thirty-ninth doctor to tell me."

"I meant no harm," he apologized.

"Neither did I." I looked at the tube that made me Siamese twin to a washtub. "How long am I supposed to stay hooked up to this thing?"

"A couple more hours ought to do it."

"Do me a favor," I asked him. "Don't tell anybody my name except Lieutenant Probcziewski out on Long Island." I racked my brains. "Five-one-six—five-three-five—two-nine-one-nine. Get hold of him and tell him the story, but stall off everybody else. It's important."

"Probcziewski, eh?" He whipped out a prescription blank and a little gold pen. "How do you spell that?"

"Oh, Jesus Christ," I said, and passed out.

The first thing I saw when I came to was Probcziewski's lugubrious mug above me. The tubes had been taken out of my arm. I felt as if I had had a long night's sleep.

"What's new?" said Probcziewski.

"Plenty," I answered. "Does anybody else know I'm here?"

"They know somebody's here," he said. "You mean by name? I don't think so."

"They think I'm dead," I said. "I wouldn't want them to know any different."

"Who thinks you're dead?"

"A big Latin American guy, and a couple of orang-outans that look like they come off the docks."

"They pitch you down the well?"

"They must have taken me down to the basement and just dumped me in the bottom. Otherwise I'd be in a body cast, if I was here at all. I'd say it was the orang-outans that threw me down. Mr. South America would have gotten bored with details. He's the engineer, though."

I pushed myself upright in bed. Probcziewski moved the pillow. "You didn't have to do that," the doctor complained, moving in from the corner. I hadn't been aware of him before he moved. "We'll crank up the bed."

"I'm all right," I said. "Can I have a cigarette?"

He nodded, and Probcziewski gave me a Lucky Strike. The doctor felt my skull to see if it was on fire. "Don't knock yourself out, now," he admonished me. "I'll be back in a little while."

"Maybe it was a lousy act," I said to Probcziewski. "Penton asked me to go down to the studio and look around, to get some idea of where his dead wife's properties were headed and what they were worth. I gave the people down there a routine about being an indulgent papa who wanted to pay for his kid making a record. It seemed harmless enough. On my way out, I was passing an alleyway between the buildings. Some guy bumped me from behind. I never even saw him. I fell toward the space in the buildings and got sapped. It was a simple mugging."

"City streets aren't safe for God-fearing people," Probcziewski maintained.

"That's right." I drew thoughtfully on my cigarette. "When I came to, there were these two apes and the big well-dressed South American. We were in a big loft somewhere—I don't know where. They started asking me a lot of silly questions and played tunes on me with an army field telephone."

"I know the rest," he intervened gently. "The doctor told me."

"If they find out I'm alive, they'll try to do one of two things," I told him. "Either they'll skip, or they'll try to kill me here. The big South American is somebody important—you could smell it all over him. He wouldn't be able to risk my tabbing him."

"A businessman?"

"No," I answered. "Army or diplomatic service—probably both. The field telephone points toward that. Everybody knows about the Goddamned things, but only somebody experienced with it would bother to go out and buy one out of surplus up here. If you put him in diplomacy, smuggling is what follows. If it's smuggling from South America, it's gold, guns, or cocaine."

"Gold or cocaine," reasoned Probcziewski. "I can't see running guns out of a recording studio. What was the place like, anyway?"

49

"The studio? Nothing remarkable. It all looked very legitimate. There were a lot of people moving around in far-out clothes and long hair and beards, but they all had very sharp eyes and a very brisk businesslike air to them. I wound up talking to some guy named Parti, Ed Parti, who was the studio director or whatever they have."

"Would we know of him?"

"I can't see why, unless he was in a drug bust somewhere. He was just a young businessman with long hair and funny clothes. I think the outfit goes with the job.

"Anyway, he seemed to think that everything I was saying sounded reasonable. Meanwhile, I was looking around for signs of the K.C. Sourballs."

"Would you have been able to recognize them? I can't tell those freaks apart."

"No, not the actual group. But Penton had the idea that the band was getting hot and was in line for a big promotional campaign. I was looking for some signs of it, you know? Posters, tear sheets from ads, maybe some correspondence I could glom onto. There was nothing like that lying around that I could see. Finally, I told Parti that my fictional son was a great fan of the K.C. Sourballs. He gave me a funny look, but I couldn't read anything in it."

"Maybe that was your miscue," said Probcziewski, "and if it was, then Parti is involved."

"Not necessarily," I objected. "He may simply have smelled a rat, or thought I was putting him on, and mentioned it to somebody else. I might not have been too convincing."

"That would mean you're not very good at your job."

"I wouldn't want to think that," I admitted, "but it was an odd feeling, talking to this guy about a boy I was supposed to have. I've never had a kid, that I know of. I was being the concerned parent trying to help Sonny get a start in life—a complete chump, in other words. I tried to figure out what kind of a kid would be involved in a setup like that, and every way I turned him he came out being a regular no-talent little prick."

"You'd have made a wonderful father," Probcziewski observed. "In my opinion, your unborn child is very lucky to stay unborn."

The metaphysics were beginning to tire my head. "Screw him," I said. "It wasn't my idea in the first place. It was Edna's, my secretary. Great legs but no brains. I jumped at it because the whole thing seemed harmless. Who's looking to get mugged at a recording studio? Who's looking for left-handed diplomats with field telephones at a joint like that?"

"Not you, certainly."

He shuffled undecidedly and gave me a deeply questioning stare. "When the doctor called the station," he began slowly, "he insisted that I was the only policeman who could help. How come?"

"How do I know if anyone got to the cops around here?" I answered. "It happens. There was money dripping all over that guy. You're the only cop I know right now that I can trust."

He didn't like the implication, but I saw him accept it. "Trust—no trust," he said. "Why should I help a private dick?"

I didn't really know what to say. I just looked at him over my bandage.

"Well," he ruminated, "I will admit that you're the sorriest looking son of a bitch I've seen this side of the Bowery. You promise to give me everything you get on the Penton outfit?"

"And more," I promised, "much, much more."

A gray-haired nurse came into the room. "Time for your medicine, Mr. Binney," she said. Probcziewski and I both froze.

"Where did you get my name?"

"Why"—she was a little flustered at the severity of it all— "I heard you tell Dr. Salt when he was talking to you. I don't think you even knew I was in the room. I wrote it down on your records."

"Billy Bones has let us down," I said to Probcziewski. "I've got to get the hell out of here."

The nurse's face spread with amusement. "I'm afraid you won't be leaving us for a little while yet," she said.

"In a pig's ear," I replied in deference to her sex. "Get me my clothes."

That, too, caused her to titter. "Don't you remember?" she asked. "You came in here as naked as the day you were born."

I began to curse and her amusement vanished. She turned very white and then very red. "Take your medicine," she snapped.

I knocked the potion out of her hand. "Get away from me," I said. "And don't bring any of that crap around me again. For all I know, somebody could have pulled a switch.

"If you really mean to help me," I said to Probcziewski with as much appeal as I could muster, "this is your moment."

He pursed his lips in decision, committed himself, and gave her a look at the tin. It was all pretty fast because he was out of his territory. His back was turned to me then, and I couldn't see what he was saying, but I watched the nurse's mouth tighten. Finally she glared at me and spat out, "He belongs in the psychiatric ward."

Well, maybe I did. I said to Probcziewski, "Throw that old bag out of here and do something fast."

The nurse left in a flurry of starch, and Probcziewski reached for the telephone. After he dialed, he said, "Send the meat wagon over to St. Andrew's. We've got a stiff going out to the Island."

He slammed down the receiver and lifted it instantly. "Get me Dr. Salt," he said.

But Salt was already on deck. He came in at a dead run, saying, *"What the hell is going on here?"* Then he wheeled on me and fixed me with that one good eye. "I know you've got troubles, Binney," he said, "but you wise off at my nurse again and you're going to be a hell of a lot sicker."

52

"Your nurse spilled the beans," I told him. "If I stay here I'll spoil your record."

"It wasn't her fault," he snapped.

"When I'm dead, I won't care whose fault it is," I said. "The guys who are looking for my name are very bad medicine."

The lieutenant took Billy Bones by the arm, and again, because his back was to me, I couldn't see what Probcziewski was saying, although it certainly looked urgent. The old man's lower lip went out in anger, and he shook his head, saying, "No, sir! Not on my service, you don't!"

But Probcziewski kept hammering away at him, and finally the pirate threw his hands in the air and said, "All right, all right. But Goddamn it, I don't ever want to see you two performers back in this hospital."

Probcziewski wheeled around and crooked an index finger at me. "Bang," he said. "You're dead."

"How so?" I asked him.

"Just lie back and dummy up," he answered. "Play dead; lie still and keep your mouth shut if you want to get out of here."

I slid down in the bed and narrowed my eyelids to slits. The nurse came in carrying a hundred and eighty-five pounds of vindication.

Billy Bones picked up the chart at the foot of the bed and scrawled something across it. "I'm afraid we've lost him, Miss Brody," he said, staring fixedly into one of her eyes. Her jaw dropped and I could see the upper plate flutter. "I guess the excitement around here has been too much for him, poor thing," the old man added with a wicked grin.

He came over to the bed and, with what I thought was indecent satisfaction, drew the sheet over my face. I didn't like the sensation, although I suppose a stiff wouldn't mind.

I didn't like it at all after that; the ghostly light filtering through the sheet was broken by incomprehensible shadows as I was lifted onto a trolley—very roughly, I thought—and

53

rolled to an elevator, which I could distinguish only by the sensation of falling into space. Then there was a draft and a steady chill; I presumed that we were waiting at the loading dock behind the hospital from which all the bad guesses are launched.

The trolley was rolled down a ramp, and I was slid onto another conveyance. All was very dark, now. The conveyance jerked forward with the unmistakable impulse of a motor vehicle being driven by a clown.

It remained dark. I dared not move. With all the stopping and starting as the vehicle apparently made its way through the city, I fell at last asleep.

Waking up was not too happy an occasion. The light filtering through the sheet over my face was the color of dead men's skin. Coming in with the light was an odor I'd smelled only once before, in a sanatorium for alcoholics—as a visitor, not a patient—and reluctantly I identified it as formaldehyde.

Obviously I was no longer in the meat wagon; but if not there, where? Was I still supposed to be playing dead? Absence of a breeze told me I must be inside a room, although the room was cold and clammy. The light, I judged, must be coming from a powerful overhead lamp. I became very conscious of my body, since I dared not move it—of how my arms lay, palms upward at my sides, how heavy my inert legs had become, pressing into the table I was lying on, the uncomfortable tingling of my cheek from the pressure of lying too long on one side of my face.

The simple progress of unmeasured time was becoming agonizing. My machinery was no help. It clattered and clanged obstreperously, but there was no beat to it at all to mark the seconds going by—and the seconds stretched out longer and longer. I felt someone's belly press against my arm and held my breath. The sheet was moved back from my head and I was staring into the filmy eyes of a very dead bald man on the table next to me.

A large hand gripped my jaw and turned my head so that

54

I was staring upward into another face—a live one, this time—a familiar one, in fact.

"Very natural," said Probcziewski.

Chapter IX

I sat up and asked, "Where the hell am I? Who's that geek on the slab?"

"Another satisfied customer of O'Malley's Funeral Emporium," said Probcziewski. "A very generous guy, in fact, who's going to lend you the suit he died in so you can get the hell out of here."

"A dead man's suit?" I objected. "I don't like it."

"You don't have to like it for long," he told me, "but you can't go running bare-assed all over Long Island."

"So that's where we are." I swung my legs off the trolley and stood up—glad, very glad, to be upright again. I stretched my legs around the layout, and the open-backed hospital garment gave me the feeling that somebody was just behind me. "What have you got picked out for me to hole up in?" I asked Probcziewski. "A graveyard?"

"There's a small motel, as a matter of fact," said the lieutenant, "that just happens to owe me a couple of favors."

"Operation sitting duck," I said bitterly. "People who owe favors to the police are usually crooks."

"We're all out of ivory towers."

The man who came into the room then had to be O'Malley, the proprietor, chief stiff shuffler, and graveside philosopher. He had a red moon face enlivened by a prosperous smile. He was the first person I ever saw making legitimate use of undertakers' gloves, and he drew them on as he approached the bald stiff on the slab.

I looked from O'Malley to the cadaver, who was wearing only a white sheet, in his restricted way. "Has he got the suit on under the sheet?" I demanded.

"Heavens, no," laughed Mr. O'Malley. "Mr. Croatalis has already been prepared for the viewing, and now we're just going to pop him into something a little more presentable."

"And permanent," added Probcziewski.

"So where's my suit?" I turned away as O'Malley began his professional fitting for the corpse.

"Keep your voice down," Probcziewski scowled at me. "The guy's wife is in the viewing room, just the other side of those drapes. The suit's being—uh, cleaned up a little."

"Great!" I said. "What did the guy die of, leprosy?" I glared at O'Malley, who was doing something nauseating with the arms.

"You've got to look reasonable when you get to the motel," the lieutenant explained. "We don't want you to draw a crowd. You're registering under the name of Simpson, George C. Simpson. I've got a car out of the pound, but it's got to go right back after you get there. Leave the keys up over the visor when you arrive, and I'll have somebody pick it up. I don't want to explain the car to anybody unless I have to. I want you to drive to the Soundsurf Motel." He jotted something on the back of a card. "Here's the address."

I took the card. It had a little map on the back with an X. It also had a New York City telephone number scrawled on it. "This isn't a Long Island number," I complained. "What's the idea?"

"That's the number you're going to call at exactly ten-fifteen tomorrow morning from the motel room."

I was outraged. "I don't make phone calls, you stupid bastard. Have you forgotten I'm deaf?"

"I haven't forgotten—and I won't forget what you called

56

me, either," said Probcziewski. "You will dial this number—
it's the number of a pay phone—and you will wait for twenty
seconds. Then you can start to talk."

"And what am I supposed to say?"

"How should I know?" asked the lieutenant. "You ought
to have something to say. Your secretary, Edna, is going to be
on the other end. We don't want any tapped conversations, do
we?"

I grinned at the tall detective. "I apologize, Einstein," I
said.

O'Malley had finished hooking the stiff into the old
slumber suit. His apprentice, or intern, or whatever they call
undertakers' assistants, came into the room with some clothes
draped over his arm. Wordlessly, he handed me the outfit, and
then he and his boss moved Mr. Croatalis into the casket. I
stared, perhaps tastelessly. I'd never seen it done before. They
wheeled the whole works out of the joint—presumably into
the viewing room, where others could gawk at the finished
product.

I became conscious of the wardrobe over my arm. The
suit was chalk white—of some artificial cloth with polyester in
it somewhere.

"A white suit," I said to Probcziewski. "Has anybody
bothered to paint a bull's-eye on the back?"

It had been so drenched in cleaning fluid that the smell of
the stuff overcame the atmospheric formaldehyde. I looked at
it and sighed. There was still a faint trace of blood—a
brownish sheen—on the lapels.

"How *did* he die?" I asked the nice policeman.

"Hemorrhage—internal, mostly. No trauma."

"O.K." The other stuff got to me, though. The ice-blue
shirt was tolerable, but the underwear, the socks, and the
shoes were a little more than I could be comfortable with. "I
can't swing it with the underwear or socks," I said. I had
recognized the inevitable with the shoes. I was reduced to
hoping that they'd be a reasonable fit.

I put the clammy pants on over my naked skin—
something I hadn't done since my pals hid my underwear at
the municipal pool when I was a kid. He must have been a big
bastard, all right. I hadn't noticed it in him lying down and
still. "Have you got a cord or something I can hold these jeans
up with?" I asked the detective. He found a roll of gauze and
peeled off a yard or so. I rolled up the cuffs of the pants and
tucked in the blue shirt. Then I had to roll up the cuffs, French
cuffs, of the shirt sleeves. The shoulders of the coat hung
down on me—who remembers the zoot suit anymore? That's
what it looked like. The shoes, black and white—I hear
they're coming back in style, but these must have been about
twenty-five years old—and big enough for me to take several
steps before I got any forward motion out of them.

Probcziewski observed me. "You're missing the final
touch," he said, and tossed me a Panama. I don't think that
anything like it had been seen on the streets in thirty years. I
put it on and managed to tilt it so that I could still see out from
under the brim.

The lieutenant drank in the full effect. He began by
looking very serious and critical. I stared back with all the
hostility I could muster, which was considerable.

"I'm trying to place you," he said, trying to keep the
smile out of his face. I glared back. "I know." He snapped his
fingers. "The sidekick in *The Maltese Falcon,* the faggot. What
was his name? They called him the gunsel."

"As big as you are, Probcziewski, and as sick as I am," I
began.

"Elisha Cook Junior!" He began to laugh; it almost
doubled him up. I took a step toward him, and the hat got
untilted so I couldn't see. I tore the hat off my head and threw
it on the deck. "I'm going—I'm going," said Probcziewski. He
held out one hand to fend me off and held his kidney with the
other. "I'm going to bring the car around for you. Take it
easy—take it easy . . ." And he backed out of the room
laughing himself sick—the son of a bitch. I put the hat back on
regretfully.

58

But I didn't like it so well alone in the room with my dead man's clothes either, and I was hoping that it wouldn't take the detective all night to roust the car. I looked at the uncompromising furniture and equipment—tubes, hoses, flasks and whatnot, each piece labeled *inevitable*. The chill went right into the marrow of my bones. Silence is one thing—something I'm used to—but stillness is another, the utter absence of movement anywhere. The room was still, patient, watching.

But something moved! The white curtain screening the drapes at the far end bulged slightly, and my heart began hammering. I told myself that it was no more than the stirring of air, although I hadn't *felt* any stirring. I moved very carefully toward the hangings and found the overlapping section, which I very slowly and cautiously pulled back.

The white curtains covered another set of heavy purple velvet draperies. I ran my hand very lightly along them until I came to an opening, and this, too, I parted very slowly, giving myself only a peephole.

Well, nerves are nerves, and only idiots pretend they've never been scared. There was no big mystery. The purple drapes merely screened off the viewing room, and yet gave O'Malley and his band of merry men the chance to look in if they thought that everything wasn't kosher.

From what I could see in the mirror on the opposite wall, Mr. Croatalis was laid out peaceably enough. They'd given him a sort of self-satisfied expression, as if he'd accomplished something. The woman who was looking at him I presumed to be Mrs. Croatalis. She appeared to be a fun-time blonde who was going to pot a lot earlier than she would want to. The fur chubby she wore gave an unfortunate accent to her belly, furthered by the tiny black hat stuck square on top of her fuzzy blond head. Her eyes were bright blue and glittered like marbles in her white pudgy face. Her lipstick was little more than a slash of red.

She was staring down at him, her feet apart and her hands on her hips. She might have been speaking under her breath, or just mouthing the words; I couldn't tell because her neck was too flabby for me to see any movement in it. Anyway, she spoke, and in deadly earnestness, she said:

"I'm glad you're dead, you bald-headed old bastard."

It was my moment to get out of there. I bit down on my lower lip and began turning away. But I'd forgotten about the gunboats I was wearing, and to save myself from falling over those oversized shoes, I had to grab onto the edge of the drapes.

It took her a few seconds to drink it in—the white suit and the Panama hat in the shadow of the draperies. The blue eyes popped right out of the old sockets. The pudgy face opened like Vesuvius, and this time I was sure that a little noise was forthcoming because her neck had swelled up like a balloon. I was riveted. The scream must have gone on for fifteen seconds. The blue eyes rolled up into her head and she hit the carpet.

Probcziewski came steaming in like he was on fire. "What the hell is going on?" he wanted to know.

I grabbed his arm. "Let's get the hell out of here," I said.

Chapter X

Welcome to Formica Land! It greeted me when I awoke and cautiously opened my eyes in response to my psychic alarm clock, the one I set every night for lack of an audible alarm. The cheap dazzle of the Soundsurf's furnishings brought back all the unreality of the last two days. Wood-grained Formica (burnproof, alcoholproof, and, no doubt, humanproof) covered the room as if it had been sprayed on by a drunken mechanic. The cold phlegmatic eye of the dead TV watched me sit up and stir around in bed. The white suit, with its light ocher sheen on the lapel, lay on the floor next to the bed—a nail from which to hang my memory. I wondered where I could burn it.

The room had the synthetic chill of air conditioning run mad, and though I was mother-naked, I refused to put on that suit once more. I wrapped the blanket around me and went to the window to turn off the machine. The gray mass of Long Island Sound, devoid of any life at all, glanced back at me through the plastic draperies. The rooms, I had noticed when I checked in, had been given names to personalize them. There were the Surf 'n Sun room, the Hilo Hattie, the Beachcomber, etc. I presumed that they had named this one the Suicide Suite.

The little alarm clock in my brain had buzzed off right on the money. It was nine-forty-five A.M., giving me a half hour to decide what I was going to tell Edna during our appointed one-way, one-shot phone call. I desperately wanted a pot of black coffee, but I solemnly bit back the desire and lighted a cigarette instead. I had decided the previous night that this was going to be a day for waiting. The DO NOT DISTURB sign hung from the outside doorknob; it marked a day of austerity and patience. The blanket, wrapped around me like a cere-monial robe, made me feel grave, wise, and magisterial. I needed only a couple of feathers sticking out of my crown and I would have been as sharp as Crazy Horse. It was his talent for tactics I needed now.

It took me nearly the full half hour, sitting at the Formica-covered kneehole-desk arrangement. The corner of the kneehole, incidentally, put a six-inch-long gash in the side of my leg. But finally, after many adjustments of the robe, I managed to cover all the necessary ground I had to impart to Edna. I checked my watch—nothing so fancy as Pro-bcziewski's Rolex, but, God help me, a thick turnip I'd bought

61

in a drugstore out of the store of funds the good lieutenant had loaned me. The turnip told me that now was the magic moment. Edna, presumably, was standing inside a telephone booth whose number was on a card I held in my hand.

My bedside phone held all the previous chill of the room, a dead piece of metal fitted up against my cheek. I put Probcziewski's card in front of me and dialed very carefully. This was not the time for second guesses. After I finished dialing, I counted to twenty, although I remembered to breathe heavily so that she would know I was on the line if she had snatched up the receiver. I began:

"Edna—just listen. As you know, I can't hear you. As a matter of fact, I don't even know if you're there. But if whoever is listening happens to be some bum robbing the paybox, I'll find him someday and cripple him.

"First of all, before coming to see me, go and see Probcziewski at the station. If he's not there, wait for him. If he's gone home, get one of the sidekicks to locate him. Above all, do not come directly to this place by yourself. Get here only with Probcziewski's help, and he'll make sure that nobody's tailing you.

"Next, I need clothes—including shoes—everything. Do not go to my apartment to get my clothes! Do you understand? Do not go to my apartment for anything. Stay away from my apartment. Go to Manny Performer's Clothing for Gents on Fourteenth Street between Seventh and Eighth on the north side of the street. Tell Manny I need a complete new outfit, including two suits, are you writing this down? Write it all down. Half a dozen shirts, two pairs of shoes, underwear, socks, toilet kit—everything from the ground up. Now, there isn't an item in Manny's shop that isn't hotter than a firecracker. He'll probably give it to you right off the truck. But he knows my sizes and he'll fill the order in two minutes flat. Tell him to put the whole lashup into a metal footlocker. Tell him to get a trustworthy cab, take the footlocker and you out the back into Fifteenth Street, and then you take the cab

62

directly to Probcziewski. If you haven't got enough money, go cash a check—maybe you'd better anyway. You won't have to pay Manny for anything. He knows I'm good.

"Now, get this very straight because it's very important. While Manny's filling the order, you tell him that I'm at a party with thirty-eight policemen and fifty of their friends, and that I'm enjoying the action. You got that? Thirty-eight policemen and fifty of their friends and I'm enjoying the action. Also tell him I said to keep his mouth shut. Also tell him to send me a performer's kit. You got that? A performer's kit.

"Don't be in too much of a hurry to get here. Don't worry about me. I'm fine and I'm safe as long as nobody slips up. If anything looks dangerous or hairy to you, just drop the whole show. Go directly to the police station. Stay there until you get in touch with Probcziewski. He'll take care of it. Keep your kisser open and don't take any wooden nickels."

I paused. I was truly breathing heavily now, signifying nothing but my own anxiety. "Listen, baby," I said, "I know this wasn't in the contract when I hired you. If it smells bad to you, drop it. If you don't show, I'll understand and I'll make other arrangements. Above all, don't take any chances. Don't let any gorillas get within a thousand feet of you." I thought again. "They don't always look like gorillas," I said helplessly. "Sometimes they come in a poor second. What can I say? Be careful." I hung up.

Would Crazy Horse have done it better? I wrapped my blanket around me, got up, paced back and forth, and sadly concluded *probably*. They were great tacticians, those guys— never lost a battle, really. How come? Terrain, I decided; they knew the terrain. And in-depth planning. Probably had contingency plans, all that kind of thing. Probably made our war department look sick.

Well, what was my terrain? As a matter of fact, who in the hell was the enemy? All that Crazy Horse had to do was look for a blue uniform and a handlebar mustache. Let him try it in Manhattan, or on Long Island or the waterfront. Head them off at the pass? In a well-known but seldom-used expletive, *pshaw.*

The mere consideration of the terrain made me feel lonely and exposed. It stretched, apparently, from Wall Street through Tin Pan Alley along the waterfront to Central or South America. Just viewing the expanse of it made me feel uncertain of myself. Even my one link with outside reality—the terrain—was tenuous. I had fixed my mind on Edna's honey-blond hair and shapely legs inhabiting a phone booth somewhere in outer space—well, not really outer space, a street corner in Manhattan, a hotel lobby. But had she been there? Alone? Had it been some thug listening and chuckling to himself, with Edna knocked over somewhere in an alley? In—I shuddered—some long dim room in a warehouse? It is not nice, talking into the long cold mechanical silence of the telephone wires. My machinery began to manufacture noise. If they had picked up Edna and were listening, they could follow her here, Probcziewski or no Probcziewski.

I lit another cigarette from one of the two packs I had providentially bought from the machine in the lobby. There was no sign of room service in any of the folders, and the cigarettes were to be my sole sustenance until Edna arrived. And if she didn't arrive? Well, I thought, we will see how long a human being can live on smoke.

I rummaged my mind for some inspirational guide to see me through the lonely hours (three, if all went well with Edna) I'd be spending in my little Formica rat trap. *When in doubt, sulk.* That wasn't very good. "Come alive, Binney," I told myself. The time had come for tactics.

The first question of tactics was priorities (how do you like them apples, Crazy Horse?). The first question of priorities was staying alive.

The combination that had put me on the end of a field telephone and eventually at the bottom of an elevator shaft seemed inescapable—Millard Penton to Ed Parti to Mr. Latin

America. My immediate impulse was to crank up and go out and get Millard Penton and shake him until his haircut rattled. He was the soft touch, obviously, and I didn't doubt for a minute that I could get all the information that was in his paper-thin skull spread out before me in ten seconds— probably just by spilling a drink on his suit.

But unless I killed him in the process, which was not something I was contemplating, Penton would still be free to blow the whistle and warn off the others after I let him go. Furthermore, there was no imminent *danger* from Penton that I could see. He might be calling the signals, but he wasn't about to wrap me up by himself.

This brought me to the keystone sack—Ed Parti, the sound engineer with the interesting clothes. While I was doing my routine as the half-witted father advancing Sonny's career, Parti must have enjoyed a spell of cold amusement. Nonetheless, he had done very well. There hadn't been a flicker of anything on his face but polite accommodation. "A record cut by your son, Mr. Maguire? No reason it couldn't be arranged. We do it all the time."

Odd to think of the face now, cold and yet sympathetic above the string tie caught by the tiny collar of his shirt. In spite of the stovepipe jeans and green suede sneakers, he gave off an aura of absolute competence—not a move wasted, not a word out of place. He had moved through the studio, with me trotting awkwardly beside him so that I could see what he was saying, like a very good doctor going through a ward, a touch here, an instruction there, all of it part of a well-oiled, expensive engine.

The question with people like Parti has always been: Why should anybody that competent screw up his life with a lot of phony enterprises? It's always a hard question to answer, but there have been too many examples of it in my experience for me to write off Parti. He had fingered me. Somewhere during that silken runaround he had dropped out to make a very fast, very accurate phone call. Parti, then, was the man with the

65

names and numbers, and while he would be one hell of a lot more difficult to crack than Penton, there was no doubt that the information would be much more valuable—exact names and addresses, numbers, relationships—hammers and nails.

But again, Parti was not of the first priority because, while I might *suspect,* even to a certainty, that he was mixed up in an attempt to kill me, I had no proof. His life and freedom were not immediately threatened by my being alive. There wasn't any need for him to come and hunt me down. And again, if I cracked him, he'd still be loose enough to sound the alarm.

I pulled my blanket around me—the room had seemed suddenly to chill again—and peered out at the unreflective Sound. What did Crazy Horse do when he wound up with a conclusion that had all the charm of getting into a clothes closet with a cobra? "Goddamn it, Binney," I said to myself. "Old Crazy Horse went out and did it."

So, through the brilliant course of my analysis, I had wound up with the solution I dreaded most. The three of them were out there in the terrain somewhere. *They* were the first priority, and one of them, the Latin American, very distinctly the absolute first because he had a long way to fall. The two mechanics did not have, so far as I could tell, any eminence, and doing time was, for them, very probably an accepted part of the whole ball game.

But the guy with the matching set of opals was an entirely different bag of tricks. Whatever he was up to meant money. And whatever his cover might be meant money and the kind of power that goes with diplomatic pouches and army connections. He had much, much more to protect, not only a racket but probably a government as well, and behind that government a lot of hard-nosed families. He was the one person who could not afford to leave me alive—if he knew I was alive, which was still problematical.

I didn't know his name. I'd never seen his picture in the paper. If it came to that, I wasn't even positive he was from Latin America! He could have been a tall Iranian for all of me.

66

Another lousy assumption! Needless to say, I have no ear for accents. My tall interrogator came from a country that has no real nationality and no firm boundaries. It is the land of the hungry, the endlessly hungry. Nail their feet to the floor like a Strasbourg goose and stuff them until their liver swells thick enough to choke them. Feed them on the richest foods in the world, endlessly, until they puke, and still they need more . . . more. I suppose it's a kind of damnation to come from that country, but it's the only race of people I really hate.

The hatred warmed me a little and stirred the blood. It's easier to work if you hate the guy, as long as you're not silly about it, or led into underestimating him. I did not underestimate him. I sat down in my blanket, facing the door of the room, and began to figure out a way to trap him—the man with no identity. I must have dozed off in my plotting, or fallen into the twilight sleep of half-consciousness, filled with long dim rooms and men with short, sharp knives. My eyes fluttered, opened blearily, and focused on the doorknob, which, I forced myself to recognize, had slowly begun to turn.

When I became fully aware of the doorknob's turning, I leaped out of the chair and held my blanket protectively around me.

It couldn't ward off bullets, but it was all I had.

Chapter XI

The door was flung back to reveal Edna's beloved posterior straining at the task of dragging a black metal footlocker across the threshold. It was, any way you want to take it, the most beautiful sight I ever saw in my life. I sat back in the chair, and the nonbulletproof blanket collapsed around me.

She got the black metal box inside, kicked the door shut, and turned around to face me. "My God," said Edna. "Are you okay?"

"I guess so," I answered, "although I almost had heart failure when you opened the door. I thought I'd locked it."

"Passkey," Edna explained. "Probcziewski gave me one so there wouldn't be any trouble getting in." She examined my costume. I became suddenly aware that I had nothing on under it. "What's the matter," I said harshly. "Haven't you ever been in a motel room with a naked man before?"

"Ugh," said Edna. "This is romance? Get some clothes on."

"Toss me some duds out of the footlocker, will you? I put on too much of a show if I dodge around in this blanket."

Out came the socks, underwear, shoes, and a shirt. "Which suit do you want?" she asked me. "Blue or gray?"

"Give me the one that weighs the most," I told her. She gave me a long searching look and balanced the suits on either arm. "Blue wins," she said.

"You get the cigar."

I took my gear into the bathroom and got dressed. It was a marvelous feeling and made complete my restoration to the land of the living. I came out with the suit coat draped over my arm. "How would you like to meet thirty-eight policemen?" I asked her.

"Not much," she replied. "What was that all about, anyway?"

I took the Smith & Wesson .38 caliber Police Special revolver from the inside pocket of the coat and broke it open. From the side pocket I removed a box of twenty-five cartridges and began loading the gun. "These are twenty-five of their fifty friends," I said. "There's a box of twenty-five more in the other pocket." She watched me with disfavor.

"I never saw you with a gun in your hand before," she said. "It makes you look ugly and mean."

"I certainly hope so," I told her. "That's half the advantage." ·

"Please put it away," she said. "It makes me nervous."

"Not half as nervous as I was without it," I said, sticking the gun in my belt. "If you ever get a look at the dandies who mugged me, you'll understand why. It's why I almost had a heart attack when you came through the door. From now on let other people have the heart attacks." I considered our position. "Are you sure you weren't tailed?"

She thought about it and gave a sad little shrug. "How would I really know? There wasn't anybody sitting on the back of my neck, and Probcziewski said he'd drive all the way behind me till I got here to make sure . . ."

"Drive behind you!" I repeated. "You mean you've brought me an automobile? You're a goddess." I went over to hug her, but she danced away.

"Oh, no you don't, buster," she said. "Not with a gun in your belt."

I retreated and asked, "Where did you rent the car? Did anybody see you?"

"I didn't rent it," she said. "Probcziewski lent it to me. He said this one doesn't have to go back to the pound right away, but don't ask questions and make sure it gets back to him in one piece."

"What kind of shape is it in now?"

"It's dirty, but it seems to run all right."

"All the attributes of civilization," I said. "It's like a miracle. New clothes, a car, and a thirty-eight revolver."

"Everything except a shave," said Edna.

I put my hand to my bandaged cheek. "I'll do what I can," I promised her.

Shaving around the wound, I saw that it wasn't going to be anything like one of those devil-may-care slashes that the Krauts were so fond of. It was just going to be an ugly hole in my face, almost the size of a half dollar, right over the cheekbone. I suppose I was lucky that they didn't start working up toward the eyes, the way the sea gulls do.

It was hard to shave around the red proud flesh that enclosed the wound, and it was even harder for me not to focus my eyes on it while I shaved. The wound became a lens through which I examined my enemies. When I had finished, I decided to leave the bandage off and give God's fresh air a chance.

Edna was upset. "How did they do that?" she asked.

"Rats," I answered. "The legitimate kind. Everyday, honest, hardworking, God-fearing rats. Nothing personal."

She shuddered.

"Let's get down to business," I suggested, "What did Probcziewski tell you?"

"Somebody brought you flowers," said Edna.

"Get well? Or R.I.P.?"

"Get well. The nurse called Probcziewski. She felt pretty bad about it."

"She ought to."

"Well, she did. She told him that this tall, suave Latin American turned up at the hospital carrying a bouquet of flowers and asking for his dear friend, Mr. Joe Binney."

"The son of a bitch."

"She sent him up to see Dr. Salt, and Dr. Salt told him you'd died. He even showed him on the chart."

"Did he buy it?"

"Dr. Salt didn't think so. The man gave his name as Rodriguez, by the way . . ."

"Spanish for Smith," I muttered.

". . . and kept asking where the funeral was to be held so he could pay his respects. They said they didn't have that information, nor who claimed the body. Salt told him it was relatives. And they think he smelled a rat . . . sorry."

"Of course he smelled a rat," I said. "Probcziewski fumbled the Goddamned ball. He should have put a phony name on the release for the body and said it was shipped to Adelaide or someplace." ·

I thought about it. "Whoever this Spanish-American bastard Rodriguez is, he isn't lacking in nerve. How did he know he wouldn't get pinched the minute he walked in the door?"

"He assumed you were dead on arrival," Edna answered, "telling no tales."

My head was ballooning with anger. It was not so much that Probcziewski had slipped up; it was just the image of that cool mustachioed operator with the bouquet of flowers in his hand—concealing what? A puff adder?

I put my hand to the hole in my cheek. "They know I'm not dead," I said bluntly. "I'd better get used to that idea right now."

Edna thought it over. "They don't know where you are right now, though," she said. "And therefore they don't know where I am, either. I can get plane tickets for us, and maybe we could lay low in—how about Hawaii?—until the police catch up with them?"

There was a lot of appeal in that suggestion. I looked at it carefully and made up my mind. "Listen, Edna; we're on a balance beam right now that can tip in either direction, depending on who throws his weight around. If we blow town, it could be years before the cops clear this up, and with the connections that this Rodriguez has got, they may never clear it up at all. I've already *been* to Hawaii, and have absolutely no desire to go back, or to go to anyplace else in this Goddamned world but to my office and resume my business. Right now it depends on who thinks of himself as the hunter and who thinks of himself as the quarry. The initiative might make all the difference."

"But what happens when both parties think of themselves as the hunter?" Edna pointed out sagely.

"Then one of them has got to be convinced otherwise."

"It's going to take a lot of convincing," she observed, "for

71

somebody who's got the brass to walk right into a hospital after his victim."

"That's what I don't understand," I told her. "Why wasn't he collared?"

"Oh, Dr. Salt tried," Edna informed me. "He tried to get hold of Probcziewski, but by the time he got through, Rodriguez was gone."

"Why didn't he call the local precinct?"

"Because you and Probcziewski told him not to," she explained patiently.

I sighed. "They wouldn't have been able to hold him anyway. Ten to one he's got some kind of immunity—enough to stymie a couple of cops with a shaky story, anyway. He must have counted on that."

I put the figure of Rodriguez into one of those dark keeps of the mind to which I make frequent, if momentary, visits. "Let's catch up with the rest of the bunch," I said. "What's Penton been doing?"

"As far as anybody knows, he's just been doing his daily rounds."

"He never inquired about me?"

"Should he have?"

It was a moot point. Ignorance indeed was Penton's bliss. "What about Ed Parti?"

"Who's he?"

"The guy that must have fingered me at the recording studio."

"Never heard of him. Don't know anything about him."

"He'll bear watching, the son of a bitch," I said. With the two mechanics, it summed up my range of villains. Then I said, "What about the kid, Larry? Any news about him?"

"He's staying with his father."

"With Penton? I thought he hated Penton's guts."

"No. With his real father."

"Jesus," I said. "I didn't even know he had one. I mean I didn't realize he was anywhere around. What's the real father's name?"

"Gil Hosier."

"What do we know about him?"

"Almost nothing. He lives on the East Side in a modern apartment. Never remarried. He's a photographer."

I filed the information under useless, although I definitely wanted to keep tabs on the kid. "Now we come to the hard part," I said. "What are we going to do about you?"

"Send me to Hawaii?"

"Why are all the girls so nuts about Hawaii?" I complained. "A lot of ratty hula skirts, some sunken battleships, and a high-priced, overcrowded beach. Even Charlie Chan doesn't live there anymore."

"You asked for suggestions," she said demurely.

"Yeah . . . well." I paused for inspiration. "Look, Edna, I don't think you ought to be on the loose with those torpedoes running around. Why don't you stay here with me until I get this cleared up?"

"You mean like a little shack up?" That girl had the most venomous smile I'd ever seen in my life.

"Not at all," I protested. "I mean you should get another room here at the motel—an adjoining one, if possible. You'll be a lot safer, and I won't have to worry about you. Also," I confessed, "I kind of need you right now."

"Who's going to be paying for it?"

"We're still on Penton's tab." It was a bright spot in an otherwise dull day. "I'll take great pleasure in melting it out of his back teeth. Are you on?"

"Well . . ." Her lower lip protruded in thought. "I have to go back and get my things . . ."

"You do *not*," I said. "With the job comes a whole new outfit, with matching bag and shoes." A smile split that pretty face. "You call up Manny Performer," I said, "and tell him exactly what you want. Don't be bashful. And tell him to have the whole kit delivered to Probcziewski. We'll call Probcziewski and have him get the bundle over here. But first make sure they've got a room."

A simple phone call to the desk assured us that the Hilo

73

Hattie room right next to mine was available. The call to Manny Performer followed as night follows day.

She was on the call quite a while. I didn't watch. But when she hung up, her face was desolate. "What's the matter?" I asked her. "Don't tell me he hasn't got what you want. What he hasn't got he steals."

"Not anymore," Edna told me. "Manny Performer's dead. He must have been killed right after I left." She was trembling. "The man who answered said he must have had a hundred little knife cuts in him."

Chapter XII

It took me three working days to find the dark one—the one with the fancy blade. I tried on the store-bought beard that Manny had sent me in the performer's makeup kit I'd ordered, and above it I placed a pair of large, very dark shades. I'd never tried on a real disguise using actual makeup before, and I felt like the world's foremost jerk with the shades and the thick beard that covered up the hole in my cheek.

With Manny's services forcibly removed, I had to buy Edna's outfit in the Lady's Shoppe of the motel—a ruinous enterprise costing at least five times what Manny would have charged. From the Men's Shoppe I bought a dozen of their cheapest shirts (which were not all that cheap)—size 14 x 30, an odd size chosen for purposes I will soon reveal.

The shirts were stock for my new occupation—an illicit one, to be sure, since an illicit occupation is the only one that looks legitimate on the docks. Hustling threads was a reasonable cover, but I didn't want to make a sale and have to renew my stock. That kind of volume at these prices could be ruinous.

I prayed for luck and drove my shabby car to Brooklyn. I covered the shifts from pier to pier, flashing a smile that matched the beard for phoniness. "Hey, hey, buddy; c'mon over here," crooking a finger to lure a stevedore to the side of the car. "Wanna nice dress shirt cheap, huh?"

"Lemme see it."

The cheap shirt in the plastic envelope is passed over the window.

"Waddayuhwant furrit?"

"Three bucks."

"Three bucks fuh this junk? Geddoddaheah."

And so it went in Brooklyn for the day. If the mark was stupid enough to consider paying that much for the rag, I was careful to point out the size. Thirty-inch sleeves? Most of these guys looked like they could touch both ends of a billboard just by spreading their arms.

But no luck in Brooklyn, which I do not think even the dead recognize anymore. The shifts came and went, the big cranes swung, and I spuriously peddled my spurious wares. By the end of the day, I felt as tired as a stevedore.

Back at the motel that evening, I peeled off the muff and sideburns and took Edna over to the alleged dining room for dinner. She was edgy from spending the day holed up in Hilo Hattie, whose barrenness Formica did nothing to fertilize. Her mouth tightened as she stared resentfully around the restaurant. "Is this the only place we can eat?" she asked me.

"There's always Macy's window."

She ordered scallops. I ordered steak. Both orders, when they arrived, looked as if they'd been filched from an airline. "I hate it here," Edna announced.

"So do I."

"How long are we going to be here?"

75

"Until I crack the egg."

"I don't really understand what you mean."

"I mean that I've got a smooth, anonymous surface to crack. I'm betting my shirt, or half a dozen of them, that the two mechanics came off the docks. I don't know their names, so I just have to look."

"Why don't you look for the boss instead?"

"Too public, too difficult, and too dangerous. I'd have to go to embassies. *Hello, there, I'm looking for a big, tall, well-dressed schmuck with an abiding affection for field telephones—goes under the alias of Rodriguez and was last seen carrying flowers. Know him?*"

"But couldn't you just stake out the embassies the same way you're staking out the waterfront?"

"You can't clean your heel on the curb in front of an embassy without the New York police and the secret police of at least eight countries getting interested. It's too exposed. I've got to locate one of the sidekicks first."

She contemplated her scallops—dourly. "It could take you forever to find a stevedore. I bet you didn't see half the dockworkers in Brooklyn today."

"Hell, I probably didn't see a tenth of them."

"You're going to spend ten days just going to Brooklyn?"

I wondered what kind of animal they had taken this steak off of. I tasted it carefully and elected a giant three-toed sloth. Sloth steak, all right, I decided. "No," I said. "Psychiatry costing what it does, I've taken against the idea of spending ten days in Brooklyn. What I'm actually doing," I explained a little more gently, "is taking soundings. I could give you a nice fancy spiel on probability justifying the whole scheme, but the truth is that I'm working by intuition. I have a conviction that if I keep moving around the waterfront I'll find my boy. Since he has outside interests, to say the least, there's a good chance he'll be screwing around more than the average stiff would be. Out for a beer—a phone call—a quick chat with a bookie, with a heister, with a fence. He'll be seen. He'll be more in evidence than the nonoperators."

We finished our meal quickly, and I wondered if we were going to be rewarded for cleaning our plates. Edna's lips had remained sullen around each morsel of scallop. "Tell you what I'm going to do," I offered. "Supposing we go into the bar and have a drink, and you can listen to the piano player."

The piano player must have been lousy. She was not appeased, not even after two scotch sours (women drink them—I know, I know). I had trouble reading her because the bar was so dark, but the message finally came through. "You talk about it being dangerous to go to the embassies—dangerous for you. But what about me?"

"Well, what about you?" I asked, honestly enough.

"You don't seem to be worried about how dangerous it is for me."

"Sure I am. Why do you think I've got you buried out here?"

"But supposing they know that I'm—that we're here?"

"They don't," I said flatly. "They don't have an inkling."

"How can you be sure that Manny Performer didn't tell them?"

"Because he died slowly and painfully," I said. "And Manny wasn't about to die any way at all, or even get his hair mussed, if he could have begged off with a little information. Manny didn't know where you'd gone. He didn't hear you give the cab instructions, did he?"

"No," she admitted sadly. "He couldn't have. We were at the end of the block before I told the driver." She shuddered. "Poor little man," she said. "He was very nice to me. It almost killed him dragging that footlocker all the way out to the back."

"It did kill him," I told her. "They must have got wise after you left by the back exit, and after a while they came in to tune him up. But believe me, they haven't got a clue about where we're at, or they'd be here. Stay in your room. Don't answer the door for anybody except me, and I promise you, in a couple of days we'll have mechanics on toast."

I said good night to her at her door like a little gentleman, repaired to the Suicide Suite, and made ready for bed, where I tossed and turned.

Edna had had to be reassured that she was safe, and indeed she was safer here than anywhere else, but safety was still a relative thing. We could not last forever in our hidey-hole, and as surely as they had tracked Edna to Manny Performer's, so they would soon enough find out that we were here. If I didn't turn up one of the ape brothers in a day or so, I'd have to start haunting the embassies. With this distasteful thought in mind, I went off to visit my nightmares.

Up and at 'em with my muff and crummy merchandise the following morning. I crawled through the plugged intestines of Long Island to arrive at the George Washington Bridge, and on over to the northern end of the Jersey docks at Union City. And did the eastern border of New Jersey smell sweeter and cleaner, or look prettier and nicer, now that the peerless leaders of its decade past were in jail? Not noticeably. New Jersey! New Jersey! The armpit of the nation! The great airborne sewer of the eastern seaboard, where but to breathe is to gag.

I edged my car along from pier to pier, trying to breathe as little as possible. It seemed that the shirts were getting soiled right through the plastic. The response did not differ much from those in Brooklyn as I wormed my way down toward Weehawken.

In Weehawken a blond young goon insisted on buying a shirt for his kid brother, and there was no discouraging him. Reluctantly I took his three bucks and let him walk away with the goods, hoping that he would fall and break his arm. But no cigar; no, no cigar. The evening sun found me on the outskirts—if they may so be called—of Hoboken, and the sight of the place discouraged me so that I resolved to start in the Port of Elizabeth on Monday, since the stevedores would not be working over the weekend. I would save Hoboken for the last as I worked north.

That evening at the sludge pot, the following repartee developed between Edna and me.

78

SHE: Did you know that your beard is getting tacky?

HE: *(Sheepishly)* I guess I've been chewing on it a little.

SHE: You're getting little red pimples with white dots in the middle of your chin where the glue is.

HE: Thank you for the information. When I am finished with this disguise, I will have my chin removed.

SHE: Maybe you ought to give up investigating and go into selling shirts in a big way. Maybe out of a truck instead of out of a car.

HE: Maybe you ought to have your face wired shut. Is that all you ever eat, scallops?

SHE: Yes. That is all I ever eat. Scallops.

That wasn't all of the evening's conversation, of course. The rest was "Good night" and "Drop dead."

And thus I spent the weekend in a secret hideaway with the luscious object of my illicit passions. We barely spoke. The quick-thawed meals congealed on our plates.

To say that Hell is a city much like Elizabeth, New Jersey, is at once to launch a metaphysical inquiry and defame the memory of Percy Bysshe Shelley—not to mention Satan. At the docks in Elizabeth on Monday morning I sat in my car and watched the small rain turn into sulphuric acid as it fell through the black billowing clouds of smoke rolling over the town from the power plants, refineries, chemical works, and a garbage dump or two. For inspiration I looked at the Pulaski Skyway, while I gnawed my beard. The pimples on my chin seemed to have rooted themselves in the bone, where they spread little tendrils, like fiery worms.

My come-on smile had slipped away, and instead of archly inviting my customers, I found that I was bellowing, *"Hey, you! C'mon over here. I want to talk to you."*

I sold five of the Goddamned shirts and snatched the money out of their hands. I think the customers bought the shirts out of the sheer relief that they hadn't been arrested. I think that everybody in New Jersey subconsciously expects to be arrested. Who am I to argue? I'd like to see it happen sometime. Arrest the entire state! What a haul!

Late afternoon found me under the gaunt shadow of the Hoboken Terminal of the Erie Lackawanna Railroad, a huge, high, mildewed-green anachronism butting on the disused ferry slip that once connected commuters with Manhattan. The ferry had gone the way of all good things, and the terminal looked wistfully in its direction.

I stared out at the glistening brick pavement that spread its circles toward the town and fingered the fifteen dollars, my day's take, that I'd stowed in my coat pocket. Fifteen dollars, I considered cunningly, would finance a respectable evening's drunk. The prospect of facing Edna empty-handed and empty-headed was more than I could at the moment endure. Also, to crawl much of the length of Very Long Island to arrive at last in Formica Land was more than any sane man could contemplate without having a few aboard.

Dimly I remembered a *gemütlich* little bar that I had visited years ago, tucked away in the corner of the waiting room. The big thriving bar that was being overrun by commuters at the moment was far too bright for me.

I crossed the waiting room and searched for the magic doorway. It was not my week for luck, I thought. The door was padlocked. Like the ferry, the bar had quietly stolen away, and with it had taken the roomy restaurant with its thick marble counters and German silver appointments. One of the troubles with being deaf, of course, is that you can't hear yourself, particularly when you deal out an expletive. A fortyish (read *dumpy*) lady looked frightened as she passed to my right—not shocked, but frightened. I stroked my molting beard and scowled at her. She hurried on.

Have I mentioned probability? It smiled on me as I began to leave the waiting room, for there, emerging from the men's room on the other side of the hall, was my dark-haired blade fancier. He was, in perfect character, still adjusting his trousers, and on his stupid face was that look of ineffable

80

contentment that follows, in some folks, genitourinary functions. Cunning Joe Binney scuttled over to the newsstand to buy a paper behind which to hide his beard and followed his pigeon outside.

The rain had stopped, but the thick haze remained, and the streetlights had come on early. He wasn't hard to follow as he headed toward the long strip of warehouses that had once served American Express. He turned up a narrow street, went into a mostly deserted parking lot, and ambled toward an automobile, apparently his own. He was just opening the door of it when I called out with an attempt at geniality, "Hey, wait a minute, buddy. You dropped something." He waited as I came toward him, happy with the nice man who recovered lost property. I held the gun behind my newspaper. The barrel is four inches long. I put an inch and a half of it right into his hairy nostril.

Chapter XIII

Looking cross-eyed down the barrel of the gun, he attempted to read my eyes. I think it was the dead, ragged beard, beginning to hang in patches from my chin, that frightened him—more, perhaps, than the gun, which was something he was familiar with, at least. The front sight on the barrel wasn't doing his nose any favors, however, and a gelid trickle of blood, almost black in the fading light, began to work its way down toward the cylinder.

"Turn around and brace on the fence," I told him.

His jaw moved, but I couldn't see what he was saying

because my fist with the gun butt in it was in the way. I guessed that he wanted the gun barrel taken out of his nose so he could turn around. Reluctantly I withdrew it, and he turned around to put his hands up high on the wire mesh fence like a little gentleman. I hit him in the mastoid with the side of the gun and he slid down suitably.

I rolled him; it couldn't have taken five seconds, and I was in a hurry. I opened his car and tumbled him into the backseat. Then I jumped in front and started the engine. My car was in a parking lot that could have been the twin to this, and was only a few minutes away. But I wanted very much to get over there before the vestigial brain cleared and called for action.

We made it nicely, with time to spare. The lot was deserted, and the two cars parked side by side made a private arena for us. I took some nylon cord out of the glove compartment and bound his hands behind him with a tight rolling hitch on his ankles. The pale glow of the streetlight from the opposite corner of the lot was not reaching the little valley between our cars, so I had to read his papers by flashlight. I hunkered down next to him to avoid attention.

I tickled his chin with the end of the gun, and he opened his eyes. He didn't like the flashlight. "Good afternoon, Mr. Moylan," I said. "I'm very happy to make your acquaintance. Robert Moylan, is that right? Robert S., in fact. What does the S. stand for?"

He was an ugly-looking bastard, all right, now that I had a good look at him. His face had sagged into shapelessness that seemed to be supported only by the five o'clock shadow. His complexion was raw and red, but whether by endowment or embarrassment, I knew not. The nose had that generous spread to it that frequent fracturing so often lends. The teeth were unkempt, the mouth thin and vicious. The eyes, dear me, were glaring out of their little red rims.

"You will remember from our last meeting," I told him, "that I am deaf, and am forced to read lips in order to communicate verbally. You *do* remember, don't you?" I smiled. "Let's start slowly, and be sure to enunciate clearly so that I understand you the first time and spare you unnecessary anguish. Reply promptly in order: What does the S. stand for in your name, and what is the name of your blond-haired partner who was up in the loft with us?"

What he replied is not to be repeated in this narrative, which was innocently brought into your home and might yet ruin the life of a pure young golden-haired child.

I stood up and peered over the roof of the car. The streets beyond the parking lot were deserted, no doubt because the population of Hoboken knew that men like Moylan were abroad. I took a roll of two-inch adhesive tape out of the glove compartment and pasted a swath of it across his ugly chops. "I don't want you attracting undue attention," I informed him. I took the hauling end of the line trailing from his ankles and threw a couple of half hitches around the rear bumper. I got into my car, warmed the engine for a few moments, and made two quick tours of the perimeter of the gravel-covered lot, accelerating nicely on the sharp turns.

I jolted to a stop at our original position and walked over to the back of the car with my flashlight. His eyes were closed, but they opened rapidly when I ripped the adhesive off. There was blood on the back of his head, and his nose was bleeding copiously. The back of his poplin windbreaker had been torn off, although the work shirt still looked good for another tour.

"Now," I asked him, "what does the S.—your middle initial—signify?"

A new expression was dawning in his little muddy eyes. Was it respect? He breathed heavily. "Stanford," he said.

"We have made a splendid beginning," I announced. "We are already on a middle-name basis. I'll call you Stanford, and you may call me Faneuil, for I am so named after the hall in which I was conceived." (I'm not really, and I wasn't, really. I was just kidding him along, you might say.)

83

"We will proceed to step two. What is the name of your blond-haired partner in the loft?"

"I don't know. I honestly don't know. I never saw the guy before that day. We got called separately. I don't know the guy from Adam."

On went the adhesive; off went the automobile for a second tour. I was beginning to learn the curves. Stanford seemed to be in real distress when we got back. When I ripped the adhesive off, he took enormous gulps of air, and it occurred to me that he was drowning in the blood that filled his nose. Most of his shirt was gone by now, and he had picked up a good bit of gravel in his back and shoulders and on the side of his face. I let him get his breath back and wiped the side of his face off so I could see what he was saying. I repeated my question.

"Manfred Schultz," he answered.

"Middle name?"

For the first time, panic began to enter his eyes. "Jesus Christ," he said. "I don' know—I don' know!"

"O.K.," I said tolerantly. "We'll let that pass. Now; where does he live?"

"The Bronx."

"Where in the Bronx?"

He gave me a street name, which I wrote down. When I asked him for the number, he said he didn't remember, which I believed.

"And now we come to the third and final step. . . ." He tensed. "Who and where is the big guy with the fancy suit and mustache who was asking me all the questions?"

He appeared to reflect. "I wish I could tell you," he began. "Believe me, I wish I could tell you. . . ."

"I wish you could, too," I answered. "It would be a great savings on gasoline."

His lips clamped shut and a real panic entered his eyes. I tore off a new strip of adhesive from the roll. "I can't," he said. "I can't."

84

We made two tours and a third for luck.

When I looked at him, he had lost consciousness, and I got the adhesive off in a hurry.

His clothes had become a few rags that stirred like Irish pennants in the mild evening breeze. Gravel had entered his body like shrapnel and, looking at the round scab of his face, I realized that he had flipped over onto his stomach once he had lost consciousness. He was still alive, all right. His breath was coming in huge gasping sobs. It needed water, but I didn't have any, and I wasn't about to go and look for some. I went back and opened the trunk of the car, where I found a two-gallon can of gasoline for emergency rations. I tossed a little on the lower part of his face, and he writhed to a sitting position, his eyes wide open.

"Can you hear me?" I asked him. He nodded.

"Either you're going to tell me the name and address or I'm going to drive around this parking lot until I grind your stupid head to a nub. Do you understand that?"

He nodded.

"What's the name and address?"

The round scab moved, but I couldn't see what he was trying to say. I wiped his face with an oil rag, from which he shrank, but there was no sense to be had from a mouth like that. My lipreading skills were stymied. There didn't appear to be much in the way of lips to read.

"You're going to have to write it down on a pad," I told him. I got out pad and pencil, and then cut the cord around his wrists with the knife I had taken from his pocket. It was a beauty, all right—a little pearl-handled number that went through the cord like butter. But his flayed hands couldn't hold the pencil. I took the rag and chafed his bloody wrists. I worked the limp fingers and clamped the pencil in his fist.

"Write it down!"

The fist left a streak of blood for every stroke of the pencil. What evolved, finally was:

DANIEL MELENDEZ

S.S. *CARLOTTA PEREZ*

"Docked where?"

The scab shook a negative.

"At sea?"

Another negative.

"At anchor, then."

An eager positive this time.

"In the harbor?"

No.

I cursed. "You mean he's out beyond the three-mile limit?"

A slow nod, yes.

"I'll get him," I said, more to myself than to the huge wound in front of me. I tied his hands again and threw him into the back seat of my car. When I'd started the engine, I looked back at him and told him, "Maybe you think you've had a hard time. Think again and remember what the bottom of that elevator shaft looked like. I'm not finished with you yet, you son of a bitch."

Chapter XIV

I had intended to ask the sergeant to put through a telephone call to Edna and Probcziewski, in that order, at the station house. But when I got past the big front door, the two of them came rushing up at me. Edna came first. "Are you O.K.?" she asked me.

"Never felt better."

It seemed to enrage her. "Then why didn't you have somebody call and let me know? I've been worried sick."

"Take it easy," I told her. "I just hit LOTTO." I looked at the lieutenant. "You haven't put out a bulletin or anything for me that they could pick up, have you?" He shook his head reassuringly.

"We were just waiting," he said. "You say you've got something?"

"The boy with the knife. He's out in the car. You're going to need a new set of seat covers."

"Let's bring him in."

"Have you got a back door to this joint? He doesn't look too presentable. I don't want anybody calling a doctor just yet."

"He isn't going to die here, is he? I don't want anything like that."

"No. He isn't going to die. He may talk while he hurts, though."

"Drive around to the back," said Probcziewski. "I'll let you in."

"Oh, boy," said Edna. "Law and order rides again." She looked to be scornful and disgusted.

"You said you were worried about me," I said mildly. "This guy is one of the reasons."

"What are you two going to do to him?"

"Absolutely nothing," I told her gently. "It's all been taken care of."

Probcziewski didn't like the looks of it while I eased my tiger up the back stairs. "You sure he isn't going to croak?"

"Not a chance," I assured him. "He may pick up a few infections, but those won't show for a while. The hospital will probably dip him in a vat of iodine."

The interrogation room was clean and neat, freshly painted, and had, of all things, indirect fluorescent lighting. It probably met the latest standards for the proper law-abiding police station, if, indeed, there are such standards. Probcziewski found a newspaper, which he spread on the chair before he'd let Moylan sit down.

"All right," said Probcziewski. "Let's have the story."

"I've got two stories," I told him. "After you've heard them both you can take your pick."

"Let's get started."

"See how you like this. I was driving over here this evening to have a word with you when I saw this gentleman dart out of the bushes by the side of the road. I didn't really feel anything in the car, and didn't realize that he'd been snagged on my bumper until I'd driven several hundred feet."

"What does that buy us?"

"That puts him in your jurisdiction."

"I need a hit-and-run victim like I need a hole in the head."

"But supposing he's not just a victim? Suppose he's running away from the scene of a crime or has been hiding out in the woods for a few days and got careless?"

"It's a thought," the policeman admitted. "Let's have the other libretto."

"He killed Manny Performer."

The red mass jerked alive in the chair. The head went back and the face moved, although I couldn't distinguish what it was trying to say. "I can't read him," I complained to Probcziewski. "What's he chipping his teeth about?"

"He says it was an accident."

"Some accident. Manny had more holes in him than a fishnet."

"He says Manny zigged when he should have zagged, and the knife accidentally nicked the carotid artery."

"Accidents will happen," I said bitterly. "He's got some peculiar ideas about manslaughter."

"Let's leave it for later. What else have you got?"

"Well, naturally, he's one of the two bastards that jumped me and played games with me up in the loft. The other one is named Manfred Schultz, and should be picked up right away before he starts getting into bad company." I gave the lieutenant Mr. Schultz's address. "I'll sign a complaint if I have to," I told him, "although I'd rather John Doe it one way or another until we're cleared up. Schultz will have to go to the cops in the city."

"What about the big spic?"

"Name of Daniel Melendez. You can't touch him."

"City police?"

"No police at all without papers from Jesus. He's on a ship anchored beyond the three-mile limit." I hesitated and smiled beguilingly. "You like him?"

"You mean Mr. Latin America?"

"Yeah. I mean, you like him for the Penton murder?"

"It's a nice idea. I'd like to talk to him. No promises, though. And if anything happens, don't call me."

"It will have to be quick," I mused. "Moylan isn't going to call anybody because you'd find out who he called. But Schultz will spread the alarm when he's picked up, and also Moylan, one way or another, will be missed."

"I don't know anything about it," said Probcziewski, "and that's official." He thought it over. "I could probably get him off the ship via the Coast Guard or the Treasury Department."

"You couldn't get a warrant in a million years, and you know it."

He shrugged it away. "Is the ship on the way in or the way out?"

"That's my next order of business. A phone call to the *New York Times* should be sufficient. Better yet, the harbormaster's office. Why don't you give them a call and find out where the S.S. *Carlotta Perez* is anchored?"

The lieutenant busied himself at the phone, while Moylan and I examined one another. "She's laying off the Sandy Hook Channel," Probcziewski told me, putting down the phone.

"I just happen to have a friend, Bob Toomey, with a beach house off the Jersey coast," I announced happily. "I'll drop by in the morning and see if it can be used for illicit purposes. Personally, I don't think it was ever used for anything else. My feeling is that the ship was on the way out, but Melendez has held up the sailing until he can find out the score."

"That would mean he'd have no evidence aboard."

"That's right."

"Screw it, then," said Probcziewski. "There's no way I can touch him." He contemplated Mr. Moylan. "What's the routine with your friend here?"

I began pacing back and forth. They both watched me. "Lieutenant," I said, "I never knew a policeman in my life who didn't have a pigeonhole with no pigeon to put in it. Now, I hate this son of a bitch, and I want to see him go up for something solid. He helped to torture me and then helped to try to kill me—not because he wanted to, or even because he got any kind of a blast out of it. He did it because somebody told him to, and because they gave him a little bit of money for it. All in a day's work. He's what they call a pro, and that's why I hate him. I hate pros.

"You've got to have something you need a patsy for. This guy couldn't prove he didn't kill President Kennedy. There isn't an alibi in the world he's got that you couldn't crack. You've got to have something to hang on him.

"And there's more," I said. "If he goes up for a job on me or for killing Manny Performer, he joins a kind of elite in stir. He's a big man. There's all kinds of privileges that go with that. I'd just as soon see him go up for something else."

Probcziewski thought it over. "If you hit him accidentally while he was coming out of the bushes between here and the motel, you must have hit him on Benson's Road," the detective said carefully.

"That's right."

"Strangely enough, that was near the scene of an interesting crime yesterday." He paused and looked at Moylan. "A six-year-old girl was seriously abused. She was raped, in fact, and she was badly injured. A few hours after she was discovered, a bank executive who had a wife and four kids, three of them daughters under the age of twelve, drove his car through the railing on a curve and into the Sound. Of course, if it is suicide, his wife and kids get nothing out of the insurance, and so they pay, you might say, for Daddy's indulgence. I'd just as soon clear up the case and stop all the speculation."

"Our client," I said, nodding toward Moylan, "doesn't exactly resemble a bank officer."

"Right now the kid would identify Billy Graham as the assailant. If I can get a make on this creep within a day or so, the kid will never deny it in court."

I looked at the tattered hulk in the newspaper-covered chair. "How do you like it, Moylan?" I asked him. "You think it's a good fit?"

It must have cost him something. He put it all together and made a bolt for the door. Nothing moved elsewhere except Probcziewski's foot. Moylan tripped over it and hit the floor.

"About time to call the doctor, don't you think?" I asked the lieutenant. "And about time to put out a bulletin on Schultz."

Probcziewski was looking at Moylan. "I know these guys gave you a hard time . . ." he began.

"But I'm a prick," I finished for him. "The old serenade. Who are you to take the law into your own hands? How dare you shoot that burglar? Remember, lieutenant, if he'd found me first he'd have killed me like stepping on a roach. Wait around and see what Melendez looks like when I hand him over."

Unfortunately, they decided to take Moylan to a doctor, rather than the other way around. Even more unfortunately, they decided to bring him down the front way while I was still trying to explain things to Edna. She looked at the wreck being helped out over the steps, and then she looked at me.

91

"Did you do that to him?"

"Yes. Do you want to know how?"

"No."

"You seem to be upset."

"I'm wondering if it was necessary."

"Was killing Manny Performer necessary?"

"It's not the same."

"Why not?"

"You're supposed to be different."

"You mean a victim?"

She looked away from me and pursed her lips. It was a very mean-looking line. "I never knew you could hate people that much."

"You never spent any time hooked up to an army field telephone, or lying at the bottom of an elevator shaft, and you haven't got a hole in your cheek," I told her. "It's O.K. with Moylan. He's a pro. You know what I mean? He'll take the fall, like it or not. He's organized. He's not crime in the streets. He's crime in embassies. I hate him. I hate everybody connected with him."

I took her by the arm and swung her around. "Let me ask you something," I said. "If a man is beaten and unmanned, what do you think he should do?"

"I don't know," her lips said.

"You don't want to know," I told her. "You think if a man's beaten, he should roll over and play dead, or dry up and blow away. Get rid of the idea. It's the way organizations think—dispensing with things. Some men come back. I'm one of them."

Edna looked very hurt. "I do not think like an organization," she said.

"Who else but an organization would order scallops every night for dinner?" I asked her seriously. "If I take you out to dinner at another place, will you promise not to order scallops?"

92

"Only if you take off that horrible beard," she said, and burst into tears.

Chapter XV

She lay low in the water off Sandy Hook, and by the cut of her in the glow of her deck lamps and anchor lights, it was obvious that the decision to leave the dock had been precipitous. The S.S. *Carlotta Perez* swung from her anchorage with a mournful worried roll that suggested her indecision. Only part of the gear had been secured. Midships and aft, the tall booms wove figure eights against the starlight—there was no moon. Approaching her from the stern, I was happy to see that they had neglected to secure the gangway and the landing stage. It dropped invitingly down toward the water—to take someone aboard? I wondered, or just the result of a fast getaway?

I congratulated myself on having things my way for a change. I had shoved off at midnight, and the luminous dial on my turnip now showed three o'clock. Two friends had provided respectively a black rubber two-man raft and an electric trolling outboard motor—slow indeed, but silent. The black wet suit was my own. The handcuffs and leg irons were a pawnshop purchase, and oh, yes, the earplugs and noseclip went along with the wet suit, since I'd just as soon not ship seawater in the large spaces within my skull.

The slovenly gangway reached down to within eight or ten feet of the water, not low enough for me to reach from my raft, but easily accessible to my grappling hook. Planning this jaunt, I had prepared myself for climbing the anchor chain—a wonderful way to lose my hands—and tossing my muffled grappling hook over the bow rail from the lip of the hawse pipe. There were so many things wrong with the idea that I had simply shut it out of my mind until the moment was at hand.

My raft glided under the stern, and I switched the motor off, propelling the rubber craft by pushing it along the side of the ship. Directly under the landing stage I slowed the raft to a dead stop in the water and threw the coiled nylon painter over the grating of the stage. I probably could have swung myself aboard with the painter, but it was no thicker than nine thread, and I was afraid of slipping and falling into the creek with a resounding splash—silent to me, of course, but not elsewhere. I tossed up my muffled grappling hook, where it caught the stage, and swung myself aboard on three-quarter-inch line. Up on the grating I lowered the hook back gently to the rubber boat and secured the painter.

Nothing is more illusory, of course, than a sleeping ship. Ships sleep with one eye open—the watch on the bridge, the watch in the engine room, and possibly the second cook and baker rising in the middle of the night to get his ovens started. Although I could not see a shadow move anywhere, except for the predictable and somehow comforting shift of the ship's roll in the swells, my first step bringing me to eye level with the deck made the old heart jump. Above all, I did not want to be surprised by an oiler coming up on deck for a smoke and a long, loving look at the skyline. I scuttled around the deckhouse, keeping well within the slice of shadow along the bulkhead. Up against the sheer forward bulkhead of the house, which rose in a straight unbroken wall to the bridge, I felt safer, and took a moment to reconnoiter. Even a lookout coming back from the bow would have a hard time seeing me in black wet suit awash in the shadows.

It stood to reason that Melendez was in one of the staterooms on the boat deck. Considering his status, it was unlikely that he would have anything but the best, which meant a corner cabin with ventilation both beamwise and forward. That narrowed it down to one of two cabins. Were there other passengers? Somehow, with the pierhead jump he had made, and out to sea with the ship's gear still flying, I doubted that they had booked a Sunday-school teachers' cruise. Under their convenient flag and their slipshod standards, I doubted that they booked many passengers at all.

The only route to the boat deck, unfortunately, lay directly through the companionway in the house, and then up the ladder to the deck above. This ladder fronted directly on the messroom, the heart of the ship, where anyone on deck would be sure to drift through.

That meant that I would have to hoist myself up to the boat deck by standing on the railing below and reaching up to the coaming on the lip of the deck above. It sounded all right to me, since the lifeboats presented plenty of cover, but when I had balanced myself on the railing I found that I was about six inches short of getting my hands on the coaming above me.

The sweat was beginning to run wickedly down my ribs inside the wet suit. There was no way I could lean back far enough to get a clear sight of the top of the coaming without toppling into the drink. What was called for was a blind leap upward and out into the space above the water.

I flexed my knees deeply for the awkward jump, and tried to hold my palms so that they would run up alongside the steel plate above me. Fright exploded inside me as my fingertips slipped just barely over the edge of the coaming at the top of my leap. I hung on with the last joints of my fingertips and tried to regulate my breathing to slow down my heart. Millimeter by millimeter I curved my hands over the edge of the steel plate until I had a secure grip at the full thickness of my palms. Fright had so exhausted me that it was a struggle to pull myself chest high to the coaming and bend my body aboard underneath the lifeboats.

I lay under a lifeboat, hoping that my gasping was not audible. It's difficult to explain the fear that seized me in my outward jump, the pure fright of falling into the unknown—not rational, although there was plenty to be rationally afraid of. I regulated my breathing and organized myself. I was much safer up here, I reflected, since crew members are generally forbidden to wander in the passenger area unless they have specific tasks to perform, which was not likely at three in the morning. Three? Not anymore. It was now three-twenty, and dawn, which breaks with startling rapidity at sea, would not be too far in the offing.

Starting forward, I tried to peer through the portholes facing the boat deck on the starboard side. They seemed to offer nothing but wells of blackness. Yet when I arrived at the last of the portholes, something clicked. I went back to the first one forward.

The blackness was relative after all, because through that first porthole I again saw something that I had dismissed at first sight—a barely luminescent glow inside the stateroom. It was at the opposite end of the room from the porthole and, as well as I could judge, about knee high above the deck. I stared at it without arriving at any conclusions, and then, remembering an old sailors' trick, I closed my eyes gently for about twenty seconds, opened them to stare out into the dim light that rained from the stars above the sea, and then looked again into the porthole, focusing my eyes just above the glow. It was a clock—a bedside clock—a traveling clock with a luminescent dial. It was obviously not part of the ship's equipment; ergo, the room was occupied. If my calculations were right, that sleek, well-barbered head should be sleeping just to the right of that barely visible glow. The bad sleep well.

The watertight door had been hooked open for better

96

ventilation. I peered into the dimly lighted companionway to see if anyone was inside, although I was very conscious of the fact that I could probably be seen myself. There was no help for it from here on in. I went to the door of the forward stateroom and tried the latch. He had been sensible enough to lock it. I took another look down the empty companionway, steeled myself, and banged on it.

"*Señor! Señor!*" I cried out in what I hoped was a reasonable approximation of Spanish. "*Radioteléfono, radioteléfono!*" The gun came up out of the elastic belt.

The bad do not sleep all *that* well, apparently. The gun was hardly comfortable in my hand when a sliver of light jumped through the opening crack of the door. I threw my weight against the door and sprang in to say good morning to Mr. Melendez.

"If you make a sound," I told him, "I'll kill you. If anybody interrupts, I'll kill you first and him second. Have you got that?"

He had prepared very carefully for bed, in his methodical diplomatic way. His pajamas were barely rumpled. His toilet articles were carefully arrayed, as if numbered, on the night table next to the luminous clock. Well, he was prepared—but not for awakening in the middle of a nightmare. He was summoning all his diplomatic cool, but his face intractably jumped in several directions.

"Dog the deadlights," I commanded. It was apparently his turn to be deaf. I gestured with the gun. "The round metal covers on the portholes," I said, "close them and screw them shut—the ones facing the boat deck first. I don't want anybody peeking in. Keep your hands where I can see them." He wouldn't have made much of a sailor. It took him quite a while. However, I was patient.

When he had finished, I told him to turn around and snapped the cuffs on his wrists. I kicked his ankles together and put on the leg irons. The ever-handy roll of Bauer and Black came out, and I slapped a strip of it over his mouth, working the tape well into the mustache. I was very aware of time's fleeting and the sun's working its way up from below the horizon. It did not take me long to go through his things. There were a diplomatic passport, letters with official-looking seals, address books (three, no less), and a very nice nickel-plated Browning .25 caliber automatic with about a thousand dollars' worth of engraving on it. I certainly was not looking for evidence of narcotics—I didn't think that even a diplomat would be fatuous enough to keep it in his stateroom. I went into the head and checked out the medicine chest—pomade, mustache wax, and a fine old straight razor—no medicine in the medicine chest.

I put the passport, letters, and address books into an oilskin pouch and slipped it into the rubber belt along with my gun. A quick look into the companionway through the gently opened door assured me that I hadn't roused the ship (maybe they were used to El Señor being wakened in the middle of the night). The boat deck still seemed to be deserted, except for us.

"Off we go, sonny," I told him. The expression in his eyes was brave and intelligent. And his eyes comprehended the meaning of my putting on the noseclip.

I slung him over my shoulder, and he was smart enough to relax, realizing that it was not his moment. We got out to the boat deck without banging into anything, although fitting the two of us through the watertight door was a strain. I went over to the space between the davits of the number two and four lifeboats and leaned him against a davit while I pulled the flippers out of my belt and put them on.

I chucked him into the creek then and followed instantly, feet first, since, if heads were to be cracked I did not want one of them to be mine. My hope was that we would land close enough together to make a single splash, and that I could grab him on the first bounce. If I didn't, I didn't look forward to his coming up for many more, not with that tape across his mouth.

There was a bad moment when I missed him on the way up, and the possibility loomed that my evening's work might go for nothing. But then I saw the white band across his mouth flash in the phosphorescence. I slid one hand beneath his armpit and with the other I ripped off the tape. I was not worried about his yelling at that point because I knew that his lungs would be otherwise occupied. His mouth opened to the size of a killer whale's, and I let him take three good gulps before I told him, "Take one more good one, the deepest you can get, and hold on to it for all you're worth. You understand me?" His head bobbed an assent in the starlight. "Take it and hold it *now*," I said. "We're going under."

Smart and brave as he was, I don't think that Mr. Melendez realized that we were going under the ship. It was my only safe bet, however, not knowing how loud a splash we had made or if anyone had called out *Man overboard!* There was an excellent chance that no one had noticed anything at all on that sleepy vessel, but it was not a chance I was prepared to look into. Our disappearance from that scene was mandatory, and the only opening was downward. I dropped my hand to the chain between his ankles and away we went.

My eyes being useless in the utter black of the depths, I kept them tightly closed so I'd have a chance of seeing rapidly when and *if* we surfaced. There were a few instants of panic when I lost touch with the hull, but I found it again with a kick of the flippers, and we continued to swim downward to the broad curve of the bilge strakes. I had been counting the seconds in my head, and while I was slower than usual with my burden, like a dead fish, behind me, I began to feel the glimmering of success as we flattened out under the ship and headed toward the massive ridge of the keel. Swimming around the waist, the thickest part of the hull, was not necessarily the easiest course, but it was the most accessible and, if I held my bearings, should bring us up directly under the landing stage, where my rubber raft, please God, would still be swinging gently and silently on the painter.

We arrived at the keel on schedule pretty well, and I flipped over to face the bottom so I could track the hull on the way up. I didn't want to broach any distance away from the ship because we would be visible in the phosphorescence that was sure to ring us when we popped above the waves. If there had been an alarm, the searchlights would be busy from the bridge, and I was not eager for the limelight.

I was very glad to feel the great sweep of the bilge strakes on the port beam of the vessel, because my lungs were not all that they should be. Too much sitting on my can in that tacky office staring at Edna's kneecaps, and too much puffing away contentedly on the pimpsticks, had taken its toll. I was no more the Joe Binney of old, demon frogman. My eyes, though shut, began to feel the pressure of little thumbs inside my head pushing them outward. I wasn't too worried about my cargo. He seemed to be a well set up kind of fellow (*well nourished,* I think, is the term the coroners use) and probably did military exercises every morning and *never* just sat around looking at kneecaps.

We arrived at the sheer strake vertical in the water, and I tried to slow us down a little so we wouldn't make too much of a splash when we broached. I let my hand trail along the steel side of the ship and felt for the ridge of the buckplates. It greeted me, to my immense relief. A pyrotechnic display was spinning nicely under my eyelids, and my lungs had become almost a justification for that carelessly used word *intolerable.*

But broach we did, and I was so grateful for that first sweet gulp of breath that I clean forgot I was holding Mr. Melendez upside down, head first, in the water. I righted him quickly, but couldn't see that it made much difference to him; however, I ripped the tape off his mouth. We had surfaced abaft the landing stage, and shifting my grip to a cross-chest hold, I towed my booty over to the raft and pushed him aboard. Then I took off my noseclip, shucked my flippers, and dragged myself after him.

There were no searchlights apparent, at least not on this side of the ship, but that did not mean there wouldn't be. All of my instincts were to rest in the raft for a while, but I forced my numb fingers to slip the painter and move the raft astern so we could hide under the lee of the fantail that jutted out over the stern.

We bobbed there for a while, secure from prying eyes, although not from the ship's screw should they decide to start the engine. While I rested, I took the time to explore Mr. Melendez. He wasn't looking too good, because while I had had control of our progress around the hull, he had been bumping helplessly behind. Barnacles, which no antifouling paint will ever quite abolish, had worked their wicked, razorlike way with him. Out of the water his face, which was all I had time to examine, was beginning to ooze blood as though it were perspiration, quite black in the no-color starlight.

I rolled him in a gray navy blanket and stretched him, head down, across the gunnels. By the time he had begun to breathe with any regularity, he had also begun to vomit. Vomiting meant noise, however slight. I pushed off from the sternpost and started my quiet engine. A peek to the starboard showed no lights of any kind reaching into the sea. The time to leave, apparently, was now, before dawn broke, or before anyone went looking for Mr. Melendez.

Heading back to shore I became aware of my machinery, humming, clanking, shrieking away inside my head at the manufacture of nothing but phantom sound. I listened to it for a while almost gratefully; it meant at least that I was still alive—a happy thought.

And I had my prize there, too, on the blunt bows of the rubber raft. He, too, was alive, although not quite as alive as I was—another happy thought. So, filled with happy thoughts, I made our way back to Sandy Hook, with the maleficent lights of Manhattan on our starboard bow. After he stopped puking, Mr. Melendez began to writhe and shudder. Perhaps he was moaning. It was to be expected. Keelhauling never improved anybody's health.

Chapter XVI

The light had broken far too soon for my taste by the time I beached the raft. I hoped to God that no one had decided on a quick morning dip, and I surveyed the hillocks of the beach for strangers. I'd brought the car down as close as I dared, and when we washed up on the sand my first order of business was to sling Melendez over my shoulder and run up to the car with him as if he were so much gear. That, at least, was the picture I wanted to give to any far-off stranger.

My legs nearly buckled three or four times trying to run nonchalantly with my burden across the sand. It reminded me that I had not spent the night in bed. But I got him over to the car, opened the back door, and dumped him on the floor. Is it habit-forming? It was the second time I'd done it in less than forty-eight hours.

"Keep your head out of sight," I told him, covering him with a blanket, "or I'll blow it off."

I trudged back to the water, detached the motor, stowed it, and towed the inflated raft across the beach and up to the car. I deflated the raft then and put everything in the trunk. I started the engine, and while it was warming, I lifted the blanket in the back to see how Mr. Melendez was faring. He seemed to have recovered very well; two shrewd and dangerous brown eyes stared back up at me.

It was not far to Bob Toomey's cabin, almost midway between Monmouth and Asbury Park. The two-room cabin was sufficiently isolated for Toomey's nefarious pursuits. I pulled the car up close to the front door and invited Melendez to hobble in. The place looked better inside than out. The front room was a kitchen–dining-room–living-room area with a stone fireplace. The back room was only an action-oriented bedroom with an adjoining bath. I hustled Melendez into the back room, just in case some friendly and inquisitive neighbors should come over to see what the hell was going on in Bob's cabin. The front door was the only one.

Leaving the still-manacled Melendez on the bed, from which he stared thoughtfully at the ceiling, I started some coffee in the percolator and, while it was jumping, got out of the wet suit and into some clothes. Rooting around in the cupboard, I found some Philadelphia scrapple. I fried it up and divided it evenly between us. By the time it was fried the coffee was done. I put it all together and took it into the bedroom.

Melendez had made no apparent shift in his position. "Nobody should have to think on an empty stomach," I told him. "Sit up and we'll have some grub."

He sat up on the bed and swung his manacled legs over the side. "If you think I'm going to feed you, you're crazy," I said. "I'm going to take your handcuffs off and I'm going to sit on the other side of the room. If you raise your hands high enough to brush back your hair, I'm going to shoot a hole in your head."

I put the food next to him, took off the cuffs, and stepped back. We both ate and drank our cups of coffee, black, regarding one another steadily across the room. "More coffee?" I asked him. He nodded. I took his cup, poured it full and set it down next to him. We shared a second cup of coffee.

"Cigarette?"

He nodded. I lighted a cigarette and threw it on the bed from across the room. He picked it off the coverlet and took a deep consolatory drag. I lighted one of my own and we smoked silently until the cigarettes were nearly butts. I put a saucer next to him for an ashtray.

"Well, Mr. Melendez," I said. "What do you think?"

"What are you going to do with me?"

"Ask you questions."

He smiled a fine brave Spanish smile. "So?"

"Look, Melendez," I said. "I'm not going to fuck around with you. I don't have any field telephones, or knives or straps or what have you. I'm going to talk to you for a little while. If I get good answers, I'll dispose of you legally, which means you stay alive. If I get no answers, bad answers, or funny answers, I'm going to put the cuffs back on you and look elsewhere for my answers until nightfall. At nightfall, I'm going to come back and take you out in the water and drown you. After I drown you, I'll take the cuffs and leg irons off and you won't be the first overly ambitious swimmer found on this beach."

"And the marks on my body?" He was indignant about the marks on his pure white body. "You think they won't be noticed?"

"The crabs will be the first to notice," I answered. "And after they've noticed, nobody else will be looking too hard. It isn't every county examiner who knows what a barnacle scrape looks like. You'll just look like a lot of crab food to him."

He thought this one over. "May I have another cigarette?" he asked me. I threw him another lighted one, which landed—I should have been so lucky pitching pennies as a kid—right in the saucer.

It seemed to impress him. He smoked for a little and asked me, "What do you mean, dispose of me legally?"

"I mean I'll swear out a complaint against you for assault and battery and attempted murder. I've got the hospital records."

"You'll tell the police you kidnaped me from a ship?"

"Not at all. I was staying in my friend's cabin looking at the beach, when guess who washed up looking like a shithouse in distress? None other than—the midnight bather who got lost."

"And you'll tell them that you held me here at gunpoint?"

"Not this gun." I waved the thirty-eight. "Bob's got a shotgun in the house—how big your eyes are, Grandma—it's in the clothes closet and it's not loaded. Make a run for it, why don't you, so I can blow your brains out. Anyway, I kept you here with a shotgun. Consider yourself detained with a shotgun."

He ruminated. "You think they'll hold me on a charge as flimsy as that?"

"Long enough to hang the Iris Penton murder on you."

He nodded sagely. "You think I murdered Iris Penton." It was a flat statement, not a question.

"It doesn't look like such a bad fit."

"What day was she killed?"

"Don't you even mark them down on the calendar? It was Thursday, the fourteenth."

"You have my passport," he said. "Why don't you look at the most recent entry?" I did so, and the date was the fourteenth, a very tight fit indeed.

"You could have arrived early in the morning," I charged, "and gone straight to her house. You could have arrived there at five or six in the morning."

"I arrived at Kennedy via Aviacion del Sud at eight o'clock that Thursday evening. Flight number seven thirty-five. You can check that and it will stand up. You will find that it is so."

"The police will check it—providing you live to see the police."

"Let's be civilized," Melendez suggested. "What else is it you want to know?"

But when it came down to the nub of the crucial question, I found myself trembling with rage, so much so that the breath was trapped in my lungs and my heart was hammering. I felt the vibration of my voice rasping in my throat.

"I ought to kill you for what you did to me, you son of a bitch," I said.

Instead of killing him, I poured coffee for us both to calm me down. To hell with Mr. Coffee Nerves.

105

Melendez himself remained calm, if interested, in the face of my threat. It was evident that he took me seriously, however. He waited and said nothing.

"Why did you work me over?"

He rolled the coffee around in his mouth as if it were vintage wine. I admired both his composure and his recuperative powers. "It was obvious that you were making inquiries about things that didn't concern you," he said finally.

"What is there about a recording studio that doesn't concern me?"

He took his time. "What really happens if I tell you?" he asked.

"That's up to the police."

"But if they let me go, how do you know I won't have you killed? The police don't hold diplomats without solid evidence, and you have no evidence except your own complaint."

"There will be a tip-off to the federal people that should keep you fairly well in line," I said. "You'll have a man sitting on your shoulders wherever you go in the country. I would think the inconvenience will keep you back home where you belong. You were very foolish and undiplomatic to expose yourself up there in the loft."

"I would not have done so except that I was certain you would be dead," he answered. "I am amazed that you survived."

"I survived because of your stupidity."

"My stupidity?" He was astonished. "How is that?"

"I wouldn't tell you in a million years," I said. "Check it out with the military the next time you have a conference on how to torture prisoners."

He was genuinely disappointed and remained silent for a while. He didn't like the crack about the military. The passport said that he was a full colonel, and he had no doubt spent quite a few happy hours strutting around in his gold braid.

Breaking the spell, I told him, "Reports will also go to

military intelligence and to your ambassador. I don't think that any of them give a shit if you're poisoning wells, but nobody likes to back a loser. Chances are the military will exclude you from further Pan American conferences, and the ambassador will keep you at home on the back burner. I think your happy days as a free agent are numbered.

"To sum it all up and answer your question, I'm not going to extract information from you and then kill you anyway, just to protect myself in the future. I don't think I have to, because I think you're going to be defused. Neither am I going to kill you for revenge or for sport, although, I admit, I was tempted. If you don't answer me nicely, however, the temptation will be overriding, and I will most certainly drown you tonight."

I had written it carefully in my head, and apparently it sounded as impressive to him as it looked to me. His brown eyes softened somewhat. He asked, "You would actually drown me in cold blood? Just like that?"

"Just like a kitten. Think about your passage under the ship's bottom for a while and see how you like it."

He thought about it and didn't like it at all. He pursed his lips. "Let us proceed," he said.

"What was there in the recording studio that I wasn't supposed to know about?"

"Are all your questions going to be rhetorical?"

"Just answer the questions one by one, and let me worry about the rhetoric."

He shrugged. "Narcotics, of course."

"Large amounts?"

The colonel was amused. "Do you think we would resort to such violent measures over a few bags?"

I regarded him. "It's hard to tell about people like you," I mused. "You have a very haughty, high-class way about money, but I think you'd set your grandmother on fire to save the cost of a reading light."

"There are millions of dollars involved, millions," he muttered.

"The recording studio is a big drop—a distribution point, then?"

He nodded.

"How is it distributed from there?"

"That is not my business," he replied stiffly. "I am not what you call—a pusher. I oversee the consignment and see that things operate smoothly from point to point."

I tried to restrain my smile, but didn't make it. "You consider pushing beneath your dignity, is that it?"

"Yes." He nodded emphatically. "I am involved only in the international marketing aspect of it."

It fetched a chuckle out of me, but I didn't want him to think I was softening up. "Let's get on with it and skip your dignity," I suggested. "Who fingered me in the studio?"

"I have no knowledge of that," said the colonel. "I received a telephone call from Manfred Schultz saying that there had been an intruder."

"Let's not be cute, Melendez. Who would have fingered me there? Who's the responsible party?"

"Very well. It would be, of course, Ed Parti."

"Does Parti run the entire distribution on his own?"

"With Mrs. Penton's help, of course."

"Then she was in it all along?"

"Of course."

"Who killed her?"

"I don't know."

"Willing to speculate?"

"It would be useless."

I looked at him carefully, and his face was veiled with that most efficient of all guards, fright. I decided to drop this line for a while and return to it later. "Why weren't you willing to believe that Penton had sent me to snoop around?"

"It did not seem logical. I assumed that Penton knew of his wife's involvement. Why would he investigate himself?"

"Very well. Who did you think would have sent me?"

"Perhaps something needs explanation here. The federal

authorities and the local police are not our outstanding worries. As you know, drug traffic is not at all a monolithic organization with one Mr. Big at the top. It is a number of organizations struggling and trying to undercut one another to get on top or to keep on top. I knew that no police of any kind would have hired you, particularly since you're so clumsy. I could only assume that some other unknown group was trying to find a wedge."

He knew more than he was saying; I knew that he knew more, and he knew that I knew that he knew more. The Philadelphia scrapple, however, had worked its inevitable magic. I felt as if I had swallowed a ton of lead. The weight of it pulled at my eyelids, already weakened by a sleepless and active night. I thought about the long drive ahead of me up to Long Island and decided to close out the interview. "Just one more thing," I told him. "I want you to speculate a little on who murdered Iris Penton."

"I already told you. I can't guess."

"Try," I urged him.

"Very well." He was not liking it. "It might have been any one of the other organizations trying to buy into her business."

"If not them, who?"

"Only two other logical suspects remain. Ed Parti"—he seemed to say this with some reluctance—"or Millard Penton, her husband. Either of them might have wanted the entire business for himself."

His expression said that he liked Penton better for it. I couldn't say that I didn't agree.

Chapter XVII

I lay in bed watching the smog seep through the blinds and examined my life in two temporal directions. The unexamined life is not worth living. The examined life, of course, is unbearable. The fact that time had slipped a cog did not make my reflections sunnier. I was floating awake in bed at the unaccustomed hour of five in the morning, having collapsed on it at six-thirty the night before.

Examining my life in the past direction, I reviewed the long deadly drive from Sandy Hook to the police station out on the Island, with Melendez chained securely in the back of the car. He did not like being booked clad only in a dirty gray blanket, and I did not like the fact that Probcziewski was out of town and not expected back until late that night. I watched them put Melendez in a cell and considered occupying the adjoining cell then and there just to get some sleep. However, I shared several pints of black coffee with the sergeant and fought my way back to Manhattan and my apartment.

Examining things in the other direction was better. I had accounted for my three immediate threats and was free to unravel some leads. The next most important threat was probably Ed Parti, and I let my mind roll over various subjects that he and I could exhaust. On the other hand, it might be a lot more interesting to see which way Parti would jump at the cue of recent events. I decided to let him incubate.

Looking over my list—Parti, Penton, and Larry—I tried to pick out an opening in any one of them that would let me begin to pry things apart. I was too comfortable. No opening presented itself. I let my mind glide over the list again and realized that it was incomplete. There was one more, now, somebody I hadn't even known of—Larry's father. The unremembered name hung in a cloud above the bed until I pierced it—Gil Hosier. For starters I would see Gil Hosier, and no doubt Larry at the same time.

After leisurely bacon and eggs, another gallon of coffee, and all the necessary ablutions, I went up to my office and arrived just as Edna was unlocking the door. I told her to make an appointment with Hosier for me that morning and settled down to my morning mail.

Gil Hosier himself came down to open the thick glass door of the apartment building for me. Edna had thoughtfully told him, while telephoning for the appointment, that speaking tubes, door buzzers, etc., did not work well for me, and that I would signal my arrival by buzzing him "Shave and a haircut, two bits."

The apartment building was richly appointed, though doormanless. The travertine walls had the proper look of marble that the moths had worried. A little red-eyed television camera spied from a molding at the ceiling. There was a lot of thick glass and gilt and heavy carpeting. A petulant closed-circuit fountain regurgitated from the wall.

Then why the old wrangler? I wondered. The man beyond the inch's depth of polished glass was totally wrapped in denim except for his high-heeled boots. He had a wrangler's handlebar mustache and a Buffalo Bill coiffure, although his hair was not white. It was that kind of thin brown hair that unfeeling young men used to call shitwater blond. I wondered if it was the high heels of his boots that threw him off balance and gave him the peculiar crouching gait that brought him to the door. It was only partly that. The rest was attitude—the fag end of beatdom—an attitude that had all the charm and immediacy of a failing candy store. His bright-blue eyes peered at me through the glass as he reached for the ornate gilt handle. The door swung open. "C'mon in, man," he said.

The moment he moved his lips, I recognized that I was in for a tough afternoon. He was a mumbler—and the mustache didn't help.

He made sure that the latch on the big door was caught after I had stepped into the foyer, and led me to the elevator. On the way up I asked him, "Larry still with you?" He looked at me, the blue eyes very different from the rest of him— sharp, appraising, very, very cool.

"Yeah."

"How's he holding up?"

"All right." We were on the eighth floor. The doors opened and he led me to his apartment—8D. The apartment was surprisingly neat for a bachelor pad—maid service, probably, an amenity I sorely lacked. The furniture was expensive-cheap, undistinguished mod, and had probably been installed by the building owners. It used to be called Hollywood Whorehouse, back before the necessity for whore-houses in Hollywood declined. Now it was just Bloom-ingdale's. The kid looked huge and pink sitting in the leather swivel chair at the end of the room. He barely glanced up when we came in.

Hosier went to the bar as if programmed. "Wanna drink?"

"Thanks. Bourbon, if you have it." The ice cubes got lost in the bottom of the big square tumbler. He began pouring the stuff over them. "Easy—easy," I said. "That's enough for a weekend's drunk. Aren't you having one?"

Unsmiling, he pushed the glass across the bar. "Nope."

"Don't you drink?"

"Nope."

"Not even with clients?"

"Nope."

That seemed to close the book, all right. I carried my drink to the other end of the room and addressed Larry. "How's it going, kid?" I asked. He didn't bother to raise his head, so I'll never know what his reply was. I saw the bottom of his beardless chin move briefly—a couple of syllables—*O.K.? Lousy?*

I took a swig from the big glass, resisting the temptation to lift it with both hands. "I hope I'm not keeping you fellas up," I said. I had to look in opposite directions to see if there was any response. Gil Hosier took the bait.

"You wanna ask questions," he said, "ask 'em."

"What about you? Don't you have any questions? Aren't either one of you interested?"

This seemed to be too much for the kid. He got up and went over to join his father at the bar. Like his father, he wore Levi's and a blue work shirt. His was buttoned up to the neck; his father's was open. There they were, the two of them, a mirror made out of time. Each could see the reflection of himself in the fun-house distortion of nearly two decades. Each of them was dressed in the laborer's uniform. Neither of them, I believed, had done a day's hard labor in his life. Workmen of the world, arise!

"What about you?" I asked the kid. "Your father let you drink?"

The kid grabbed one of the big glasses and poured scotch into it. He must have been very familiar with the equipment, because he never took his eyes off me. His eyes stayed on my face while he took his first belt of scotch, too, but while it was going down, they seemed to get a bit filmy.

"Aren't either one of you interested in whether I've made any progress?"

"Progress?" said the kid. "Fixing things up for Penton? That's progress?"

"I'm not fixing anything for anybody," I told him. "That's not my job. Never was."

"What is your job, then?" Hosier asked me. I was very happy that the two of them were side by side in front of me at the bar. It saved me from the tennis-match syndrome.

"Primarily it's to investigate Iris Penton's interest at

Groupe records so that Mr. Penton doesn't get screwed when it comes to getting everything due to him after the will is probated. Indirectly, it is also to see that the kid doesn't get screwed either. Even more indirectly, Iris Penton's primary interest at Groupe or anywhere else was just like ours— staying alive. I don't mind finding out who did her out of that particular interest."

The kid poured another scotch for himself, flooding the bottom of the glass with a reckless hand. "Even if it's Penton?" he asked.

"Even if it's Penton."

"What do you get out of it if it's Penton?"

"Penton pays the bill."

The boy laughed. "That would be great." He couldn't drink. It didn't surprise me. His father took the glass away from him and looked at him.

"What kind of questions did you want to ask us?" Hosier said, looking at me.

The boy took the glass and poured a lighter but still lethal drink. Hosier smiled at him.

"A little more background," I said. "I'd sort of over-looked the fact that Penton isn't the boy's natural father."

"Penton isn't a natural anything," said Hosier. He sighed. His natural-born son was looking pretty cockeyed and was having trouble adjusting to the tiny rail on the bar. "Let's get comfortable somewhere, and I'll tell you all I can."

We went down to the far end of the long room, where Larry had been sitting when I first came in. This time Hosier assumed the deep black leather-and-rosewood chair, and put his feet up on the ottoman. Larry sat in a leather British officer's chair. I found a spindly, comfortless, modern rocking chair. We sat and stared at each other, all three of us. Finally Hosier said, "Where do you want me to start?"

"You and Iris Penton," I said, "and how Larry got born."

"What do you mean how I got born?" Larry asked with his lower lip stuck out. "Jesus Christ. What a thing to say!"

114

Hosier gave him another of those constricted smiles that somewhat resembled the expression of a gas pain. Then he turned to me and delivered. "North Beach," he said. "Vesuvio's. City Lights next door. Mean anything to you?"

"Not much."

"It was both the early and the late time," said Hosier. "You know—I mean you've got to know—everything has happened before it happens. Right?"

"Depends on how you mean," I said.

"I don't mean the Vonnegut bullshit," said Hosier. I saw the kid stiffen slightly, a big generation gap between his teeth. "What I mean is that North Beach had already happened by the time Iris and I were arriving. We were tailgating." He lapsed into a minute reverie, his hands clasped in his lap and his eyes on the ceiling. "We came in," he continued, "just as the genuine scene was ending and the horseshit was coming on. Everything that was happening had happened. We came in while the vultures were circling. You know San Francisco?"

"Probably a different one than yours," I said. "You know the Three-O-One Club? Pete Popodopolous, Prop.? The California Bar? Turk Street? The Jockey Club?"

"Never heard of them."

"There you go." I rocked back in the skinny chair. "Different worlds."

"What were you doing in San Francisco?"

"Drinking and screwing. What were you doing?"

"Painting." He scowled, and then he smiled. "And drinking," he said. He smiled again. "And screwing." It was the first time I'd seen him really smile. He got up. "Let me fix up your drink for you." I handed him the *vase*.

He fixed me the kind of drink I used to fix for eighteen-year-old girls when I was nineteen, a deep caramel shade. I sipped it cautiously. The boy appeared to be nailed to his British officer's chair by liquor or the Haroun al Raschid reflex, I knew not. Hosier lighted a Camel and made a lot out of the first draw.

115

"You remember a singer in San Francisco named Stan Wilson?" he challenged me.

"No, I don't."

"He was one of the best. Used to sing at the hungry i, places like that. Folk singing had really come into its own. Hell, Odetta was singing down at the Tin Angel, and Iris was singing with her little tiny voice in little tiny bars."

"Ma was a folk singer?" asked the kid. "I didn't know that. She never told me that." He was ready to accuse the dead of omissions, but stopped himself and peered into the huge opening of his glass.

"It was nothing she wanted to brag about," said Hosier. "She used to come on like Susan Reed, you know? But she didn't have the zither—she had a pretty standard guitar—and she didn't really have the steam, although she sang louder than Susan." He paused and stared at the cigarette. "Also, she was very esoteric. It was great for a small audience, but the audience kept dwindling."

"This would have been about . . . ?"

"In the late fifties. Everything that was really going to be done had been done—Kerouac, Ginsberg, Ferlinghetti, Corso—jeez." He sat back reflectively. "A long time ago.

"I was painting," he went on. "I thought I was good. Some people told me I was good, but it was a funny time. Sometimes good didn't really mean good. Sometimes good just meant being with it. But I was full of piss and vinegar. Living was cheap, if you knew how to live. Iris and I shacked up . . ."

"You mean you weren't married?" said Larry.

"That's right."

"Were you ever?"

"Ever what?"

"Ever . . . uh . . . married." It seemed to bother the kid—am I a bastard, daddy?

"Sure, nineteen-sixty-two. Why not? It was a hell of a wedding. Iris was as big as a house. It was a gas."

116

"You mean you had to get married," Larry said. "I mean, because of me."

For the first time, there was absolutely no approval mixed in the look that Hosier gave him. "Nobody has to do anything, Larry," he said. "We thought it was a gas, like I told you. What difference could it make to us?"

"But did it?" I asked him.

He pursed his lips in thought. "Yeah," he admitted with a short laugh. "I guess it did. It kind of changed Iris around."

"How was that?"

"Well, she popped the kid about a month after the marriage, and by the time she was all caught up, you know, two months, three months, she figured her career was shot to hell."

"Sometimes women get depressed after they have babies," I said.

"Naw, it wasn't anything like that," he answered. "She didn't get sad; she just sort of got cold, you know, businesslike. She gave up on her own career, and then she started worrying about mine. She stopped posing for me, too. It was funny, a kind of paradox, you know? She was worried about my career, but the hottest item I had was the nudes of Iris, and she closed 'em down. I never did figure that out."

The kid said, "You sold nude paintings of my mother?"

"Those paintings bought the beans," said Hosier.

As you must realize *ad nauseam* by now, I have to look at peoples' faces while they talk—not just their lips, but their eyes, their foreheads. I'm pretty good at reading expressions. It's hard to hide a lie from me. But the look that Larry's face was wearing was a whole gallery of expressions. It would take me months to sort them out. They flitted over his face—shock, anger, incredulity, prurience, shame—all because he really didn't know *what* to feel. Never reluctant to exploit an opening, I asked him, "What's the matter? Haven't you ever seen one?"

117

"No," said the kid.

Hosier looked at him. He said, "Well, you must have seen the photographic study I did."

"No," said the kid. "I never saw anything like that."

"It's hanging right over there by the window."

Larry's jaw dropped. "That's her? That's my mother?"

"Sure."

It was a big room, the showpiece of three apparently, and it took the kid several steps to get over by the window. From where I was sitting, I could see only the huge, protuberant abdomen projected and the swollen, unwieldy breasts arrayed to support their weight. The head had no more meaning than a grapefruit jammed on a stick.

"She got a job in an agency," said Hosier, "and started showing other singers the ropes, but she didn't bring home much in the way of money. I wasn't bringing home anything at all. She was the one who suggested that I could make a buck with photography. I'd always done photographic studies before starting on a painting, and Iris began telling me that maybe my photography was better than my painting." He shifted in the chair. "That hurt." He smiled; his blue eyes very clear and sharp. "I couldn't argue, so I went along and I started getting assignments for ads. It's a tough racket. Iris got in with a giant outfit down in L.A. We sort of split up. No hard words. She took Larry with her."

Larry walked back from the wall. "What did you photograph her like that for?" he asked.

Hosier appeared to consider the subject. "You think pregnant women are ugly?"

"No," said Larry defenselessly. "Of course not . . . only . . ."

"A bod's a bod," said Hosier. "Some girl they shot in *Playboy* said it . . . . 'It's only skin.'" Larry sat down.

I got up and walked along the wall. There were other photographs—of animals, mostly deer, a bear, a beaver, and some small animals I couldn't identify, probably otters, weasels, things like that. The photographs were magnificent. They had an intimacy I had never seen in animals before. I sipped a little more bourbon. "Then what happened?" I asked him.

"We had no connection at all until last year, and then it wasn't really a connection. I accidentally ran into Larry at a party. I still hadn't seen Iris, and still haven't seen Iris. She'd only known I was in New York for the last few weeks, and then only because Larry had told her. She didn't call me; I didn't call her."

I stopped in front of an eight-by-ten of a young woman holding a guitar. "This Iris?" I asked him.

"You mean you don't recognize her?"

"Not really," I answered. In fact I had just been making conversation. However, I looked again, sharply, and thought fast, combating the bourbon. "It's a beautiful print," I opined. "You develop it yourself and print it yourself?"

I looked back at him, and he nodded an assent.

"I wonder how you get that texture," I said. "Do you ever flop the negative over for tones, shadows, things like that? I mean, I'm a complete ignoramus."

"The only time you flop a neg is either by accident or for layout purposes—you know, so the model is looking into the page or something like that. It doesn't change the texture at all."

"Live and learn," I said. I moved back to the animals. "These are great," I said. "I take it you did them?" I turned around to look at him.

"Yeah. I got into animals about two years ago. The market still isn't big enough, but when it comes in, I'll own it. Nobody does them that good."

"You mean nobody's got a lens that good?"

"Lens?" He got up and came over to the wall. "Screw that. You don't do it with a lens. Every clown has got a lens. That's why you get the blank looks in those people's studies. I get in close. The animal knows I'm there. He doesn't really

119

know what I am or what I'm doing. He's interested. He's curious. He's a little bit afraid, but not really threatened. It's not like I had a gun. You ever think about that? That maybe animals can smell guns? Not the man himself so much. What the hell, man is just another animal. But guns—you ever get a whiff of Hoppe's gun cleaner?" I nodded. "You think the animals don't get it? It smells like nothing else. You can smell it a mile away. It's unmistakable. It means gun—loud noise—bang! You're dead."

I looked back at the furry animal on the wall. His eyes were bright, intelligent, interested. "Hell," I said. "I don't even know what the animal is called."

"That's a marten," said Hosier. "Interested as hell, ain't he? That's what makes him look alive. You know—he knows something's happening. He's not sure what, but he's game. He's alive. It's not like a telephoto. In those shots the animals are just one jump ahead of being asleep. But when you get in up on them—slow—slow—the right moves—nothing lateral—you just grow on them, you know? All of a sudden they know you're there. And that's when you get 'em."

I looked back at the marten and cautioned myself against Hosier's spiel. It was a great sales talk, but I wondered why he was selling me—practice? "You sure didn't photograph him in Central Park," I said.

"No—up around Menominee."

"Where's that?"

"In Michigan. I went up to do the old hotel in Mackinac. Whenever I go out on a job with expenses, I like to take another day to go out in the local woods and shoot what I can."

"And when you're in town?"

"I go up to my place in the Catskills." He nodded toward the boy. "Going to take Larry up there one of these days."

Larry stirred. "You've been promising that for months now."

120

"Been busy."

"Busy sitting on your ass," said Larry.

"You drink too much—for a kid," Hosier said mildly.

"And you suck too much," Larry said.

There was a lengthy silence.

"What's your problem?" Hosier asked finally.

"My problem is listening to you get it off with this professional fink," Larry said. "You think he gives a shit about animals or taking pictures? He's laughing at you, and all the time he's jerking you off."

The bright-blue eyes bored into Larry. "I keep wondering if I was anything like you when I was your age," he said. "I've looked at it a lot. I don't think so."

"You didn't know shit when you were my age," Larry said. "That was back in the dark ages. They didn't even have acid then. Everybody had a brain like a keyhole."

"And now everybody's got a brain like an asshole," Hosier said. "An expanded asshole. If you're all expanded and everything, what are you so uptight about? You're pissing yourself like a high school girl."

The rage built up in Larry's face, more than crimson, nearly purple. He grabbed the scotch bottle and reared back to fire.

"That's not cool," said Hosier. The kid's eyes bulged, and then he wheeled and pitched the bottle at the photograph of his mother on the wall. The Little League had done a lot for him. The glass starred and refracted the pregnant body in a hundred directions. The kid snatched a denim jacket off the chair and headed for the door.

"Where are you going?" Hosier asked. The kid stopped and turned a clenched-fist face to us. "Stay away from the studio," Hosier told him.

"Fuck you," said Larry. I felt the vibration of the slamming door.

"What's the matter with the studio?" I asked Hosier.

"I don't want him screwing around down there getting in everybody's way, that's all."

121

Hosier was beginning to let the irritation leak out of his seams. "Anybody complaining?" I asked.

Hosier took a deep breath. "I've about had it with you for the day," he said. "The party's over. Good-bye."

"Thanks for the drink," I said.

I let myself out. Hosier was picking pieces of broken glass out of the frame when I left. The photograph was torn.

Chapter XVIII

It didn't surprise me at all that Probcziewski was sitting at my desk when I got back to my office. I had expected him earlier in the day, before I'd left the office to see Hosier and Larry, in fact. He had his long legs elevated and his feet planted not at the edge but in the very middle of my desk. His hands were laced behind his head. He was staring intently at Edna's kneecaps.

If you can hear, of course, you can notice a sudden silence just from the end of the buzz. When you're deaf, you have to sense it. I sensed it. Edna was flushing very prettily. Probcziewski, I think, had been making time.

"Looking for a partnership?" I asked him. "Start at the top?"

I pulled his feet off the desk and tipped the swivel chair. He got out. I sat in the chair and put my feet on the *edge* of the desk, the way my mother taught me. Probcziewski sat in the client's chair, which was only right.

"I came to thank you for the wonderful favor you've done for me," Probcziewski said. "I haven't really decided how I'm going to repay you yet, but I'm thinking hard."

"Along what lines?"

"Like having you kidnaped and sent to a certain interested party in South America."

"Oh, Melendez, eh?" I answered warily. "Cause you some trouble, did he?"

"Melendez didn't give me trouble," said Probcziewski. "The chief gave me trouble, the federal narcotics people gave me trouble. The State Department . . ."

"The State Department!"

"It seems they were negotiating. Also, the State people were very upset because Melendez had his hair mussed. They kept stroking him and cooing at him."

"The State people like heroin?"

"They like promises kept. They like diplomatic immunity, things like that."

"They like foreigners putting wires on my balls?" Edna jumped. "I'm sorry, Edna."

"What the State Department wants is for nobody to interfere with the making of money or the making of deals."

"And what do the narcos want?"

"They wanted the credit for making the arrest."

"So give it to them."

"Give it to them they arrested a diplomat in a police station?"

"They can't have everything."

"They can have my head on a platter."

"What about the chief?"

"He wants the State Department and the narcos to get the hell out of the station and take Melendez with them. Also, he wants my head on a platter."

"Doesn't the chief want to clear up crime in this God-fearing nation?"

"Not wealthy crime."

"How did you tag Melendez?"

"I got a positive identification from Schultz. I also told

123

them that I'd get an attempted murder charge from you if they wanted it. They didn't want it. They took him out."

"And?"

"They're shipping him back—mustache wax and all."

I was suddenly very interested. "That doesn't mean he can come back in at will, does it?"

"No. I don't think so. The narcos would love to grab him, and the ambassador looked pretty pissed off with Melendez."

"You didn't even mention the ambassador before."

"He was just another indignant friend of the suspect. I never pay attention to indignant friends of suspects."

"How are they shipping him back?"

"On the S.S. *Carlotta Perez*."

I thought about it. "They'd better hurry up," I said, "or I'll go out there and keelhaul that bastard all over again."

"You'll stay put," said Probcziewski. "If you even take a bath I'll arrest you. What's more," he continued, "I want to question you."

"About what?"

"About why you're still on the case."

"I'm on the case because Penton is paying me."

"Maybe it's time you got off."

"Have you found somebody to pay me for getting off?"

He gave me one of his long ferocious scowls, and I took the opportunity to light a cigarette. "You know a guy named Herb Rauscher?" he asked me finally.

"Deuce Detective Agency, down on West Twenty-third? Yeah, what about him?"

"Did you know that Mrs. Penton hired him before Penton hired you?"

"Nobody said anything to me about it. Did she have him checking on Penton?"

"Not exactly," said Probcziewski. He reached inside his coat and took out a folded photostat. "She had him draw up one of these." He handed me the paper.

It was a sworn affidavit, duly notarized, and signed by

Herbert J. Rauscher to the effect that that premises owned and occupied by Mrs. Penton had been thoroughly and professionally searched for evidence of narcotics and that no such narcotics had been found. The notarized date was just one week before I had found her in the pool.

"You remember Penton saying anything about this?" I asked Edna.

"Not that I know of. I never made a note of anything like that."

"You think Penton knew about this?" I asked Probcziewski.

"The whole idea, I guess, is that he shouldn't know about it."

"How'd you come across it?"

"Rauscher mailed the copy after he read about the drowning."

"Brownie points," I said.

"I went down to see him," said Probcziewski. "Maybe you already know everything he told me, maybe not. I'm going to tell you anyway, because then I'll know that you know, and you'll know that I know you know. O.K.?"

There was something very dangerous about the big cop now, and there was a little perspiration collecting on my forehead that wasn't entirely from the effort of following his you-know-I-know-you-know routine. "That will be very nice," I said. "Edna? Maybe you'd better take this down."

Edna flapped her book open and looked expectantly at Probcziewski. He smiled—wolfishly, I thought. Edna crossed her legs. We both smiled.

"What Rauscher told me is this," said Probcziewski. "Mrs. Penton needed a clean bill of health because Penton was trying to blackmail her through her son Larry."

"That's not news," I interrupted. "He was actually trying to get me to plant some narcotics in the place and then 'discover' it. I told him no. I made a report and dictated it to Edna. You can have a copy if you want. He finally settled just

125

for me to go over and look around on the off chance I might find a stash somewhere."

"Or a dead Mrs. Penton, with her husband carefully established in his office."

"I have a very lively appreciation of that theory. Keep moving."

"After the very real blackmail threat from Penton, Mrs. Penton told Larry to move out for a while—a week at most. He went and stayed with his father."

"She threw him out?"

"No; nothing like that. She told him that the police were snooping around for a possible bust and that she wanted the place clean. He understood. They got along."

"What was she trying to accomplish?"

"She suspected that Penton would try to plant some junk in the house. And, of course, she was right. With the affidavit of sanitization, and with the kid demonstrably living somewhere else, she would have trapped Penton in his own scheme."

"Nice," I said. "Nice people."

"Desperate," Probcziewski told me, "very desperate people."

I was suddenly very irritated. "What the hell is desperate about living in a quarter-of-a-million dollar lash-up on Long Island, owning your own recording company, and swimming up to your chin in hot-shot brokerage clients?"

"Not a thing, as long as you're clean," said the big lieutenant. "But Penton isn't clean."

"Aha!"

Probcziewski looked down at me. "Is this really news to you? Don't you ever look into your clients?"

"My clients pay me to investigate *other* people, not themselves."

"If I find out you're kidding me," warned Probcziewski, "I'll tie your legs in a bow."

"Did the police-loving all-American boy Herb Rauscher investigate Mrs. Penton?"

126

"Not that he mentioned."

"There you go," I advised him. "Proceed."

"I hardly have to tell you," Probcziewski said, "but just for the record"—he nodded toward Edna—"Penton decided to become wealthy in his own right by investing other people's money in sure-fire speculations. He not only bought, he bought on margins that aren't really legal. He pulled every stupid trick in the book, I guess, and he wound up in a hole so deep you couldn't even see him at the bottom. It was boom or bust with Penton, and he busted."

"I knew he was a jerk," I said. "But a jerk's money is still money."

Probcziewski took out a thin cigar and got out of the chair, a good, old, golden-oak office chair that has ironed out many a bottom. He lit the cigar, rubbed his behind, and grimaced at me.

"That chair tends to keep interviews short," I told him.

"I'm surprised you have any interviews at all."

"Be sure to get that insult on the record," I instructed Edna.

"Penton came home to his wife and put his head in her lap," Probcziewski continued. "The only out he had was for her to let him borrow on the record-company stock. He'd always figured this as his ace in the hole, I guess. Mrs. Penton wasn't having any."

"If he didn't realize that, he's even dumber than I thought."

"I don't know if it was stupidity or what," Probcziewski said. He was still standing, but he looked guardedly at the chair, sighed, and sat in it again. "If a guy can kid himself into thinking he can make a killing on the market, I guess he could fool himself into thinking he could manipulate his wife."

"He didn't do his homework. She's been building up that company for fifteen years. It meant a lot to her."

"A guy like Penton can't understand that," Probcziewski adjudged. "He can't understand anything in the world being more important than his particular problem at that particular

127

moment. Sometimes I think that's the best definition of the criminal class there is."

Edna paused with her pencil and shook her pretty head. "What's the matter?" I asked her.

"Criminal class," she said. "Penton's no criminal."

Probcziewski and I nodded cheerfully and smiled at each other. "Empty the prisons," I suggested.

Probcziewski gave Edna a long, loving look. "What makes you think Penton's not a member of the criminal class?" he asked sweetly.

"Well, he doesn't go around hitting people on the head."

"That we know of," Probcziewski offered.

"Oh, come on," she said. "You can't really see Penton doing anything violent, can you?"

"As a matter of fact" Probcziewski answered, "I think Penton would saw your throat open with a rusty tin can if it would get him out of the hole, or keep him out of jail. But that's beside the point. . . ." He forestalled her with an upraised palm the size of Achilles' shield. "You don't have to hit people on the head to be a criminal. Most of the real pros I've collared wouldn't dream of mussing anybody's hair. On the other hand, if somebody blows his brains out because a pro is blackmailing him, if somebody loses everything he worked for all his life because a pro has swindled him—the pro just shrugs. 'That's life, buddy,' says the pro. There's the assumption that *everybody* would steal, swindle, and blackmail if only they had the brains or the guts. It's the thieves' philosophy—'If I don't take it, somebody else will.' The only thing that separates Penton from the pros is that he's dumber than most."

"A highly prejudiced portrait of my client," I objected. "Be sure you get that down, Edna."

"Is he still your client?" Probcziewski asked me.

"Why shouldn't he be? He hasn't been convicted of anything. I've been sitting here taking in a lot of injurious hearsay about him, that's all."

"You really need money that much?" The sneer was on Probcziewski's face, so I suppose it rang out in his voice as well. Being deaf has probably spared me a lot of insults.

"I like to eat," I admitted. "So does Edna, and besides, she's madly in love with Penton" (daggers from Edna). "I couldn't break up anything as beautiful as that. Maybe *she'll* give him the money to get off the stove."

"You're disgusting," said Edna.

"There's another thing," I told Probcziewski. "I've sort of taken to the idea of Penton paying for the investigation into his wife's murder, particularly if he turns up holding the sack. If he has run out of holding money, I can always tap the estate."

Probcziewski was all policeman now. "Watch it," he warned me. "Officially Mrs. Penton was an O.D. We haven't proved a damn thing otherwise."

"That's not where I'm standing."

"You've proved it, but we haven't?"

"Good enough proof for me to operate on," I said. "For one thing, those needle marks were all fresh. You want to see tracks, take a look at her kid's arm sometime."

"So she was playing around with the needle, first time around. Happens all the time. So do O.D.s, first time around."

"When I was up at her ex-husband's apartment today," I told Probcziewski, "I saw a photograph of her, a publicity shot, really, in a homespun dress with long hair hanging down, playing the guitar and singing. She used to be a folksinger, you know."

"No, I didn't know, and so what?"

"She was strumming the guitar with her left hand, and her right hand was on the frets."

"Oh," said the lieutenant.

"Oh—what?" demanded Edna.

Probcziewski turned resignedly to her. "The needle

129

marks were all on her left arm. Since she's left-handed, they should have been on her right arm."

It was Edna's turn to say, "Oh."

I looked at Edna. "She was almost certainly murdered," I said, "in a very dirty way. I like Penton for it, even though he was safely established in his office. I think he got frustrated and hired a couple of goons, probably the same boys that had their fun with me."

I turned to Probcziewski. "All this stuff about Penton stealing," I asked him, "anybody mind if I brace him with it?"

"The shop he works for would mind, and the insurance company would mind, but would the police mind? No."

"I don't understand," said Edna to the detective.

"The shop and the bonding company want the money back. Penton, while making license plates in the can, will be earning about thirty-five cents a day. What money he gets from the house and the estate would be spent on his defense at the trial. Lawyers have a wonderful way of sizing up what a person owns and writing a bill to fit that exact amount. That means that his employer and the bonding people don't get a nickel back to defray the repayment of the fraud.

"Now the police are being very nice about this. Nobody has brought charges yet, so they're sitting on it. But if Penton should do something stupid, like run for it, the police can put him in the jug." He smiled at me. "You want to brace him, so brace him," he said.

This seemed to satisfy Probcziewski's lust for conversation. He got up from the chair, yawned, and stretched, his fists nearly touching the ceiling. I saw Edna's eyes follow him up, as though she were watching a balloon ascension. Probcziewski looked at her and said something that I couldn't see. She seemed to enjoy it, whatever it was. She colored prettily and nodded. "I'll have to get back," he said, turning back to me. "When I do, I'll check out that left hand, right hand with the coroner's office."

"You don't have a full report yet?"

"They're in no hurry to write up O.D.s in expensive houses," said Probcziewski, "even less a woman being murdered in her own swimming pool. I think they like a nice, quiet, accidental drowning. I'm going to blow them up." He scratched at the dark shadow on his chin as if he were enjoying the prospect. Then he said, "How come the Deuce Agency?"

"What's that?"

"How come it's called the Deuce Agency—Rauscher operating all by his lonesome?"

"He used to have a partner up until five years ago."

"What happened?"

"Perforated."

"Shot?"

"Ulcer."

"Oh." He nodded understandingly. At the door he said, "You can make Penton hop if you want to. But don't make him hop right out of the pond."

"I understand."

He left as though he were stepping into another world. We were forgotten the minute his hand touched the doorknob. "What's with you and the lieutenant?" I asked Edna.

"He wants me to help him type up some papers he's putting together."

"At the station, way out there?"

"Uh, no. I told him he could bring them over to my apartment."

"Just like that, eh?"

She has that kind of very clear skin that looks as though neon lights are flashing when she blushes. "Do you want to investigate *me* now?"

"Not in any way that's legal."

"Joe?"

"Yeah?"

"Do you think that's true, that every crook just assumes that everybody else is a crook too?"

"Not really. Thieves know that there are a lot of people

131

who aren't, but they consider those people to be freaks or half-wits—victims—apples, marks, they call them. They think that the real population of the world is made up of crooks and sharpies, right from the six-for-five shoeshine man to a president of the United States. Noncrooks exasperate them. Difficult noncrooks infuriate them. Amateur crooks, like Penton, amuse them.

"Get Penton at his office, will you? And tell him I'm coming over with my bill. I want to get the bill on record before the lawyers take over."

Chapter XIX

I hadn't seen the Penton house since that afternoon I'd discovered the owner in the pool. Even now I wasn't here by choice, only because the shop had told Edna that "Mr. Penton is no longer associated with this firm. We believe he may be reached at his home."

"Don't reach him right now," I'd told Edna. "I'll go out unannounced."

The house looked now like its former owner—lifeless. If it had had a FOR RENT sign out in front it would have looked normal. I parked the car on the street, walked up, and pushed the chimes.

It was obvious that Penton hadn't seen me come up the walk. It took him a few moments to recognize me, and even after that it seemed an effort for him to make the right associations. He was wearing shapeless flannel slacks and an old turtleneck. He needed a shave and had that look people used to call "unbuttoned," which really meant that he hadn't changed his underwear recently.

"C'mon in, c'mon in." He gestured vaguely to a dim, dusty-looking interior. There was a glass in his hand that had acquired a thick residue of film inside it. The dregs of the drink sloshed in the base as he waved me in.

I had seen interiors of homes like this before when I had visited lonely invalids or the blind. There had been a minimal effort to maintain the niceties, but dust and dirt had built up in the corners. Stray socks peeped out from under the couch and an empty pork-and-beans can, from which a meal had been made, sat next to a piece of Sevres on a Hepplewhite table. The fork jutted out of the can. It seemed just as much at home in the living room as the piece of Sevres.

"I thought we'd better get together and compare notes," I said to Penton. I wondered if I would have to maintain that stilted a tone for the rest of the conversation. Above all, I didn't want to panic him.

He nodded wordlessly, an expression of profound conviction on his face. His eyes were vacant under the furrowed brow. Suddenly animated, he said, "Let me fix you a drink. Bourbon, isn't it?" And before I could reply, he vanished into the kitchen.

While he was gone, I looked through the French doors into the backyard. The pool, where I'd found his wife, apparently hadn't been touched. Leaves sailed idly on the surface, along with twigs, small branches, and other less distinguishable bits of flotsam. Most of the lawn furniture had been tipped over, either by the wind or by Penton's falling down, I guessed.

A big sycamore up by the high paling fence in the back brooded over the yard, and its shadows announced that the afternoon was late indeed. The door to the cabana had been left ajar.

Penton came in and handed me a drink. It was not a glass I would have accepted in Red Hook, but I accepted it from

133

Penton, hoping that the alcohol would kill the bugs. "Let's sit down," Penton said. "Let's sit down and talk. I'm glad to see you."

I tasted the drink—and for the second time that day, somebody had handed me a bomb. It was straight bourbon. It's very odd how people pour out enormous quantities of liquor that they don't drink—Penton being a scotch man if I ever saw one. The bourbon set fire to my mouth, and I struggled to swallow it right way down. I set the tumbler on the floor in front of me, delicately, so that it wouldn't explode. "How've you been making out?" I asked him.

"Fine, just fine," he said, sitting forward. Again, he reminded me of an invalid in his conscious effort to respond. It was as if he had pushed a button to start the mechanism in his brain. After he had spoken, his eyes went dark.

"I'm afraid I haven't got very much to report," I told him.

"You think they're hiding something?" He was difficult to read. The expression in his face didn't match the words his lips were framing.

"I'm afraid I can't even tell you that," I said. "I've been busy with other problems in the case."

"What problems?"

"Problems like making sure I stay alive to collect my fee."

It inspired some animation in him. "Someone has been threatening you?"

"That's putting it pretty cool," I said. "I got mugged when I walked out of the studio after I'd gone there. I got worked over and spent some time in the hospital. As a matter of fact, the scar I've got under my eye wasn't there the last time you saw me."

"Scar?" He got up in the fading light and walked, as if he were stepping over broken glass, to my chair and stared at my face. I realized that I was sitting in a pool of shadow. "That's very ugly," he said, his face very close to mine. He hadn't been brushing his teeth. "I'm very sorry." His eyes had nothing in them. They were dead, dull, bronze buttons. "It looks as if someone gouged you," he said.

"I won't bore you with the details."

"Please," he said. "I'd like to know. Did someone try to stab you?"

"No. They tossed me in an elevator shaft, and a rat joined me for lunch."

"They? Did you ever find out who did it?"

"Oh, yes; it's all taken care of."

"Good." There was absolutely no change of expression in his eyes or mouth. Then he said, "Have you seen Larry recently?"

"Very recently—today, in fact."

"Is that so? How is he?"

"He seemed pretty disturbed."

"Disturbed." Questions are framed by eyebrows hoisting upward. His remained level.

"Not psychiatrically," I reassured him. "I just mean upset. There seems to be a little friction between him and his father."

"That's not surprising. Larry hates any kind of authority."

"Did he hate his mother, too?"

Now the dead eyes stared into mine as if, perhaps, it were Penton who was deaf instead of me. "No," he said finally. "He didn't hate his mother."

"Did he obey her?"

"Up to a point."

"What point?"

Penton heaved a huge sigh. "Up to the point where he couldn't help himself, I suppose. You know, he couldn't just stop taking drugs like that." His fingers fumbled at a snap in the air.

"But he didn't mind doing what she told him generally," I commented. "It makes you wonder about authority."

He thought this over. "I guess he loved her," he said. "I guess that makes a difference."

"A hell of a difference," I agreed. "From what I saw this morning, he doesn't exactly have the same feelings toward his

135

father. He was going to bean him with a scotch bottle."

"They had a fight?"

"It never got that far." I tested the drink again, hoping that some of the proof had evaporated. False hopes, easily dispelled. "He slung the bottle at the wall, finally. Something in his old man's eye turned him off."

"What were they arguing about?"

"It seemed like an old, long-standing thing. He blew up when Hosier told him to stay away from the studio. I couldn't figure out why Hosier wanted him to stay away. When I asked him, he sort of told me to get lost."

"Ed Parti." Penton spoke the name, nodding sagely. "Ed Parti. I wonder how much Hosier really knows?"

I sat up straighter. "How much is there to know?"

"Plenty." He drained his glass and waved it at me. "Finish your drink," he ordered, "and I'll fill you in."

Afraid to disturb the camaraderie, I swallowed the drink. By the time I handed the glass over, my face felt as if it were made of plywood. Penton disappeared into the kitchen, and I got up and paced back and forth to shake off the spell of the alcohol.

He shambled back into the darkening room with the drinks slopping over the rims of the glasses and held the two of them up to me. "Can you tell which one is the bourbon?" he asked. "I've forgotten."

I took the wicked-looking glass from his left hand, tasted it, and winced. "This will do," I said and tottered back to my chair.

Penton inhaled a large amount of his drink and began. "Did you know that Iris was going to fire Ed Parti?" he asked me.

"First I've heard of it."

He nodded sagely again, his mouth drooping knowledge-ably. "That's right. She was just about to fire him before she died. You want to know why?" I evinced interest. "Because she knew he was running narcotics, that's why."

"Don't a lot of those people use drugs?" I objected. "If you fired everybody with a habit, the music industry would shut down."

"Not just using," Penton said. "Dealing. He was dealing in a big way. But even that isn't the main reason. The main reason is that he turned Larry on. He got him started using heroin. He did all the supplying, everything. He got Larry hooked. *That's* why Larry thinks Ed's the best friend he ever had."

"Did you know this when you hired me?" I asked him. He nodded an assent. "Why didn't you tell me then?"

"I thought it would be better if you found out for yourself," he replied. "Be honest now." He leaned forward. "Would you have believed me if I'd accused them right off like that?"

"Maybe not," I said, "but I would have been a little more on my guard, and I might not have been bowled over the way I was."

"I am really very sorry about that," he said.

I fingered my scar. "Do you know how the set-up worked?"

He leaned back and took a long, long swig. "You have to know something about the business to understand the set-up," he said. His lips were stiff, and I was having trouble reading him in the darkening room. I hunched up closer. "The stuff was being delivered by the K.C. Sourballs."

"That's the outfit Mrs. Penton was keeping her eye on?"

"That's right. Whenever they went on tour they'd drop the stuff off at various points along the way."

"Stupid," I said. "How stupid can you get? Didn't they know they were primed for a bust? Jesus. They've gotten real stars on this kind of thing. Busted them right in the dressing room."

"I don't think they had much of a choice," Penton told me. "They were in the hole pretty deep to the company."

"I had the impression they were making money."

"Only on one side of the ledger. The expenses out-balanced the earnings. It happens to most of the groups—the same way it happened to fighters. They go on tour and they earn a mint. They're happy. Full houses, a lot of chicks, coke, anything they want, right? But when they get back to the apple, it's another story. They get to peek at the expenses—and the expenses are astronomical, way over what they made, or even what they thought they made. It crushes them. They find out that they're poorer than when they started. They owe for everything, and they owe it all to the company. They're not overly bright, you know. A lot of them can't even read music, let alone double-entry bookkeeping."

"Are all these expenses legit?"

"Legitimate?" He tasted the word. I got the feeling he thought it might be Swahili. "Legitimate." He repeated it again, for the novelty of the thing. "That would really depend on what you mean by legitimate." He smiled his little thief's smile.

"What I mean by legitimate," I clarified, "is was the Groupe Record Company stealing money from these kids by making false entries in their accounts?"

The modish haircut had grown over itself, ragged and unkempt. The ends of it flared out as he shook his head. "If you understood cost accounting you wouldn't ask questions like that," Penton advised me. "You wouldn't use words like *stealing* and *false entry*. You don't use words like that about these kids. They're not that important."

"They're not important because they don't know how to squawk, apparently," I said. "What happens if they learn double-entry bookkeeping and start checking up on you?"

"Then they're replaced. Who wants troublemakers?"

I sat back and savored the stew. "Something I haven't mentioned," I began. "Aren't these kids supposed to have a manager who looks after these things?"

I saw his face shift slightly, but I wasn't able to read him. Finally, I said, "Penton, it's getting very dark in here, and I

138

really can't see what you're saying anymore." It evoked a dull glimmer of teeth as he grinned. "Could you switch on the lamp?"

The backyard outside the window dissolved into blackness as the light he had snapped on shone against the windowpane. In the harsh electric glare his profile was outlined against the black sheen of the window. Gray, puffy, and sagging, he made a silhouette of manic despair.

"Iris," he said, and the thief's grin flitted across his face. "Iris was their manager."

"So the fox was counting the chickens," I observed. "It was Iris all by herself who cooked the books on them?"

The observation provoked him. The ragged mop over the gray face shook wildly. "You sit here making all kinds of judgments," he said. His fist hit the arm of the overstuffed chair. "Do you know how much money you have to invest in those snot noses to get them any kind of a name? How do you think anybody's going to make any money?"

"Money?" I asked him. "Or a killing? Are you talking about investment or speculation?"

"Investment is for grandmothers," he said impatiently. "Ten percent, fifteen percent, twenty, twenty-five, thirty percent, it's never enough. All investment is good for is to get the money from some suckers all in one place so somebody with some brains can use it."

"Brains like yours," I said. I couldn't help it; it just slipped out. "Do you think the group ever tumbled to what was happening?"

The thought arrested him. "It could only happen in one way," he said slowly. "First, you have to realize that they really trusted Iris. I mean, she'd brought them along from being just a bunch of kids practicing in a garage to being a name, you know? They weren't going to question Iris about expenses. But it could be—it just might be—that Ed Parti was trying to get them away from her, and Ed Parti could have shown them the numbers."

139

"How they were being cheated, you mean?"

He hated words like *cheating* and *stealing*. He waved me off impatiently. "He could have stirred them up against her, all right," said Penton, "the son of a bitch."

"How do you think they would have reacted?"

He shrugged. "Who knows what goes on in those coked-up skulls? You'd have to ask Ed Parti about that."

I hauled out my notebook. "I'll try," I promised, "but just for safety, I think you'd better give me their names and any other information you have about them."

I jotted it down as he filled me in. Names: Joe Dodds, Benny Willicz, Bernie Schwartskop, and Eddie Seguarez. Where from? Great Neck, every one of them. Descriptions? Pretty shaky, but I took it all down. I thought about the transfer of allegiance. "One more question," I said, putting my notebook aside. "Was Iris involved in distributing the drugs?"

He shook his head very slowly. His eyes were almost closed. "No," he said. "Iris hated all that stuff. She'd have no part of it."

"Are you sure?" I asked him. "Are you one-hundred-percent sure? It's important—really important."

There was no answer from him. I got up and went over to his chair. He was passed out colder than a mackerel. His head had not moved very much, simply sunk a little deeper toward his chest. Should I wake him? I wondered.

I looked at his face. Apart from the sag, it was almost placid—a very quiet ruin. I wondered how it would look in prison, where there would be no easy escape through the neck of a scotch bottle. Maybe a prison regimen would paste him back together again, but I doubted it. Bad food, gray days, and gray nights wouldn't help to repair Iris's pretty toy.

I decided to leave him as he sat, debating briefly whether I should turn off the lamp. I decided against it. Waking in the dark not knowing where you were or why you were sitting upright in the midst of sleep would not be pleasant. I tiptoed away and let myself out the front door.

I was all the way down to the street before I reached for the absent notebook at my breast pocket. I cursed a nice round oath and started back up to get it from the chair arm, where I'd left it while ruminating over sonny boy.

The lock on the front door had not been snapped, and I reminded myself to set it for self-locking on the way out. I tiptoed back into the room, not wanting to frighten him, and spotted my notebook on the chair.

He had tipped far over, as drunks sometimes do, but with the spastic attitude of his body and the fresh smell of blood, I knew that he was dead.

The blood was still draining from the emptiness of the temple that faced the floor. A round, substantial entrance wound was on the other side. The size of it just about matched the hole in the dark window where the bullet had passed through.

I suddenly became very cold, as if all the blood had stopped in my arteries. I snapped off the light and jumped back from the window. Then I ran into the hallway and locked the front door. I looked at the telephone on its stand in the foyer. There was no question, now, of my running next door to rouse the neighbors. I picked up the phone and called the police, repeating the message and the address over and over again into the dead machine until I felt sure it had gotten through. I stayed in the foyer until the police arrived. By the time they got there, I was shaking pretty good. After they arrived, I finished the second drink that Penton had fixed for me.

Chapter XX

"Calm down," Probcziewski kept telling me. "Pull yourself together."

I was wandering in that awful countryside between drunkenness and shock. "I'll be all right," I mumbled. "I'll be all right. Just give me a couple of minutes." I was shaking very hard.

"How did you manage to get this loaded?" he asked me. The cops who were moiling through the rooms were giving me stares of very frank disgust. I had thrown up in the foyer. Somebody had dropped a bath towel over the mess, but it hadn't helped things much.

"The air," I told Probcziewski, "the air hit me." Somehow, being forced to explain things helped to calm my nerves. The trembling began to slow down. "It seems everybody I talked to today was handing me one-thousand-proof tumblers of whiskey. I was all right here until I stepped outside and caught the fresh air. You know how it hits you when you've been drinking in a stuffy room?"

The big lieutenant nodded.

"It didn't really catch up with me until I got back into the house. I came back for my notebook," I explained, "and saw Penton with his brains on the carpet."

"How long were you out of the house?"

"It couldn't have been more than two minutes. Just down to the end of the front walk and back. I came back in and first I just thought that he'd slipped down in his chair. Then I smelled the blood and saw the carpet, and the first thing that jumped into my head was that Penton had done the Dutch act. But there wasn't any gun. Then I saw the bullet hole in the window and I panicked."

"I can appreciate that," Probcziewski said gravely.

"The son of a bitch could have killed the two of us like clay pigeons," I said. "I realized that I was standing over the victim's body, a real live witness, lit up like a Christmas tree."

They had pulled the slug out of the wall—a big meaty-looking bastard that had buried itself in a stud half-way between the floor and the molding of the ceiling. They ran a string from the bullet hole in the wall to the one in the window.

"Do you want some coffee?" Probcziewski asked me.

"Yeah, yeah. Make it black." The cup and saucer rattled as I got up and began to experiment with my legs. I walked up and down, sipping the coffee and spilling not a little of it on my tie.

They had passed the string through the hole in the window, where another cop led the end of it out and down the slope of the backyard.

The backyard was now crisscrossed with floodlights, some of them from the house itself, and some of them brought in by the police. I watched the plainclothesman with his piece of string back carefully away from the window, keeping his string in a straight line. The shallow hypotenuse took him to the cabana door, about forty yards to the rear of the house.

"Nice shooting," I said to Probcziewski, and then I started to shake again. I put the cup and saucer down.

"Easy target," Probcziewski answered. "Silhouetted under a lamp—dead still. Nothing to worry about. Got the side of the cabana to steady his gun. I don't think it's so great."

"It's a real bull's-eye, though," I commented. "A surgeon couldn't have put a better hole in his head."

"Let's talk about something else for a minute," said Probcziewski. "Why do you think Penton was shot?"

143

"To keep him out of the witness chair when his case came up."

"How could he hurt anybody?"

"Let's sit down again," I said. "Groupe records was distributing drugs all over the country. Penton knew it. He also knew how it worked."

"He tell you?"

"Yes. Ed Parti, as we'd suspected, is running things. He turned Iris's kid on, among other things, and she was going to fire him just before she died. Now Parti was into the K.C. Sourballs—who were managed by Iris, incidentally—to distribute drugs while they were on tour. He had a lock on them because they were deep in the hole to the company, and this was the only way they could bail themselves out. Do you like it?"

"I'd like it better if it hadn't come from Penton," the lieutenant said. His massive blue-stubbled jaw went out in thought. "Maybe Penton was running the ring and was just trying to set up Parti for it."

"Then why was he panic-stricken about his losses?" I objected. "You ever see a heavy pusher worried about money? Penton wanted in, that's all."

"Then maybe he was shot for wanting in."

I shook my head. "You wouldn't have to shoot Penton to scare him off. If they'd just sent somebody around to step on his toes it would have been enough. It would have been enough to keep him from talking, too, but it wouldn't have been enough to keep him from talking in a witness chair under a subpoena. They needed the silence, the real silence, and they bought themselves a piece of it."

A patrolman came in with a brass cartridge on a handkerchief. "That it?" Probcziewski asked him.

"Looks like it, lieutenant." The young patrolman was bucking for a stripe. He was very cool, yet with a large streak of being thrilled about it all flashing out of his eyes. "We found it twenty-seven inches away, at an angle of thirty-six degrees to the right and behind the front corner of the cabana."

I whistled. Probcziewski grinned. "You'll swear to that in court?" he asked the patrolman.

The young man held up a notebook—as if it were a crucifix to ward off evil spirits. "I've got it all down here lieutenant."

"Good," said Probcziewski. "Don't lose the notebook. You see any footprints out there?"

"It's all lawn, lieutenant. There wasn't anything."

"O.K.," said Probcziewski, dismissing him. "Don't let anybody clown around out there. Seal things up, and I'll come in and look around in the morning."

"Yes, sir." The young man left in a cloud of aspiration.

Probcziewski looked at the cartridge. "Forty-four magnum," he announced.

"Jesus Christ," I said. "Why didn't they use a field mortar?"

Probcziewski got up and went to the telephone. I watched him dial and talk into the handset. My mind was an absolute perfect blank, grabbing as much rest as it could. He was quiet for a long time. Then he nodded, put down the phone, and came back to me.

"You were right," he told me. "That was a good piece of shooting. They're only accurate for seventy-five yards, and they're usually carried with open sights. It's doubtful that anybody would bother to mount telescopic sights on one of them. He'd get a different kind of rifle."

"What do they use them for, ordinarily?" I asked. "Hunting whales?"

"No, it's a deer rifle," Probcziewski said soberly. "A brush gun. You know, most deer are taken at less than fifty yards."

"It makes you think," I observed.

"Think what?"

"The guy was probably going to come into the house and

145

take Penton up close. Then he saw the perfect target through the window, lined up, and let go. He had a lot of self-confidence."

"Who do you like for it?"

"Under other circumstances," I said thoughtfully, "I would have named you six suspects. But now I can only see two."

"Give me all six, and let's see what I can shake out of it."

"There are four kids in the K.C. Sourballs," I said. "Names on demand; they're in the notebook I came back to get. Iris had been robbing them blind, and Penton told me that they were distributing drugs to recoup. I was going to look them up, because it was just possible that they might have killed Iris. But this kind of knocks the idea."

"Why?" asked Probcziewski. "They could have shot Penton to keep him from spilling the beans—just the way you said before."

"Uh-uh." I shook my head. "Whoever shot Penton knew that I was deaf and wouldn't hear the shot. If he hadn't known, he'd have waited until I drove away out of earshot, or else waited until I came back in, having heard the shot, and nailed me too. As it was, the guy saw me leave the house, figured he could forget about me, shot Penton, and split, probably over the backyard fence."

"Why not straight out the driveway?"

"There would have been the risk of running into me. It all happened pretty quick. He must have been gone by the time I got back, or he probably would have shot me too. Why not? Shoot one, shoot two. Like they say, they can't hang you twice."

"They don't hang you at all anymore," Probcziewski said, flexing his hands. "So you figure it couldn't have been the rock stars?"

"No," I answered. "And that leaves us with the other two—Ed Parti and Larry."

"I don't have any evidence on either one of them," Probcziewski complained.

"That doesn't mean that I can't drop in on them tomorrow morning," I said. "Shoot one, shoot two. Shoot tonight or shoot tomorrow. I think I'll keep close tabs on these boys, and I think I'm going to stay in a motel tonight—*not* the Soundsurf!"

Chapter XXI

I got up the next morning feeling strange in my strange motel room. I bought a toothbrush, toothpaste, and a razor from a coin-operated dispenser and achieved the smile of beauty, if not health. A small man with a bludgeon sat on top of my brain and banged against the interior walls of my skull. He also twisted the knobs at the back of my eyeballs in a futile attempt to adjust the tuning.

In the coffee shop my hand shook as it raised the large glass of orange juice. I forced myself to eat a substantial breakfast and absorbed endless cups of black coffee over the morning paper.

I drove to my apartment and parked the heap in the parking lot, where I pay an exorbitant monthly fee for the privilege if not idiocy of keeping an automobile in Manhattan. The street was full of people, and I felt better about approaching my door. You just *don't* expect to get shot in the morning surrounded by neighbors, although I've seen it done. The apartment, which I entered in a way that made me feel foolish afterward, was essentially unchanged. When I was satisfied that no one had been there in my absence, I changed my clothes and prepared for the day.

It was a pleasant walk to Nassau Street, and the fumes of

Manhattan bit deeply into my lungs. I stopped at the gun shop I had singled out (you were permitted entrance only after the clerk coming to the glass door had looked you over) and made a few inquiries. Together we made the arrangements I had in mind, with the promise that the goods would be waiting for me on the following morning. The fine tuning of the eyeballs had ended by this time, and we were all satisfied with the vertical hold. I took the subway up to the Groupe studios.

All that I was looking for on this healthful morning was a preliminary little minuet with Ed Parti—nothing heavy, nothing even alarming. But when the elevator doors opened on the reception room, my whole plan was shot to hell by a kind of triple vision—three faces, more or less alike, all beautiful and all belonging to the same woman.

There was the haunting white face I'd seen in my delirium up in the loft, which now swam up through my awakened memory, a poster on the lobby wall that was obviously the source of that mysterious image with the dark hair streaming cometlike behind it; and the actual face itself made flesh— very, very beautiful flesh.

She had been bent over the receptionist's tiny desk looking at some papers when I came in, and she looked up— not inquiringly, *she* was certainly no receptionist—but with that level stare that guesses your weight and prepares for all eventualities. It was the stare of a celebrity who has been put upon once too often. In a second or so it changed slightly into puzzlement. At some time during my first visit she had probably glimpsed the comic figure I had represented, and was now trying to put the two images together. I hoped fervently she never would.

I stared at her, slack jawed. She gave the impression of being a large woman, although she was not really extraordinarily big. It was the sense of vitality about her, glowing through her skin, a *muchness,* an abundance of energy and strength kept in taut physical control. When she stood up, I saw that if she were wearing high heels, our eyes would be on a level.

"Is Mr. Parti around?" I asked her, feeling stupid.

She took her time about answering. She wasn't happy in the role of office help; that was obvious. Again she looked me over with huge deep blue eyes of the type that the slang expression *lamps* has been coined for. They really were lamps, astonishingly large, although not out of proportion, with delicate shadings of blue at the edges of the whites. Her face hardened. She decided to be rude.

"What do you want him for?"

I could be rude too. I felt challenged. "A client of mine was shot last night," I said sharply. "I want to talk to Mr. Parti about it."

She considered this while going through a sheaf of papers, and then she looked up again. "Would Mr. Parti have known your client?"

"I would think so," I said stiffly. "It was Millard Penton."

Her face changed utterly. All the defenses softened into real concern. "Oh, no," she said. "Irey's husband? Is he hurt badly?"

"He was killed," I said.

She had dropped the sheaf of papers back on the desk, and now she came around to sit on its angular edge. There was no hint of celebrity to her now. The poster mocked her. She bent her head and mumbled something.

"I'm sorry," I said, "but I can't understand what you're saying unless I look at you. I'm deaf."

Her head snapped up at that, and she looked at me again, as if seeing a different human being. "Deaf?" she repeated. Her face was unbelieving. "I—I had no idea . . ."

"That's fine," I smiled. "You're not supposed to, really. I try to get by reading lips."

She stared at me again, and then shook her head sharply, as if clearing away a troubling vision. "How did it happen?—I mean with . . ."

"Did you know Penton well?" I asked her.

She seemed to turn the question over in her mind as if there were a thousand different facets to it. Finally, she said,

149

"Look, this is no place to talk. Ed is out for the day, so you wouldn't be able to see him anyway. Why don't we go down and have a cup of coffee? The stuff they've got in the coffee maker here is undrinkable."

Somewhere behind my intelligence there flashed the idea that this was a scam, that she wanted me *out of there.* But in fact, if she had said, *Let us now join hands, climb up on the windowsill, and fly to the moon,* why, that would have been Joe Binney, all right, up there on the ledge.

She remained resting for a stunned moment against the surface of the desk as I looked at her and the poster above her. *Felicity Bowers,* it shouted, *Tonight!* She was wearing a white silk blouse of the kind that looks simple but you know somehow is very complicated. Her legs filled out a pair of skimpy, pale blue-green, silklike britches that came halfway down her calves. Below them she wore crushed leather piratical-looking boots. "I'll be with you in a minute," she said, and disappeared from the lobby. My suspicion that this was a scam was reinforced by the alacrity of her return. I have *never* known a woman who said, "I'll be with you in a minute," and actually meant it. But Miss Bowers had meant it, going back only to snatch a light suede jacket and a shoulder-slung purse of dimensions that might encase a small motorcycle.

She came back shrugging on the jacket and taking from the purse an enormous pair of sunglasses. When she had put them on, they covered half her face and completely obscured the startling eyes. It was only then, as if the sunglasses had made things bearable enough, that she reached over to touch my cheek.

"That's recent, isn't it?" she asked.

I nodded, not knowing what to say. I also cursed the sunglasses, which were going to make Miss Bowers very difficult to read. The receptionist came in and settled at her station. While I had remembered her as something of a dish, comparison to Miss Bowers in this small cramped room reduced her to the status of a high-school girl.

We went down in the small elevator together side by side, at attention and staring straight forward, but when we got to the street I might as well have been on a leash. She hit the celebrity stride immediately, a pace just barely slower than a trot, which is calculated to get the personage through traffic without hindrance—fast enough so that the passerby might stop and remark, "Say—isn't that . . . ?" by which time the personage would be lost in traffic and forging happily into the distance.

After breasting the crowds a few blocks eastward, we arrived at a coffee shoppe (yes, yes, a *shoppe*), where she was apparently well known, and we were taken immediately to a leatherette booth in the back. When we had ordered our coffee, she said, "Tell me about it. Why do you want to see Ed?"

"First of all," I told her, "if you wear those glasses it's going to be almost impossible for us to talk. I have to be able to see your face as well as just your lips."

You might have thought I was asking her to undress in public. She fingered the temple bars of her glasses gingerly. Finally, slowly, she removed them and looked at me. "This isn't a put-on?" she said slowly. "You really can't hear anything at all? You really have to watch people talk to understand them? You can do that? Just by watching?"

"Yes," I said. "It's all true."

The thought seemed to overwhelm her. "I've never met a deaf person before," she said. "I'm sorry. I mean, I've heard about it, of course, but I guess I never believed it. I mean, I guess I couldn't really conceive of it."

I waved it away. "There's a lot of it around," I said. "You'd be surprised."

But it seemed to have taken the wind out of her sails, for which I was grateful. She had come on with such a tremendous air of authority that I was worried that the play would be taken away from me. I said, "I'm sorry to have broken the news

151

about Penton like that. Did you know him well?"

"Oh, no," she responded quickly. "I'd only met him a few times."

"You seemed to be—uh—rather upset at hearing about it."

A quantity of pain and bewilderment shifted in the depths of those dark-blue eyes. "I'd be upset to hear directly that anyone was shot and killed. Wouldn't you?"

I reflected on this and remained silent.

"It's just that . . ." She gestured above the table. "Coming so quickly after Irey—it just seems so terrible."

I decided that this was the moment to take charge. "Just what is your relationship to Iris and Millard Penton?"

Again the blue lamps turned on me, searching my face for clues. Her face expressed wonderment. "This really *isn't* a put-on," she said slowly. "You really don't know who I am, do you?"

"Well," I began. I guess I was sputtering. "I saw the poster. I know your name is Felicity Bowers and you—you're some kind of entertainer, like—uh—the K.C. Sourballs, for instance."

It was the prettiest thing I ever saw. Her face began to break up radiantly. She threw her head back to laugh, and all the beautiful upstairs part of her shook with merriment. Her head came back down, and she exclaimed, "The K.C. Sourballs!" and off she went again into a beautiful gale of laughter. "I'm sorry; I'm sorry," she apologized, still laughing. She seized my arm on the table and the mildest of thunderbolts went through my shoulder. She sobered down. "I'm a little different from them," she said, still smiling. "A little bit different."

"I can see some of that already," I said, appreciatively, I hope.

She settled down and smiled. My heart broke. She said, "It's funny. I've been through this a million times with smartass reporters who always know the answers to the

152

questions before they ask them. They know all about me, and I know all about them—not that I care. But you, I don't even know your name. What's your name?"

"Joe Binney."

"And what do you do?"

"I am the legendary private detective you've heard about. The scourge of the underworld."

"A private detective." She rolled it around. "And who are you private detecting for?"

"For—" I began. "—I was doing it for Millard Penton. But now I don't know."

"Millard Penton," she repeated. "What did he hire you for?"

"To check up on Iris and the kid and Groupe records."

"That son of a bitch," she said, and stared off into space.

"You're all over the place," I complained. "Start at the beginning."

"At the beginning." She pondered. "Well, Mr. Binney . . ."

"And call me Joe, please."

"Aha," she said. "Very clever. And what then shall you call me?"

"Miss Bowers?"

She stared at me and then made up her mind. "My friends call me Sitty," she announced.

The reading left me nowhere. "Now I'm in trouble," I admitted. "It doesn't always work. You mean like in 'Sioux City Sue'?"

She smiled. "Oh, yes," she said. "Like in 'Sioux City Sue.'" Her smile got broader. "So you do know some songs."

"Yeah." I leaned back and took out a cigarette. "I know some songs all right. But they're pretty old by now."

"Then you weren't—pardon me for asking—you weren't born—"

"It happened when I was nineteen," I told her. "In the Navy."

She thought it all over and then dismissed it. "Irey and I go back—went back—a long way. Fifteen years." She stared into space again. "Nineteen," she mused. "When I was nineteen, I'd just met Irey. She caught me at a roadhouse with a pickup band. I was a wreck. I was on just about every chemical improvement you could think of and was wandering back and forth in my mind in the—the"—she suddenly smiled triumphantly—"'The Landscape of the Lost,'" she said.

I was blank. "'The Landscape of the Lost'?"

"You never heard of it?" she pouted. "My first song," she said, "I mean, I wrote it."

"You'll have to forgive me," I apologized. "These things have passed me by."

She gave me what is called a searching look. Not every woman has eyes in which you can recognize the *roundness* of them—that they are genuinely *orbs*.

"Anyway, Irey got me out of there." She was speaking into the air above my head, as if she were constructing the past on the ceiling—a magic-lantern show. "She got me a few gigs, and I had a reasonable success. She got me off the better-living-through-chemistry kick and kept me clean—and I've been clean ever since. . . ." Her head snapped down challengingly when she told me this, and then returned to the magic-lantern show. "Then I made 'The Landscape of the Lost' with Irey, and it turned a mint. First a gold and then a platinum—right off the bat. It really helped establish the Groupe studios, their first big one. So in a way Irey and I made each other. I loved Irey. I can't bear to think that she's—she's . . ." And suddenly there were tears coming down from those improbable eyes. I got out the handkerchief and touched her very gently on both cheeks. It was like brushing a flower. She took the handkerchief and blew her nose. Her throat worked, and then she stopped it all.

"The next one was 'Dry Cries,' another single, and it made even more. And then the album made even more and more. It got to be a mania." Suddenly she looked at me and

154

smiled, a smile that turned into a light laugh. "Some mania. You never even heard of it, huh? You never even heard of me."

"I wish I could have," I said honestly. "It's just not in my line of things."

"A funny world," she mused. "A tiny, crazy world, really, where you think that every living soul gets up in the morning and rushes down to buy *Billboard* to see how you're doing on the charts. And really, ninety percent of the world doesn't know that you exist."

"Not knowing that you exist," I said warmly, "was one of the major omissions in my life."

She put her hand on mine. It was warm, white, soft, and gentle, and yet it felt as lively as a trout. "You're very nice," she said. "It's good for me to talk to you. It's different. It's strange—please note that I didn't use the word *weird.*" I must have looked puzzled. *"Weird."* She spelled it out: "Double-you ee eye are dee." She paused. "It's a word I'm very sick of."

"Tell me how it's strange," I prompted gently.

"In this business," said City, "we don't really look at each other too much, I mean to see each other. Even when we talk, we tend to mutter, to look away. It comes with the music, with the style. Everything is cool, understated to the point of vanishing. And now I'm sitting here with my shades off—I *always* wear shades—and you're devouring my face with your eyes. I know you have to do it to understand me, but it's very strange. It makes me feel—you'll pardon the expression"— and she laughed heartily—"naked."

"It's not just you," I reassured her. "If it makes you feel any better, I've been punched in the mouth for staring at people, trying to read them. Nobody likes that kind of concentration much."

"But it's good for me," she insisted. "I'm seeing myself through your eyes."

"You should be very happy with what you see." I smiled.

"I don't know about that," she answered. "Using your eyes, I see a lot more than you do. You're seeing a surface. I can see thirty years. Mostly I see back fifteen years when I was spinning around wildly, escaping, escaping."

"What were you escaping from?"

"My life—the wreck I'd made of it. The absolute utter mess."

"A wrecked life at nineteen?"

"Oh, God, yes. From the smartest little girl in high school, from the prettiest little girl in high school, from Daddy's little girl in high school, to—to—well, to what Irey scraped up off the floor in a roadhouse."

I remained silent. She brushed it all away with a gesture in front of her eyes. Then she addressed me directly. "You're going to find out who did it to Irey?"

"I'm going to try," I said. "I'd like you to help me, but I have to warn you that some of the questions will be rough. I don't want you to get sore at me."

"I won't get sore," she assured me.

"All right." I decided that for this I would be all business. I put my hands on the edge of the table. "When Penton hired me, he intimated that Iris might be playing around, might have been having an affair with another man."

"Bullshit," said City. "Iris married Penton for the exact reason that she wouldn't have to play around. And if he'd been holding out on her sexually, she would have dumped him."

"O.K. Number two. Would Iris have used, bought, sold, or dabbled in narcotics of any kind?"

"Never. She hated everything about it. It almost killed her when Larry turned up with a habit."

"All right. Now we get to the toughie. Iris started you off, right? Does that mean that she was your manager?" City nodded, puzzled. "Well"—I cleared my throat—"are you sure that she always gave you a fair shake? I mean was anybody watching the store?"

156

Her face was utterly uncomprehending. Then, finally, she understood. Her eyes got even bigger. They blazed.

"You promised not to get sore." I put up an admonishing palm.

"Did Irey steal from me? Is that what you're implying?"

"I just asked . . ."

"My God. Irey *made* me!"

"That's not what I'm asking."

"O.K." She, too, decided to be businesslike, and reduced the candlepower. "Irey"—and then she flared again—"for your information—never stole a dime in her life."

"Easy," I said. "Easy."

She calmed down. "Irey could drive deals that made big, stout businessmen break down and cry like babies. She was always very sweet and soft-spoken, and they always assumed that she was a pushover, but sooner or later they all came to the sticking point. What everybody likes to call the bottom line, another term that's going to make me throw up one of these days. And when they got to it, you could hear them scream. . . ." She threw her hands into the air. "*'But where's my end? What's the advantage?'* And Irey would just go on and on, just as sweet, just as soft-spoken. But she was as straight as a ruler."

I considered what she had told me. "So Iris never stole from you," I stated. "But let me ask you something. When I mentioned the K.C. Sourballs, you got practically hysterical with laughter. Why?"

"Because they're nothing," she said with a contemptuous curl to her lips. "They would have been better off staying in their garage. God only knows what Ed wants with them."

I looked at her inquiringly. "They're Ed's babies," she explained. "Once Irey found them she turned them over to Ed for a toy."

"What makes them so different?" I pursued.

"They're not part of music or of performance, really." Her face was earnest. "They're part of the audience, part of the so-called scene. Disco—juice bars, you name it—you know, where some little pisspants in a vinyl jacket stands out by the door and tells you you can't come in because you haven't got the shine."

We'd gotten into our second cup of coffee, but mine had long since grown cold in the cup without being touched. I was suddenly very hungry. "Look," I said, "we're way past coffee time. Can I buy you some lunch?"

"I'd love it," said City. "I'm starved."

Did she like seafood? (Somehow it seemed impossible that anybody would actually eat lunch in this shoppe.) You bet. Would she like lunch at the best seafood restaurant in New York, and maybe in the United States of America? Lead on.

We got out of the booth, and automatically she put on the sunglasses. "Why do you wear them?" I asked her, smiling.

"Privacy," she admitted. "Somewhere I read that the eyes are the visible part of the brain."

What I said was heartfelt. "You've got the most beautiful brains in the world," I told her.

We were out in the street trying to hook a cab. I was thinking about Ed Parti and how he fitted into the scheme of things. "Mr. Parti," I began tentatively. "Does he manage anybody else besides the K.C. Sourballs? You, for instance?"

"Oh, no. Not me."

"Then you don't really have any kind of relationship with him at all?"

The enormous shades reflected all the traffic flowing behind me. She was staring at me, her mouth slightly open with surprise. Finally, she said, "I keep forgetting that you don't know anything about me. I'm Ed's old lady. I've been living with him for over a year. Everybody knows that."

Chapter XXII

I contemplated the masts and spars of the *Peking* through an immaculate window of Sweets restaurant. They were the first things to come clearly and consciously into focus since the red haze of rage had gripped me stepping into the cab with City. In the cab there had been no attempt at conversation, and coming into Sweets it had been limited to very perfunctory comments. City had caused the expected commotion at the headwaiter's desk, and we had been shown to a very visible table at the window overlooking South Street and the Brooklyn Bridge in its massive leap beyond.

She had disposed of a crab Louis and now was regarding me with considerable amusement across the remains of her grilled sea bass. I, in my quiet fury, had put away my soft-shelled crabs in ruinous haste, for which, I knew, I would pay a digestive penalty. I also had made a number of lightning calculations on the contents of my wallet and realized that, if I followed my budget, I would be living on toast and peanut butter for the remainder of the week. Sweets is very good, but it is not free. Cold cash is the medium there, sir, no credit cards, no feasting on the never never.

I heartily wished that I were aboard the *Peking* and some several thousand miles at sea a hundred years ago, when she had plied the nitrate trade to Valparaiso. I was conscious of being a complete and irredeemable idiot.

City touched my shoulder, and I turned to look at her.

"You're mad," she said. It was a word I qualified for in either definition.

I gave her back the stock reply under full sail of stupidity. "Why should I be mad?"

"You're mad because I'm Ed's old lady."

"It's none of *my* business," I said in a flash of repartee, feeling more isolated and more foolish than I had ever felt in my life.

"If you could only see your face," said City.

The lucky lunchtimers were long since gone from Sweets. We had the joint pretty much to ourselves. One or two waiters lounged by the kitchen door. "Are you going to have dessert?" I asked her.

"Oh, yes," she assented. "I'm a growing girl." The waiter, summoned by telepathic communication, glided up to the table and City ordered pêche Melba. "Actually, I'm very flattered," City said to me.

The waiter brought her dessert, and coffee was poured for both of us.

"All right," I admitted. "I'm sore, but I'm also puzzled." The huge eyes were fixed on me above the spoon. "You say that getting clean and staying clean meant a lot to you—a turning point in your life, and yet you've got yourself fastened to a guy who's up to his ears in junk."

She continued to eat her dessert until she had finished every last bit of it. Then she laid the spoon in the dish and said, "When you live in Siberia, it's hard to find somebody who hasn't been snowed on. Just about everybody I know uses something. Almost everybody in the business does. The more I look around," she concluded, "the more I think that everybody in the whole world does."

"Not everybody deals," I said.

She shrugged. "In a way they do, and if they don't now, they will. They go to a party. The host puts out the coke, and everybody has a snort. But when the host comes to your party, you're supposed to lay it out so he can have a snort."

160

"And if you don't?"

"Then you've broken the circle. You don't get invited to any more parties, and you don't get to meet the wonderful people who are going to make you rich. It's all commercial. It's all business. It's all dealing."

"But you?" I pressed her on it. "You supply it?"

"I don't snort, and I don't supply," said City. "I *am* rich. I'm not looking for deals. I'm looking for my next song, and I'm not going to find it in a rolled-up hundred-dollar bill." She gestured as if clearing something away. "Besides," she added, "Ed gives the parties. Ed takes care of all that. I'm not really needed."

"Ed," I continued cautiously. "Does he use it? Use it a lot?"

She looked at me again and then turned her face full profile to stare out over the harbor. She said something.

"I'm sorry," I complained gently, "but I don't know what you're saying when you don't look at me."

She turned her head to stare at me full face. "Yes," she said. "He uses it a lot."

I mulled things over carefully before proceeding. "Would you like to top this off with a cognac?" I asked, bidding farewell to the luxurious idea of peanut butter on my toast.

She nodded absently, the dark blue of her eyes very remote and abstracted. I signaled the waiter and ordered the cognac. When it was served, the afternoon light picked out gold reflections in its depths. We both took a sip. "Doesn't it get to be something of a drag?" I prompted her.

Again she looked off, and then returned to me. "Yes, it does," she said. "So much so that I'm leaving him."

I kept my face absolutely rigid, although I had no control over the blood supply that seemed to rush away from my brain and leave me floating, light-headed. She wasn't really looking at me, however. Her eyes were focused beyond me.

"You'd really have to know a lot more about me and Ed to understand what I'm saying," she offered.

"Supposing you tell me a little about it then." I tried to keep the note of beggary out.

"I wouldn't have had to explain to Irey," said City. "She would have understood. I was going to tell Irey, when I made up my mind. But now—" She paused and looked out the window. When she looked back she said, "I have to tell somebody. I have to talk to *someone,* don't I?"

I nodded, still trying to keep my face in order.

"Start with me," she began. "I grew up in Indianapolis— *nice . . .*" She grimaced around the word. "Nice, nice, sugar and spice; Daddy's little girl. God, there was even a song, a sickening song, called 'Daddy's Little Girl.' Not that I didn't love my father." She looked up suddenly, protesting, as if challenged. "But I was given a lot to live up to." She brushed it all away. "When I started growing up, budding, sprouting, whatever you want to call it, when I got into—not high school—*junior* high school, I discovered a very central fact in my life. I discovered that I liked boys."

She took a tiny sip of her cognac and set the glass down. "Every lousy magazine you pick up today has an article on how it's perfectly normal to like boys," she reflected. "But when I was changing from a little girl to a woman, I learned the core dictum to Middle American life. All the ten commandments, all the social cant, the entire society was boiled down to three words that might as well have been branded on your forehead—*Don't Put Out.*

"And all the dancing lessons, the piano lessons, the tennis lessons, the teeth-straightening sessions, all, all were aimed at keeping you from putting out, to keep you so Goddamned busy, so exhausted, so worried, so anxious about living up to everything, that you'd never have the chance or inclination to get horizontal with a boy."

She took another sip. I remained perfectly still. "And I'm not knocking it," she said. "It worked pretty well, or it used to, anyway. They had a lot of help. A lot of girls simply didn't like boys. I mean, if they *did* put out it was a kind of social

162

thing, you know? To be—what? Jesus Christ, *popular!*

"The trouble with me was that I was already popular, and yet I still liked boys. I even had the energy and self-assurance left over that I *could* have gotten horizontal—as I so deeply and dearly wanted to. But to do that, I would have had to somehow betray Daddy. That's the way they set it up.

"I used to come home from dates with my guts absolutely tied in knots. You know, you'd always get the old story from the boy you were out with—'Gee, you can't stop now. I'll get the stone aches, you know? I'll get sick.'" She grimaced. "I never knew if they were serious or not. But they could have told me that the whole works was going to drop off, and I still wouldn't have been able to do it for them. And yet, *I*"—she pointed to her beautiful chest—"I was the one who had the stone aches. I was the one who came home with my nails digging into my palms and my perfectly even teeth grinding away—lying in bed with my arms stiffened out by my sides and my body as tense as a bridge.

"So I didn't put out," she concluded. "But the prohibition on grass and on anything else that came down the pike didn't seem nearly so serious. I'd started playing the guitar in a little high-school band and doing some vocals for them, and somehow, just like it always is, the stuff was available, and I started getting stoned." Suddenly she laughed. "I don't want this to sound like 'The Fatal Glass of Beer,'" she said. "But of course what happened was that I got stoned, horizontal, pregnant, and busted, all in the same night."

I had taken out my cigarettes and lighted one. She reached over and pensively drew a smoke from the pack. I lighted it for her.

"The bust got publicity and a write-up in the papers," she said. "Daddy dear struck back for his betrayal. I pretty much got thrown out. They sent me to a private school in Kansas City, but that didn't last. I took off, and kept on getting gigs with this group and that, and always let Daddy dearest know where I was so he could send a check, which he was willing to

163

do as long as I didn't show up in Indianapolis.

"So I started my career on better living through chemistry and how to improve your sex life by playing in scrungy-ass pickup bands. And the thing of it was, I still liked boys, when and where I could find them, although that wasn't easy."

"Wasn't easy?" I said incomprehendingly. "You? You had trouble finding boys?"

"Oh, my, yes," said City. "My goodness, yes." She reached down to seize the rim of the seat of her chair and hitched it around so that her back was completely turned to the restaurant and the waiters, who had been eyeing us warily. "You don't mind if I talk to you, do you? But I don't want the waiters to see or hear." I nodded my nearly paralyzed assent.

"I said that I like boys, men, and I like them the same way that men are supposed to like girls. I mean I like the way they look, the way they walk and move around. I like the way they feel, I mean in my hands and inside me. Now, if a man said this to you about women, you'd assume that he was crazy for even having to tell you that. In other words, it's normal. But when a woman feels it and says it, somehow she's *abnormal*. See what I mean?" I nodded rigidly.

"Yes," she continued, "and they all reacted the same way you're reacting. I can hear the twang of your umbilical cord right back to parochial school. They wanted me, all right, but when they found out I wanted them, they were frightened. And after a while, I could tell right off the bat which ones would be so frightened that they'd be impossible—and they were the majority. There were only a few, a very few, that I could trust enough to love even for one whole night, and a lot of those would turn on me by morning."

She settled back in her chair, her soft mouth pursed, her deep eyes distant. "Irey got me off chemicals, but she couldn't do anything about men except tell me once flat and forever that I wasn't the one who was wrong. It was the men, or the would-be men who were always talking up a great game and falling apart in the clutch.

164

"But with Irey, I survived and hobbled along with the hits I wrote and waxed and sold. I got some of my old self-esteem back without any of the cuteness—I hope"—her eyes widened in a quest for reassurance, and I nodded reassuringly—"and then, three years ago, she hired Ed Parti as a sound engineer. He did 'Bad Time Girl' with me. Technically, it was the best record I ever cut."

City blew a cloud of smoke into the still air of Sweets and studied it. "That was three years ago," she said. "I had just gotten used to being thirty, a very sharp angle for any girl. Ed had a wife and kid out in Queens, where he came from originally, and he had been coming along in good shape in the business. But when Irey hired him, it was the big break, and he knew it. We stayed on a very professional basis for a while, but when 'Bad Time Girl' began to take off and turned out to be such a hit, there was a wild feeling of achievement that you don't get any other way, and it went to our heads. We got"— City laughed—"you'll pardon the expression—carried away.

"Well," and here she heaved an enormous, quite visible sigh, "Ed was different for me and I was different for Ed, and we wouldn't stop, we couldn't stop. He had tremendous control of himself in everything else, his work, his attitude toward life. I thought I'd found the bedrock, you know? The place where I could anchor myself, and he saw his whole future—and I mean his emotional future, Ed was no para- site—wrapped up in me. He asked his wife for a divorce. I still feel pretty shitty about that and I probably always will. And he told her that she could have everything—no worries about the house, car, money, child support, nothing. It like to kill her."

A wave of sorrow passed over City's face. She put out the cigarette. "And now it's all for nothing," she said. "That lady got caught in the road with a steamroller coming on and she got flattened. And now it's all for nothing."

She took a deep breath and continued. "We decided not to get married right away, a very sensible idea, as you can plainly see. And I moved into Ed's apartment. It wasn't much

165

of a move for me because all my gear is what I put on my back. I'd always lived in hotels. And we were happy fixing up the apartment, although I haven't got any more decorating sense than a cowbird.

"But after we'd been together for a little while, Ed started making plans for me, even though he wasn't, and never would be, my manager. He didn't want to control me emotionally, or it never would have happened at all, but he did, somehow, want to control my career. I'd told him a million times, once and forever, my career was Irey's to control. But Ed kept insisting that all he wanted to do was help, and he'd get sore when I told him it looked like we didn't need any help. What he kept doing was trying to explore the other side of the business, the talent side, the part he really hadn't paid much attention to before." Her face softened with remembered tenderness. "Ed knew—knows—everything there is to know about the technical side of it, all the electronics—spaghetti—acoustics, what-have-you. But he didn't know anything about the jungle, I mean where the talent and the agents and the producers and the managers all hang from the trees with one hand and scratch their bellies with the other.

"Let me have another cigarette," she demanded suddenly. When I lighted it for her, she drew so strongly that the tip glowed like a stoplight. "He started hanging out with—what do you want to call it, the scene?—and started going to their parties and coming home coked to the gills. I didn't mind. I didn't go to the parties because I've already had all that. But then he started having parties at our place, like I told you, and I didn't mind *that,* because it's his house too. I did mention to him that he was running a pretty high tab for the coke, but he swore he could handle it."

Suddenly, as if to stop an unspoken argument, she put her hands up, fingers outspread except for the two that held the cigarette. "Look," she said, "even though I don't use it, I'm not a ninny about coke or anything else. If somebody wants it, fine. It's part of the atmosphere. But one day I was trying to

166

work in the apartment, where I do a lot of my work now when I'm not performing, and I came across something in the kitchen that I hadn't seen before. It was a free-base kit that some dealer had given Ed as a present. That was"—she looked ruminatively at the ceiling—"a little less than six months ago."

She paused again as if to summon the strength to confront what she was going to say. "You know what free-base is?" she asked me. I nodded. "Yeah, well," she continued, "you know, you reduce the coke so you can smoke it to where you can get a hit like a wrecking ball. A skull crusher. And Ed started on that. *Why?"* she suddenly demanded of me with a ferocity in her expression that made me jump. "Why did he want to blow his brains out through his nose? Everything was going for him—for us."

She sat back, one elbow cradled in her palm with the cigarette aloft near her temple and pondered her own question. Finally she pushed it away. "Of course he couldn't handle it. Nobody handles it. It's stupid. You might as well buy shit off the street.

"For the last three months it's been like living with a stone junkie. He can't take a pee unless he's wired. I get the full benefit of his advice on how I can improve my career—on how I can really become somebody—somebody like those assholes he hangs out with now. And when I turn him off, he rants and raves. And now he says because I won't improve my career, I'm ruining his career. Because I won't give up and change what me and Irey built together all these years, because I won't go along with him, he says I'm wrecking his career. And he's getting physical."

This snapped my head back. "He's belting you around?"

There were a lot of small muscles jumping in my shoulders and the back of my neck—I didn't even know I had 'em—when she nodded. "Oh," I said. I don't know what was happening to my eyesight. Everything looked far away and hazy. My lips felt cold.

"So I'm going to leave him," City concluded. "It's killing me. He was the first and the best I ever really found, and now it's all going away and there's no way I can hold it back, and there isn't even Irey to talk to now."

I suppose that my voice was very small. "There's me," I said.

She looked at me with a slow, sad smile that I couldn't really interpret. "Yes," she agreed. "There's you."

"You see that ship out the window there?" I gestured to the *Peking*. "You ever been aboard her?"

"They let you?" asked City.

"Costs three dollars," I said, "but it could take your mind off your troubles. Want to walk over?"

"I'd love to," said City. We stood up after I'd put the heart-stilling amount of cash in the little tray. As we stood up we bumped together, and suddenly she seized me by the arm and leaned close to tell me something. Her breast was pushed up hard against my ribcage. "For a deaf man, Binney," said City, "you're a hell of a listener."

Chapter XXIII

But aboard the *Peking* it was City who did the listening. I had hold of her hand and pulled her down below into the fo'c'sle to show her where the men had lived before the mast, then back topsides to the quarterdeck to see how the ship was run, all the while discoursing learnedly on ships and seafaring. "It's one of the great old Flying P windjammers," I told her grandly, "that's been around the Horn more times than most

168

people have been around their bathtubs." We were leaning against the fife rail, and she was staring into my face as though it was she who had to do the lipreading. There was the ghost of amusement on her lips. I suddenly became very self-conscious.

"What's the matter," I said. "Do I sound funny?"

"Oh, no!" she assured me. "It's just that you're so different here. I hardly recognize you. I mean, you're really not what you were like in the restaurant. Being here on this"—she swept the vista of the long graceful deck with her arm—"it changes you." She searched my face again. "Why?" she asked.

"I come here a lot," I admitted. "I like it a lot. Maybe I fantasize, you know, dream a little."

"Fantasize—you mean like being one of the sailors? On a voyage?"

I nodded. "Sure," I said. "Wouldn't you?"

"And live on something like this for weeks—months? You'd have to be crazy to do something like that."

"A lot of men did it," I countered, "and they were very proud of it. Proud of themselves. If you'd been around the Horn, you'd done something. You were part of something very good—very special. It didn't really mean anything to anybody else. The meaning was all inside you."

She looked at me. "You talk like you've done it yourself."

"Only in my head," I told her. "It's been a long time since I was part of anything. But I know what it means. Not everybody even knows what it means."

"Tell me what it means."

"When they sent me back from Korea—Yokosuka, the naval base in Japan, actually—they had to send me back by ship because they were afraid of what a pressurized cabin in an airplane might do to what was left of my ears. There weren't any naval vessels going back just then, so they sent me as a passenger on a merchant ship. It was very different from the Navy, but I got a feel of what it would be like to spend my life

169

as a merchant seaman. Hell, I couldn't hear anything, and I could hardly walk, but I sat down in the messroom with the crew and somehow got the feeling of being part of something—it's very difficult to explain. In a way, I've always thought about what my life would have been like if I could have kept going with that kind of life—a part of a crew. It's why I keep coming back down here.

"But the funny thing is I've pretty much stayed the same while this place is changing almost day by day. I thought it was great when they brought the old ships here, the *Wavertree* and the *Peking*, but with it all has come a kind of Disneyland development. The old Seamen's Church Institute is gone; only the beacon light is left, sitting there on the corner like an abandoned idiot. But the place—South Street, what it was and what it meant—is disappearing in the worst possible way, not even vanishing but being prettified, like a corpse. I don't come here as much anymore. They don't know what they are anymore." I stared out glumly across the river.

City put two fingers alongside my jawbone and watched me gravely. "But you," she said, "you know what you are, huh?"

"Yes," I said. "I think I do."

There's a word that keeps cropping up in certain books I've read that never seemed to apply much to life until now: *transfixed*—like a butterfly being pinned in the case. I stared at her, unable to move. The setting sun shot over the southern tip of Manhattan and picked out the auburn lights in her dark rich hair. It tinged her face with a deep rose-coppery color that made her glow like a flower. The silk blouse under her open jacket clung to her, and from the open throat of it there was arising a scent and a warmth that made me dizzy. The spell was broken when she turned suddenly away, and then back to me. "The man is calling," she said. "It's time to go."

At the bottom of the gangway I was suddenly desperate. "Don't go away now," I said. "Come over to my place. I've got some more cognac. It's very good cognac."

170

"I'm sure it is," said City.

It was a short cab ride that took us through several worlds. I would have walked it with her, but I was afraid that, somehow, she might slip away from me. A cab was safer, even if it didn't give us time to savor all the richness of passing from the old City Hall into Chinatown, which melted imperceptibly into Puerto Rican areas and then into the solid base of the Jewish establishment of the Lower East Side that still clung tenaciously to its roots.

"My God," said City. "I didn't know that anybody actually lived here." She was referring to the Lower East Side neighborhood, I guess, not specifically to the building in which I have a floor-through apartment, up over a Puerto Rican furniture store. I paid the cab with the last few remaining dollars in my wallet, and we slipped in through the little door at the side of the furniture store. The hallway is narrow and not too brightly lighted, but it is conspicuously clean and the steps leading up the one flight to my apartment are topped with marble. I opened the door to my apartment and the lights went on.

"Who turned on the lights?" asked City, scared.

"It's automatic," I assured her. "I'm not crazy about walking into pitch-dark rooms." She seemed hesitant about entering, and I ushered her in. "Make yourself comfortable," I told her, "and I'll see about that cognac."

"Where's the bathroom?" asked City. I gestured toward the connecting hall, but suddenly found myself pointing toward the reading lamp, which was flashing in lengthy sequence. "The bathroom's the second door to your right," I said.

"Why is that lamp going on and off?"

"That's my telephone," I said, stepping over to the machine. "I can't hear a bell, so this is the signal. It flashes in the same sequence as the telephone bell." Privately, I was cursing Edna, and also myself for not having checked with her earlier in the day. I picked up the phone and looked at the

171

little red light on my Code-Com. It flashes: .-. / ..- / - - - / -.- at me. "I'm O.K., Edna," I told the telephone. "I'll see you tomorrow."

I hung up. She hadn't moved. "Edna," said City.

"My secretary," I explained. "She was wondering how I was getting on. That Morse code was just the letters R, U, O, K. It's a nice simple system." In truth, I was wishing the whole thing were in hell.

"And you told her you were getting on all right, huh?"

"Yeah," I answered artlessly.

City took a while to make up her mind. "You said second door on the right?" I nodded. "Any little surprises in there? Whoopee cushions or anything?"

"No," I told her, embarrassed. Understand, I'm not wild about turning my apartment into a funhouse. Since my career had extended beyond bookkeeping, however, I had thought it was just as well for me to put in a pressure switch on the door for the lights. I had resisted the Code-Com until three months prior to this, when Edna had insisted and it had seemed churlish to both her and the telephone company not to install one. It works as a simple system of communication for the deaf and speech impaired.

I had not been kidding City about the cognac. There was, somewhere in my apartment, a bottle of very good Otard that a grateful client had given me with every assurance. It was not for me to judge. I am not a cognac fancier. I looked in the likely cupboards and shelves of my front room, but the bottle was not to be found there. I surmised that I had stuck it in one of the kitchen cabinets.

But when I got to the end of the long hall to the kitchen, City was already there, looking around bemusedly. "You look surprised," I told her.

"I am," said City. "I didn't expect it to be like this."

"Like what?"

"Clean."

"I am very clean," I assured her.

172

"Jesus Christ," said City. "The men's places I've been to all look like garbage dumps unless they're rich enough to have help. Do you have help?"

"No help," said I. "It's a matter of record that I enjoy doing the dishes and taking out the garbage." I turned away. "There's a bottle of very good cognac cunningly secreted in this kitchen," I announced. Finally I found the little bugger hiding in the farthest corner of the lower cabinets. In the upper cabinets I had glasses, but they were not snifters. Two double-shot glasses were all that the Binney establishment could put forth. I had the bottle in one hand and the shot glasses in the other when I turned around from the cabinet. Well, now, will the sexual history of the United States be written in terms of kitchen decor? Granted that kitchens are small, but what is it in them that switches on the old libido? When I turned, I found my chest pressing against her chest— not that it was any contest. I bent just a little and kissed her. Then I put my laden arms around her, set the bottle and glasses on the counter, held her, and kissed her again. Her blouse was a complicated affair, but what I found underneath was not. It was all warm, scented, beautiful, lively, resilient City.

"Not here," said City, after she'd pulled my head up for air. "I still want that drink you promised me."

She preceded me down the hallway to the front room, the loose ends of her silk blouse trailing out behind her. When she got there, she went to the big club chair, sat down, and curled her legs under her. The lamplight cascaded across her breasts. She held out her hand. I opened the cognac, poured a shot glass full, and served it to her. After she'd sipped it, she smiled and said, "It is very good." I was about to throw myself on her, but she commanded me, "Over there—sit over there." And so I retreated and sank into the couch, I hope invitingly.

City carefully scanned the room, the ceiling-high book-stacks, the odd bits of furniture and junk I'd collected, the magazines and journals scattered across the big round coffee table. "So this is the glacier," she said.

"The what?"

"The glacier where the mastodon was kept."

"You think I'm a mastodon?"

"Very like a mastodon," said City. "And only very recently thawed. I've never really ever met anybody like you, or seen a place like this. It could be a glacier for all of me."

"I don't understand."

"Don't be offended, but I've never in my life seen an apartment without a stereo. That's one thing that makes it strange. You don't even have television."

"I do too," I replied, aroused. I marched over to the high stack of *Scientific American*s on the shelf in the corner and extracted my ten-incher from behind it. I held the tube aloft, like a trophy.

"But not really," said City.

"No," I admitted, letting my trophy descend forlornly to its home behind the stack, "not really."

She flung her arm toward the shelves, which did something to her breasts that made my heart beat backward. "You do it all with books, huh?"

"Yeah," I replied, "I do it with books." I don't know if the words sounded like a gasp, but they felt like a gasp coming out of my throat.

"I'm surprised the floor doesn't collapse. I've never seen—personal bookshelves—where you need a ladder."

"Well, yeah." I suddenly felt very defensive. "I've gutted all the book clubs. And I march through all the Fourth Avenue stores, where it doesn't seem fair not to buy *something*. I always buy a book or two to pay for the entertainment of browsing."

"And you've read them all?"

"Oh, no, but they're always there for me to get to, and sooner or later, I manage to get around to them. It's like putting away freezer food, you know, for a rainy day. You'd be surprised how many rainy days there are."

I tried to formulate a better explanation. "There's another thing. People don't think about it too much, but books beat time. I mean they pull it into line so it's all in the present. The whole wall behind you is happening right now. All the voices in there are talking, muttering, mumbling, arguing, cursing, crying. You can hear them. It never stops. It never fades away. All the voices for hundreds and hundreds of years . . . ."

"Not for me." She smiled. "I have to hear music."

"Oh, I hear music all right," I told her.

"You do?" She was startled. And then she looked wise. "In your head, huh? You remember songs?"

"Sure," I said. "It's just that my jukebox got busted in the fifties. But I can still hear Patti Page singing 'Tennessee Waltz,' and the big sobber she did, 'I Went to Your Wedding.' Teresa Brewer did a number called 'Till I Waltz Again with You,' and a girl named Joni James had a song called 'Your Cheatin' Heart.'"

"Christ Almighty," said City, sitting up. She extended her glass, and I filled it carefully. "Tell me some more."

"Everything was getting schmaltzy then," I said, replenishing my own glass, "and things tend to run together in a certain sound I can play in my head." I took a sip; my client had been right.

"But what doesn't run together," I told her, "was what I heard up in Seattle just before I went over. Louis Armstrong and his band were touring the West Coast then, and I went to hear them at—I think it was called the Palace. They were there for, I think, five nights. I know I went every night. There was Louis, and there was Jack Teagarden, Barney Bigard played the clarinet, 'Fatha' Hines on piano and Cozy Cole on the drums. I'll never forget one minute of that. I'll never forget Louis Armstrong coming out on the stage and waving

175

his arm outward, like royalty, and saying—'*Aah, I see all you cats out there.*' And then they'd play. I heard all that. I got it all in. I'll never lose it."

City was smiling. "You heard it all," she said. She opened up her arms. "Come over here."

I stood over her tentatively, looking down, restrained, not wanting to spoil things now. She took my hands. "Did you ever hear any of the records of Bessie Smith?" she asked me.

"I heard of her, but never really heard her sing," I admitted.

"They say that she'd be on stage, singing, and she'd fasten her eyes on some guy in the audience, and he would just rise up out of his seat and sort of float down the aisle and come right up on the stage, standing next to her, without knowing how he got there. She called it 'walking a man.' I'd like to be able to do that."

"Consider it done," I said. City laughed. Her hands slid up my arms and her head fell back. Her eyes were half closed, the laugh subsided into the open curve of a smile.

I was still apprehensive because I had never in my life been up against so much *woman* as City. I don't mean to sound virginal; I'm not. But neither am I a cocksman. I don't know how anyone could have found more woman than City, relaxed as she was then in the big chair, glowing. I put my hands under her arms and drew her up. Her stylish britches were fastened only with a drawstring, and when I pulled it, they collapsed at her calves. Under those, she had only the briefest of bikini panties. We were both trembling, clasped together, when suddenly she broke away from me, kicked off the britches, shrugged off the open blouse and went over to the end table. She shakily poured herself a drink in the glass I'd been using. I collapsed in the chair with surprise. City spilled a good deal of valuable cognac on the surface of the table. "Give me a minute," she said.

"I'll give you forever," I answered. "I'll sit here forever." I was drowning in the sight of her body.

She threw the long fall of dark hair over her shoulder, and her face became austere. "It's all going back, now," she said, "back to years and years ago when it was all wrong to do this—and that is a long way back. Back to when you were somehow betraying some phantom of an idea. What right had anybody to make me feel like that? But now they do have the right. Now I really am betraying somebody—no phantom. I'm doing it because I have to do it—to be free again.

"Oh," she exclaimed suddenly, with a different expression on her face. "I've hurt you. I didn't mean to hurt you."

My chest was full of gravel. "I understand what you said," I told her. "I know what you mean."

"Do you? Do you?" she demanded. Those enormous eyes were dark pools of a deep-blue glimmer that fought against the soft glow of the lamp. "I may actually love you," she said. "I may, I may." Her hand with the small glass in it shook as she finished the cognac. She stood for an instant facing me, and her body drank in all the light in the room and then radiated it outward, as if she alone controlled the light.

She said, "Do you know that now I feel like I haven't got any strength in my body at all? As if I was all made up of water? These stupid pants"—she snapped the waist of the tiny briefs—"I can't—I can't take them off. I can't do it." She glided to the chair in front of me. "You," she said. "You do it for me."

I took them off and she knelt in front of me by the chair. She took my shirt off and ran her finger across my shoulder. "I don't think I ever saw skin so white and thin," she said. "I can see all the veins in your shoulder."

"I burn easily," I told her. God only knows what the words could have sounded like.

She pulled the rest of my clothes off and we fell on the floor together. She was more woman than I had ever known, doing more things than had ever been done, and engaging me in more than I had ever done. We would surface for more

177

cognac and then plunge to the floor again as if we were diving into the depths of a magical sea.

I don't remember what I said to her except that I was promising my life away. She had become the universe and all the constellations by which any man could chart his fortunes. When I awoke next morning, sprawled naked on the couch, she was gone.

Chapter XXIV

Disorientation was becoming a way of life for me, I fear. It is one thing to wake up disoriented in a strange motel, and quite another to feel the same sensation in your own front room. But that is what I felt, levitating buck naked and still redolent of City's perfume from my couch. I wandered through all five rooms of my apartment, checking the bedroom and guest room in the hope that City had collapsed in bed. But the beds were severely pristine. The kitchen, where I had kissed her first and unfettered all the delight she'd kept inside her blouse, was utterly empty. My dining room, which also serves as a workroom, showed no signs of her ever having been there. I picked up the empty cognac bottle by the couch, thinking to throw it away, but in the end I reverentially put it back in its old position in the cupboard.

I took a shower, as hot as I could stand it, and after I had scraped my face and whisked the fur from my teeth, I fixed breakfast, daring the bacon grease to ruin my robe. But the disorientation remained and clung to me throughout the weekend as I remained holed up in my apartment trying to fit the disparate parts of City's life and mine together.

On Monday morning I dressed, not too carefully, and went off to search for my tan London Fog. There had been no prediction of rain, but I had devised an ulterior purpose for the coat. I'd bought the coat during a Sinatra boom, but unlike Sinatra, I could never get it to hang artfully over my shoulder. I'd even thought of taping it to my shoulder so it wouldn't slide off but that is another story, having no place here.

I walked over to Nassau Street, which was in the throes of the Labor Day sales, and picked up the purchase I'd made before. Then, after stowing my purchase suitably, I hailed a cab for the Groupe studios. I counted on Ed Parti's ignoring Labor Day. On the way into the building, I carried the raincoat by the loop so that it hung down over my back and banged along companionably.

I didn't expect to see City at the studio, and I was right. She was, I hoped, sitting at home and ruminating happily on the events of a prior evening. Working on instinct, I swept past the empty receptionist's desk with a very brief wave, headed for the president's office—Iris's, really—and walked in without knocking.

Ed Parti was seated behind Iris's big desk. He looked up impassively through his shades. Larry was standing near him, looking out a window. I laid my raincoat on the couch full length, as if it were going to be photographed for an ad. He hadn't had a couch in the other office. This was his big step up.

"Something I can do for you?" he said. The shades were an irritant, but I couldn't very well ask *him* to take them off. I never did understand why anybody wears them indoors under fluorescent lights. His lips made the mechanical movements, and I read them as best I could.

"For openers," I said, "you might want to pick up some of my medical expenses."

He smiled a good healthy smile with a lot of strong white teeth framed by a fine firm mouth. He had a broad face that

179

looked sullen, ordinarily, but the smile must have played hell with the ladies. "Wrong office," he said. "Blue Cross is down the street."

I was a little irritated. "Blue Cross didn't set me up," I said.

This amused him. His little shrug sketched a laugh, and the smile got bigger. "You'd better fill me in," he said. "Tell me what happened, or at least what you think happened." He indicated a chair. "Sit down and rest your ankles." As I sat down, he stood up and moved next to Larry.

"I got sandbagged about a block away from here just after I left."

"Oh, yeah." The smile reached the maximum. "I remember you now. Wanted to set your kid up with a record, wasn't that it? How's he doing?"

"Better than Larry," I said. "At least he doesn't exist."

Larry turned slowly around from the window, and the smile on Parti's face began to dwindle. "You're actually trying to blame me because you got mugged?" he asked me. "There's a mugging every eight seconds in this town. Ask anybody. You must have had a concussion or something if you're running around bothering people about something like that."

"I got a lot more than a concussion out of it," I told him. "I got a hell of a lot of information."

"Is any of it any good?"

"I think so. I think it ties you in pretty solidly."

"And who's been giving you the funny stories?"

"Melendez for one. Schultz and Moylan."

"Never heard of them," said Parti. He pursed his lips. "Melendez," he repeated. "A Puerto Rican? They're all over the place. They get blamed for everything. You shouldn't be prejudiced."

"He's a Latin American diplomat, in fact," I said. "Didn't you know?"

180

"Never heard of him," Parti maintained. "You're quite a guy if you're getting mugged by diplomats."

"It's funny you don't remember him," I replied. "He told me a lot about you, after a while."

"There's liars, there's Goddamned liars, and there's diplomats," Parti commented. "But keep talking."

"The way Melendez has it," I said, "you smelled a rat the minute you saw me and called him. He put Schultz and Moylan on me."

"I'm surprised he didn't say I mugged you myself. It would make just as much sense. I never heard of any of these people. Why should I be calling a Latin American diplomat?"

"To protect your interests."

"My interests are here in the studio. We don't even have a Latin American line." He smiled his broad smile again. "Been thinking about it, but I just can't stand the word *corazón.*" He winked at Larry.

"There seems to be a general agreement," I said, "that your interests include a lot more than cutting records."

"Agreement where?"

"Among the police, Melendez, Penton, and myself."

He looked over at Larry again. "You hear that, kid? I'm a kingpin. Big deal, huh?" he said to me. "You people are all alike. Recording studios are very visible. A lot of the people connected with them look funny and act funny. It's a setup."

"A lot of them use drugs, too," I objected mildly.

"Like who?"

"Like your outfit the K.C. Sourballs."

"The K.C. . . ." He leaned down and hit the desk with his hand. "How nuts can you be? They're not even with us anymore."

"Since when?"

"Never mind since when. That's what you call proprietary information."

"Stop playing stupid, Ed," I admonished him. "Contracts

can be looked at anytime. When did you get rid of them?"

He smiled an abashed, boyish smile. "Friday," he said.

"Who'd you sell them to?"

"National Managing Controls. That suit you? They respectable enough for you?"

"I stopped believing in respectability a long time ago," I answered. "But I admit they're big, and probably legit." I tried to puzzle it out. Finally, I said, "What I can't understand is how you got Penton to put his name on the deal."

"Penton?" The smile opened up again. "So who needs Penton?"

"Anybody who wants to make a legitimate transfer of property at Groupe, I should think," I answered. "What other ownership authority do you have?"

He decided to lecture me. "First of all, it was a corporate decision, carried out by the management, which is, at this moment, me." He pointed soberly at his broad chest. "Even though Iris had final say, the contract was in my hands."

"In a company that Iris owned," I objected.

"But which in her absence I operate."

"She's absent, all right," I agreed.

"Now just to make everything kosher, as a matter of fact, we did get a signature authorizing the sale."

"From Penton?" I was astounded.

"No, of course not. From Larry here. He signed it over."

"You must be stupider than I ever guessed. Larry's a minor. His name isn't worth a nickel."

"It is with his father's up against it."

"Gil Hosier," I mused. "That's the way it is, eh?" I sat back in my chair. "It will never stand up, Ed. They'll tear it to pieces in court."

He leaned back against the casement of the window and put his hands across his belly. "I don't agree," he said, the feathers of the canary still dangling from his mouth. "I think we can make it stick."

182

I decided to shift my ground. "What made you decide to sell them—Friday?"

He shrugged. "They're hot. They're big—too big for us to develop properly. NMC has been sniffing around them for quite a while. We decided this was the best price we'd ever get. Strictly a business deal. Do it every day."

I laughed. "It's a great story, Ed. Would you like to hear the Binney version now?"

"I haven't got all day."

"This won't take long. We'll start from last Thursday and work back. Incidentally, where were you last Thursday?"

"Where I always am. Right here."

"What about the evening, seven or eightish?"

"Still here."

"Anybody with you?"

He cast his eyes up. "Seven or eight? No. Everybody'd gone home by then. I'm the first to arrive and the last to leave." He paused, beginning to think. "What's this all about, anyway?"

"Nothing," I lied. "I'm just checking something I heard. But getting back to the Binney version, first of all, I don't think that the K.C. Sourballs were hot at all—not in the way you meant it—and I think the sales charts will back me up. Secondly, I don't think that NMC was sniffing around them for a long time, because what they sniff around for thirty seconds they get in the next thirty seconds. I think you unloaded that outfit for a cup of coffee, and I think a subpoena to NMC will reveal the price."

He spread his arms. "You think I'm crazy? Why would I do a thing like that?"

"Because the Sourballs tie you directly to the center of a nationwide narcotics distribution ring. It had Melendez at the top, you in the middle, and the rock group running around the country making drops. In the light of recent events, I think

183

you saw that they had gotten *really* hot, and you wanted to break this association."

"You're really serious about this." It wasn't a question. His face was blank and bleak.

"Try me."

"Even if your story were true, not for a minute that it isn't really a wild fantasy, how the hell do you think anybody would prosecute? If it were true, do you think that group would go into court and hang themselves?"

"Melendez will make a deal."

"Don't make me laugh," said Parti. "When was the last time you ever saw a diplomat give evidence?"

"I'm trying hard not to make you laugh, Ed," I told him. "But let's try this on as long as we're at it. It might loosen up Larry, too." At the mention of his name, the kid stirred, something like a dog at a fireplace, and came over to sit on the corner of the desk.

"Try it this way," I said. "Iris found out that you were shipping drugs around the country through her company, and she told you to quit. You said O.K., but kept right on going. However, to get some leverage on her, you introduced her son, this upstanding lad, to the joys of heroin—about as tough as hooking a goldfish in your front-room aquarium. You kept the kid on ice, so to speak, well supplied, but ready to use when you needed him.

"Iris picked up rumors that the shipping hadn't stopped, and she braced you with it. You showed her Exhibit A—to wit, her one and only son, with a set of tracks like the Penn Central. Your plan was to cut her in, both to implicate her and to have her protect Larry.

"Iris had a much better mind than yours, and she figured out ways to get Larry off the hook and can you at the same time. Larry relayed this information to you. You had a show-down with Iris and gave her a deadline to come across. She didn't meet it, and you sent two gorillas out to the house to brace her. They took her upstairs and played games with her

184

and shot her up with something like a barrel of horse.

"Then they took her downstairs and threw her into the pool. She was dead before she hit the water, and you, as you have pointed out, are now operating Groupe records for fun and profit.

"How do you like it?" I asked him. "And furthermore," I asked, swinging around to face Larry, "how in the hell do *you* like it?"

Larry got off the corner of the desk and walked around his mother's office. He took up his old position at the window and stayed there for a while. When he turned around, finally, he said to me, "I don't feel good about it, naturally. But I think you're full of shit. Penton killed my mother—or had her killed, the way you say."

"Penton is dead," I told them.

There was no immediate sensation between them. There was a spark of curiosity in Larry's eyes. I wasn't able to see Ed Parti's, but his mouth hadn't changed. At last Parti said, "How come?"

"He was shot," I said, "through the window facing his backyard. Somebody picked him off last Thursday. Haven't you seen the papers?"

It appeared that Parti read only *Billboard*. Larry read nothing.

"What time did this happen?" Parti asked me.

"Between seven and eight in the evening."

"So that's why you were asking."

"Yes, that's why I was asking, and that's what the police will ask. I like you a lot for it, Ed, and so will they."

"Can I ask why?"

"Sure. You figured Melendez would never testify. You figured the group wouldn't dare testify, and you figured the chump, here"—I nodded toward Larry—"would never catch on or let himself believe it if he did."

"That isn't a hell of a lot," said Ed Parti.

"I've got more," I told him. I went over to the couch and

took the corner of my raincoat. I jerked it upward so that the carbine spun in the air and subsided finally on the couch, black, shiny, and dangerous. "The police gave me this when I went over there this morning," I said. "It's the murder weapon, and they traced it to you."

He came around the desk to stand next to me. I noticed for the first time how truly big he was. "Stop the bullshitting," he said.

"They picked it up at your apartment this morning after you left," I told him. "They traced the rifle number back to the point of purchase, and your name is on the register. They picked up a pair of shoes of yours, and they match the tracks in the backyard. They matched the cartridge of the murder gun to a cartridge ejected from this one and the marks are the same. We loaded the gun up, and they showed me how it works. See these?" I held two cartridges in my hand for him to inspect. "The marks on the side are from the same ejection. One is from the murder weapon and one was ejected from this. This is the murder weapon, and it's yours."

He was breathing very heavily now, and the shades hid less than usual. "You're bullshitting," he said. "Stay here a minute. I have to go to the can."

He was out of the office before I had a chance to move. I looked at Larry. "Where do you think he's gone?"

"To the can, like he said."

I didn't like it at all. I liked it even less as the minutes ticked away, far too much time for any normal occupation of a toilet. I didn't like the way Larry was staring at me from the window—there are better views in Manhattan than staring at my kisser. I stared back at him. He was a big kid, in spite of being so young, and I didn't want any funny moves. Because I was watching the kid, I didn't see Ed Parti come back into the office. When he did cross my line of sight, it was obvious that there was something different about him, a different carriage of the body, a different way of putting his feet on the floor. I

186

wondered if he was carrying, but I couldn't see any bulging evidence of it.

He spoke to Larry. "Did City call here this morning?"

"Not that I know of."

"I called home. She's not there. Nobody's there."

I assumed my best dummy expression and kept my mouth firmly shut. It was a stroke of good fortune I had no right to expect. I blessed my good luck and City, wherever she was, in equal portions.

Shades or no shades to screen his eyes, it was obvious that Parti had done more than take a pee and make a phone call. He was high enough to be on circus stilts. "Now," he said, "let's have it about this here gun again."

I held out the cartridges again. "These both came from this gun," I repeated. "One was used to kill Penton, the other one we ejected for comparison." I picked up the gun, ejected a round, and put it back on the couch.

"Take the gun and eject a bullet, Ed," I instructed him. "Go ahead—it's got a full magazine of ammunition. Eject a bullet and look at the marks on the cartridge."

He stepped next to the couch and stared at the carbine. His hand strayed near it, and suddenly he snatched the gun up and pointed it at me.

"I was only trying to demonstrate," I complained.

"You'll get a demonstration, you son of a bitch," he said. "You were supposed to be dead a long time ago, and there isn't any reason you shouldn't be dead now."

"Just eject a cartridge and look at it and tell me what you see," I repeated stubbornly.

"I'll tell you what I see." His lips were very tight around the words. "I see a frame you could hang in a museum."

"You're not doing yourself any good with this kind of attitude," I told him. It was a line I'd picked up along the way, it having been addressed to me many, many times by various

187

authorities and functionaries. It was, at that moment, the only thing I could think of to say.

"I don't know what you've got cooked up or with who," Parti said, "but I'm nobody's patsy. Move over there." He gestured with the gun, and Larry stepped fluidly out of the way. "Up against that outside wall. These inside walls are just cardboard and insulation."

"I don't understand," I said.

"I don't want the bullet to travel through the studio rooms, stupid," said Parti.

"Are you really going to shoot me here?" I asked him. "Aren't you in enough trouble?"

"Nobody will hear," said Parti. "You outcuted yourself, wiseguy. No hard feelings."

His finger tightened on the trigger. The knuckle turned white and the muscles leaped in his jaw. He swore some unformed expletive, and I gave him the good old-fashioned G.I. disarming maneuver—nothing fancy—twisting the barrel of the gun, forcing it out of his hands, and bringing the stock up smartly into his mouth. It put him away with a lot of blood and teeth on Iris's rug, but you can't have everything. I turned the gun around to hold the kid, but Larry was gone.

Chapter XXV

Edna was just putting down the phone when I walked into the office. She turned toward the opened door and said, "Hail the conquering hero!"

"Hero of what?" I asked her.

"You got your man."

"I got *a* man," I corrected her.

"Dick says he wishes you would just once bring in a man who doesn't need surgery."

"Who's Dick?" I sat down behind my desk and started going through the mail. There was a thick envelope underneath a stack of bills—thousands and thousands of bills. Among them, however, was a check for a hundred and fifty dollars that had been owed to me for eighteen months. "I'll take you to dinner," I announced. "Who's Dick?"

"Lieutenant Probcziewski, silly," said Edna. She had a look on her face that is usually described as sappy.

"Maybe I won't take you to dinner after all," I said disapprovingly. "I don't like first-name terms with the police."

She dismissed the remonstrance with a gesture. I had a feeling she would have dismissed the news that the Empire State Building had collapsed on the lunch-hour crowd exactly the same way. I returned to my mail. The thick envelope turned out to be the new lease for my office. The increased rent was outrageous. I put it in my inside coat pocket to teach them a lesson.

"Tell me how you did it—how you trapped him," Edna demanded.

"Why don't you get Dickie boy to tell you?"

"Don't be that way," she said, pouting. "Why do you think I work in this lousy office, for the money?"

"It's the glamor, eh?"

"You bet it is."

"All right," I said. "We'll do it both ways. I'll tell you, but you'll have to take it down." Edna got out her notebook.

I put my feet on the desk and kept one eye fixed on Edna's apparently susceptible calves. "Events of last Thursday night have been described in a signed deposition with Lieutenant Dickie Probcziewski," I said. Edna grimaced and had the virtue to blush. "This morning I made preparations to induce the suspect to reveal himself. Before going to the suspect's

189

office, I stopped in a local gunshop to acquire a purchase I had made last week. It was a rifle, a carbine, actually, identical to the weapon alleged to have shot Mr. Penton—a Ruger forty-four magnum carbine. I loaded the weapon with a full magazine and concealed it in my raincoat. When I arrived at the office, I put the raincoat on the couch with the weapon inside.

"Larry Hosier was in the office with Ed Parti. I charged Ed Parti with the following crimes: One—Ordering my illegal apprehension, assault, and subsequent attempted murder. Two—Operating a distribution ring for the nationwide sale of narcotics. Three—Receiving illicit narcotics from abroad for distribution. Four—Contributing to the delinquency of a minor by introducing Larry Hosier, his employer's son, to the use of heroin. Five—Ordering the execution of Iris Penton by hired assistants and providing them with sufficient illicit narcotics to introduce a lethal dose of heroin into her bloodstream. Six—Murdering Millard Penton on Thursday night last by firing a rifle bullet through a window at which Penton had been sitting illuminated by a lamp."

"Wow," exclaimed Edna. "You let him have it? Just like that?"

"It was a little more drawn out than that," I admitted shyly.

"Like the jail sentence he's going to get?" said Edna with unseemly relish. "I'll bet the jail falls down before they let him out."

"Don't bet on it. Jails are built for durability in these parts. They've got one upstate that was built in eighteen thirty."

"I bet anyway," said Edna, rearranging the knees. "Keep going—about the gun and all. . . . "

"When I charged him with these crimes," I continued, resisting the hypnosis of the knees, "he denied them seriatim. However, his denial of the drug dealing was less vehement than that of the murders. He hypothesized . . ."

"Spelling," said Edna.

"Where did you go to school?" I demanded irritably. "In a detention home?"

"Saint Lucy's Academy for Secretarial Skills," she replied placidly.

"Where, in God's name, is that?"

"It's not farre from Wilkes Barre—that's what the ad says, anyway."

I gave up and spelled it out. "He hypothesized that even if he were brought to trial, there would be no evidence to convict him and no witnesses."

"Crap," said Edna, rejecting the remorseless training of St. Lucy's. "There's witnesses all over the lot."

"It was his conjecture," I battled on, " that even if there *were* witnesses, they would be either reluctant to testify or protected from having to give testimony. The first instance applied to a group known as the K.C. Sourballs, and the second to one Colonel Daniel Melendez, who is a member of the diplomatic corps."

"What about the two gorillas?" she interrupted.

"The question of the two assailants is so patentably answerable to Mr. Parti that he did not even bother to mention it," I told the notebook in Edna's lap. "The direct contact to Moylan and Schultz was apparently Colonel Melendez, the Latin American diplomat, who will in all probability be unavailable for testimony. Secondly, both of these gentlemen have rather unprepossessing . . ."

"What kind of a word is that?" objected Edna.

"Strike *unprepossessing*," I said instantly. "Substitute *unappetizing*."

"Unappetizing," she repeated, and wrote it down studiously.

"Demeanors and appearances," I plunged ahead, "aggravated by long and malodorous careers, well certified in the lists

191

of criminal law, on the waterfront of New Jersey, where Alexander Hamilton, the first of many victims there, was slain."

"Who are you making this memorandum for?" demanded Edna.

"Posterity," I assured her. "It is very clear," I continued, "that the testimony of these two worthies, should they swear that the sun had risen that morning, would be instantly subject to challenge, discredit and disbelief."

"Tell about the rifle," insisted Edna, "how you got it away from him and all."

"Mr. Parti grew increasingly distraught as I pursued the subject of Millard Penton's murder by shooting," I continued imperturbably. "At what I thought was the right psychological moment, I revealed the rifle I had picked up that morning and told him that the police had found it in his apartment. I said its sale had been traced to him and that, furthermore, they had discovered shoes in his home that matched the footprints at the scene. I ejected a cartridge from the gun, showed him the marks on the side, and invited him to do the same."

"Who told you that was the right kind of gun?"

"Nobody told me—not even Dickie boy," I answered irritably. "They discovered the forty-four cartridge out near the cabana and marked its position. Now there are three major brands of forty-four magnums: Winchester, Marlin, and Ruger. Both Winchester and Marlin are lever action. The Ruger is automatic. I figured it had to be an automatic."

"How come?"

"Because with the other two he would have had to work the lever to eject the cartridge. Since he made a clean hit, first shot, there was no need to work the lever. The Ruger automatic, on the other hand, ejects the cartridge just like it says—automatically. Chances are that he was looking around for the ejected cartridge—the light was bad, you know—when he saw me returning to the room and split. Also, the position of the cartridge showed that it had been ejected with some force, and the force of an automatic discharge is considerable."

Edna pursed her lips and looked up from the pad. "I'll never understand you," she said.

"Well, you just don't understand the difference between a lever action and an automatic action . . ." I began.

"Not that," she interrupted. "I mean I'll never understand how you can be smart enough to figure that out and yet dumb enough to bring a loaded gun into a place like that. I mean, you were practically sure the man was already a murderer! You bring in the gun—a loaded gun—and actually ask him to pick it up. I mean, you even showed him it was loaded."

"Oh, that," I said modestly. "It was nothing."

"Nothing! It's a miracle you weren't shot. You were begging for it."

"Not really. I made a few arrangements before going in. You may as well put this down so I can read about it in my old age. When I went to the gun shop and bought the rifle, I got into a conversation with the clerk about handloading."

"Handloading?" The eyebrows went up.

"Making your own bullets by loading the powder to the precise weight you want and then fitting the cartridge and the bullet together. According to the way you fix the charge in the cartridge relative to the weight of the bullet, or slug, you get a difference in muzzle velocity and things like that. Now, handloaded ammunition is something dealers love to talk about, because if they can get hold of a handloading freak they can sell him a truckload full of equipment, particularly when he's just setting up. I had the salesman demonstrate a press for me, and in no time at all I had a handful of forty-four magnum cartridges. That's what I loaded the rifle with. They were just the case, primer, and bullet. There was no charge in the cartridges. They were empty."

"Like blanks."

"No; not like blanks. Blanks are very dangerous. There

was no powder in these cartridges at all. The only way one of these rounds could have hurt me would have been if he'd made me swallow one."

"And that's why you weren't shot." Her eyes had gotten very round. She was disappointed. What, indeed, do women want? "They were empty bullets."

"A needless precaution, as it turned out," I told her. "He couldn't have shot me readily if those rounds had been fully charged and the bullets tipped in cyanide."

"You're bragging now. . . ." She made a little moue. "That's not like you."

"Braggadocio has nothing to do with it," I said. "He wouldn't have shot me because he didn't know how to operate the rifle. He'd never seen the gun before in his life or anything like it. He snatched it up, pointed it, and got himself in a position to kill me—boom, boom—just like in the movies. But he didn't know where the safety catch was. I don't think he even knew there was such a thing as a safety catch. I don't think the guy had ever picked up a rifle before in his life. He hauled on the trigger until I thought he'd break his finger off. All that happened was that his eyes bulged out. He didn't even think about a safety catch or look for one.

"If he'd had the slightest familiarity with weapons, he'd have guessed at it. He just didn't know. I belted him with the rifle just to keep him from getting ideas about doing the same to me. If he'd thought *that* fast, I might well have been killed, but with the other end of the gun."

"But then how did he shoot Mr. . . . "

"Who said he did? I said he was a suspect. I wanted him to prove otherwise, and he did. That doesn't mean he isn't guilty of narcotics distribution, though. His little routine up in the office with assaulting me with intent to kill gives the police a reason to hold on to him and whistle while they work."

"But if he was innocent, why did he try to kill you?"

"He thought he'd been set up—framed. He thought that

194

his buddies had decided to throw the cops a fish just to keep the heat off. He really believed that the gun had been found in his apartment. Mysterious things were going on that he didn't know about. People weren't where they should be. Telephones weren't being answered. The paranoia index was running off the chart. All he knew was that *he* hadn't put the gun in his apartment. On the other hand, *somebody* had. It suddenly got to be very cold weather for Mr. Parti."

"What was Larry doing all this time?"

"He was watching, up to a point, and then he split."

"Was he afraid of Parti?"

"I don't know," I told her. "We'll find out tomorrow when I bring him in."

Chapter XXVI

You don't notice the climb until you go through the circle to ascend Long Mountain Road that skirts the southern border of West Point. True enough, there are hills that slope upwards on the Palisades as you move imperceptibly west of the Hudson, but somehow, by the time you've absorbed the trees, the sky, and the rest of the child's picture-book scenery, you've forgotten that these hills do not come down again, that you have been entering the highlands that soar above the Hudson. But on Long Mountain Road you know you're climbing because not all the cars can make the pace, and about halfway up there's a funny feeling in your ears that's probably translated into a *click* for people who have eardrums.

When you reach the summit of Long Mountain, the

Central Valley stretches out for miles and miles. It is a peaceable kingdom, and it spreads a carpet to the Catskills.

"The Catskills" is a vast area that includes valleys as well as mountains, and also includes a number of lesser ranges, less famous mountains, that make up the time warp of New York's upstate territories. These territories are woven out of time as well as real estate, some of them with houses built and still inhabited reaching back to the middle of the seventeenth century, when the Dutchmen had it all, and with mountains whose second growth is secondary only to the virgin forests of three hundred years ago.

I was headed for one of the lesser ranges, having discovered that when Hosier spoke of the "Catskills" it was only a manner of speaking. His place was tucked in one of the mountains between the Hudson range and the Catskills themselves. Am I a geographer? No. No. I had it all spelled out for me by Charley Braithewaithe (via Edna, of course) on the telephone.

Because when Edna had called the Hosier apartment and had gotten no answer at all, and when discreet inquiries among the neighbors had revealed that Hosier had been seen carrying camping gear to the elevator *(Yes, now that I think of it, that young fella was with him),* I put it together that he had headed for the bush. Many long years of tracking deadbeats from county to county had put me in touch with many a county seat. And in one of those county seats sat Charley Braithewaithe. "Hosier, hmn?" he had asked. "Let me take a look and I'll call you back."

When he called back, it developed that Hosier's cabin was about thirty miles inland from the Hudson on a mountain of lesser fame. The property abutted a state park that extended along the trail of the summit. Was there a way to drive there? Well, yes, but not easy. Edna wrote down the interminable instructions.

It was a beautiful day, two days after Labor Day, in fact, when all the tourists had gone home and the territory was

196

drawing a deep, deep breath. I avoided the big highway and took the old road up to Goshen, where I stopped in the Occidental Hotel, reminiscent of Dan Patch and the Hambletonian, for a consoling noontime beer.

Onward and upward. In another thirty minutes I had hit the road near the summit and was making a tortuous "now left—now right" progress onto the dirt roads that Charley had prescribed. My old heap bucked and groaned.

The only sign of habitation was a crude sign nailed to a tree. It said KEEP OUT. The dirt path curving down from it did not invite. I parked the car and eased the gun in my belt. When I got out of the car, I took the keys with me and left the door slightly ajar so there would be no warning *thunk* of the door slam, beloved of Fisher Body. I picked my way carefully down the path.

The path leveled off at a clearing that looked down on the cabin squatting in a niche in the mountain. It was a true mountain cabin, built of rough heavy timbers with a massive stone chimney. The roof was a very low, snug one pulled down over the windows—a cabin built against the cold and the icy winds that roar through the mountains in the wintertime. From where I stood, the path dropped down to the clearing at the door and then stopped. Beyond the clearing only the trees rose along the ascent of the mountain. They were thick, and they obscured the view of the barren summit ridge I'd seen from the road coming in. There was no one in the clearing.

I didn't bother to knock. The door was unlatched. Hosier's back was to me as he worked at something small that I couldn't see on the rough table in the middle of the room.

"Afternoon, Gil," I said. "The boy around anywhere?"

He turned around slowly and stood up. "Out there, somewhere," he said, "screwing around." Then he said, "I've been expecting you."

"It figures," I replied. "Mind if I sit down?" With a nod, he indicated an old kitchen chair near the wall between the table and the door. His blue eyes were very sharp. In fact, he

197

looked very much *in place,* and the clothes that were out of place on the East Side of Manhattan were exactly right up here in the mountains. There was a recognizable, authentic aura of the West about him. Up here I was the outlander.

"Who's going to tell it?" I asked him. "Me or you?"

He turned the chair around from the table, and I saw that it had been a small camera he'd been working on—the pieces carefully laid out as in an exploded drawing. "Might's well hear your end of it," he said.

I drew my chair up closer to the table. "That hoedown you met your son at—it was at Ed Parti's, wasn't it?" I began. He nodded amiably. "And it wasn't only the first time you'd seen your boy in New York, it was the first time you'd met Parti. That's right, too, isn't it?"

He nodded. "A chick took me up there," he said. "It wasn't really much of a party."

"But there were drugs," I suggested. "Hash, coke—pretty much anything anybody wanted, wasn't there?"

He shrugged. "No different from any other party I've been to in the last twenty years."

"I think there was a difference," I said. "I think that at this particular party you were looking for an outlet. I think you were the link to Colonel Melendez. I think you had the pipeline to a good supply and you were looking for a distribution outlet."

"Not bad," said Hosier. "I knew Melendez when he was a playboy out on the coast. I met him again when I was covering a Pan American trade meeting. We got to talking. You know how it is."

"So when Larry introduced you to Ed Parti, it all fell into place, huh?"

"What made it click was Iris," said Hosier. "I thought it would be good for a few laughs."

"How long did it take you to find out that Larry was mainlining?"

"Same night." The blue eyes clouded a bit. "And I saw

that Parti was the supply. But I also saw that Parti was no heavyweight. He was a casual user, then, and a sort of fringe dealer. People like that are always looking for something—some leverage somewhere. That's what got me interested."

"So you got to talking—I know how it is."

"Yeah, well, Parti wanted Iris's outfit. He had that written all over him."

"Did Larry know that?"

"Larry had only one enemy in this world—Millard Penton. He couldn't see anybody else as a threat at all. Ed's story was that he'd keep the company out of Penton's hands. Larry ate it up."

"How did you get to Parti?"

"He was a lightweight. I told him he'd be screwing around in a control booth for the rest of his life if he didn't get ahold of some money. The only way he could get next to any ownership was by having some money. In the long run, it's the only kind of clout."

"And you? Was that all you saw? Set up the distributorship, pick up your end, and go home?"

He grinned under the mustache. It was not a terribly pleasant grin. "That never works, does it? You make a pile, so you got a pile. You put it down somewheres, and it sits there and rots. Money melts like snow. You've got to get it into something, and you've got to get it in good. No. I admit it. I figured if Parti could take the company, then I could take Parti."

"Just like that?" I shook my head. "It doesn't add up. If you were an operator, you wouldn't be doing what you're doing. You'd be manipulating something—would have been all your life, just like Penton."

"What do they say about an idea whose time has come?" The eyes were getting very remote now. "It probably doesn't fit, anyway. But look, I wasn't getting any younger, you know. A man has to look at himself. I'm sweating my balls off and living on top of the telephone just to get assignments. You think I'm rich? I was looking, and I was hungry. And then there was Iris. Just the *fact* of Iris. When the kid told me about the big house out on the Island, I couldn't believe it. Where did she come off getting that kind of loot?"

"She worked for it, I'm told."

He dismissed this as if batting down a fly. "Everybody works," he said. "But she had it all. She had it all, and I had nothing."

"It looks to me as if you've got a professional career going for you."

He sat up rigidly in his chair and the eyes snapped. The silent, shouted words wrote themselves out for me.

"I'm a painter, Goddamn it! A *painter!* She faked me out of the one thing that ever meant anything to me, and then she left me. And then she went on to make a mint while I was sitting on my ass and starving."

I leaned back in my chair. "You know," I began, "the other morning when I dropped in on Parti—the kid has told you?—" He nodded. "I put it to him that he had called Melendez to set the dogs on me. He was pretty noncommittal. I've been thinking it over. Parti never had a line to Melendez at all, did he? He called you, and you opened the gates to the zoo."

He was laughing now. "I guess you got it pretty good."

My words must have sounded like a growl. They came from very deep in my chest where I could feel the vibrations. "I'm not the only one who got it pretty good . . . ."

"No—no," he protested. "I mean you got the story pretty good. Parti had never even heard of Melendez. I wouldn't trust Parti to walk my dog, if I had a dog. He looks cool, but he comes apart pretty quick—as you probably found out."

"Yes," I said. "I found out. That's why I don't really believe that he set up Iris for the murder. I don't believe he would have thought that through."

A look of extreme patience stole over Hosier's face. "Nobody set Iris up for murder," he said. "People tried to talk to her, and she wouldn't listen."

"Who was she supposed to listen to?"

"All she had to do was sign a lousy Goddamned piece of paper."

"What was on it?"

"A partnership."

"With you?"

He laughed again. "That would have been too rich for her blood. Even I knew that. No. It was a partnership with Parti. She didn't even know I was still alive. I—I asked Larry not to mention it to her."

"You sent over those same two lads that worked on me?"

"Yes. What's the difference? They were available."

"You knew they were going to play games with her?"

"I knew that Iris had a neurotic fear of both needles and heroin. There wasn't much else she was afraid of. I thought if they waved the needle under her nose she'd sign anything. I mean she fainted when they drew blood for the VD test before we got married. And heroin—even the idea of heroin was like a loaded gun to her. She wouldn't even let people talk about it in front of her. I always thought maybe she had a secret yen for it that she was frightened of."

I let out a long, long sigh. "I was wondering what kind of instructions you gave them," I said.

"Just to scare her a little. And if she got snotty to give her a taste of the needle. I figured if they went ahead and did it, she'd collapse and sign anything."

"They did it seven times," I said. "Up in the bedroom, after they took her bathing suit off. They gave her a heavy jolt, and then they stuck her six more times with an empty needle, to panic her a little more. She wouldn't have known it was empty. She could have died of panic, but she died of anaphylactic shock. That make you happy?"

"Too bad about old Iris," he said. "She always was a hardheaded bitch."

"I still don't know," I mused, "why she stayed home that day."

"Oh, that wasn't hard," said Hosier. "I had Moylan call

her and tell her that her son was in trouble with the narcs, but that we could save him and her a lot of trouble. She saw an easy way to trim off the edges after getting things under way with Penton. But we wouldn't make an appointment, because we didn't want anybody else waiting for us there. So we just told her to stay home all day. She was just killing time, swimming around in the pool."

"And me, if I'd been there how much earlier, an hour—a half hour—?"

"You'd be dead. It would have been a break for us because maybe we could have set you up for the whole thing."

"Maybe and maybe not," I said. "I'm not a middle-aged woman in a bathing suit."

He grinned again. "You never can tell," he said.

"Why did Penton have to go?"

"Too many complications. Too much testimony riding on the top of that wet brain of his. The unpredictable. You know, if he hadn't've been in all that other trouble, there would have been a chance of making a deal with him. But he seemed to be frightened crazy—I mean all holed up and drinking himself nutty like that. There was no way to reach him. . . ."

"Except with a bullet?"

The grin got very wide. "That's right Mr. Detective," said Hosier. "The same kind of bullet that's aimed right at the base of your skull right this very minute. Sit very still and don't make any kind of a move at all."

He reached over and took the revolver out of my belt. "You can relax now," he told me.

I turned my head very slowly in the chair. Larry was standing inside the open door, the gun held loosely but accurately over his forearm. It was a Ruger forty-four magnum semiautomatic, and it certainly wasn't the one I'd bought on Nassau Street.

Chapter XXVII

"Been out shooting?" I asked the kid. I shifted my chair back a little so that I could see the two of them. The muzzle of the Ruger followed me almost indifferently. The kid nodded soberly. "Anyone I know?" I asked again, smiling pleasantly. The kid scowled. It was almost as nasty as his father's grin.

"What did you mean by that?" he asked.

"I wondered if shooting Penton had given you an appetite for the sport."

"I never shot anybody," said Larry.

"I'm relieved to hear it," I told him. "That means your father shot him."

"He had it coming," said the kid.

"For what?"

"For what he did to my mother."

"Such as?"

"You ought to know," said Larry. "You found her. And then you took his side."

"I was hired before I found her," I said mildly. "After I found her, I wasn't on anybody's side." I tried to edge away from the muzzle, but it followed me as if there were a magnet in my head. "If you've never shot anybody before, what makes you so ready to shoot me?" I complained.

"Who said anything about shooting you? You're just not supposed to get any funny ideas, that's all," said the kid. "I saw what you did to Ed Parti."

"A once-in-a-lifetime move," I assured him. "It could

never happen twice. Besides, I haven't come to hurt any-body."

"Not much," said Gil Hosier.

"What if I could prove to you that Penton had nothing to do with your mother's murder?" I asked Larry.

"I wouldn't believe you."

"What if I showed you a transcript of the confession of the two goons and it implicated your father?"

"I wouldn't believe them either." But for a split second the muzzle wavered off true north.

"Think about it," I urged him. "The two men who did the actual murder are facing life if they don't come up with goods. You think they're going to play games? You think they're worried about protecting anybody now? They sang, and it's all down in black and white, very legal, very regular, with every police procedure observed to protect the validity of the confessions. Think about it. Separate confessions, obtained separately. Both implicating Gil Hosier. Everything matching up perfectly. You want to see it? I'll show it to you."

Like his father's, the kids eyes would cloud up when he was puzzled. His jaw tensed.

"I've got it with me," I said, "but I don't intend to get cut in half reaching for it. May I open my coat?"

They both nodded—the kid because he was surprised, Gil Hosier because he didn't know what else to do.

I opened my coat to reveal a heavy legal document in my inside pocket. "Now watch carefully, and don't get nervous," I said. "I'm going to pick this out of my pocket with just two fingers. I'm not reaching for a weapon and I don't want to die—at least not by mistake. All right?"

Again they nodded in unison, but blankly. I focused their attention on my two fingers, which I held up, and then I dipped the two fingers into my coat and pincered the edge of the document. It was so thick and heavy that I had trouble holding it between my trembling fingers. I held it in the air.

"Exhibit A," I said softly.

They were both hypnotized by the document, and both moved toward it simultaneously. For once the muzzle of the gun had moved way off course. I grabbed the wood of the Ruger with my other hand and drove the barrel into Gil Hosier's crotch. His two hands, one still holding my pistol, went where they were supposed to go—to protect his genitals. The kid, still clinging to the stock, came tumbling after and collided with Gil. The document plummeted to the floor, and I bolted for the outside.

But outside, a wall of solid green with no opening path confronted me. I darted to the side of the house, grabbed one of the low-hanging eaves, and swung myself to the roof, where I flattened out prone. And not a second too soon. They came tumbling out together—Gil Hosier with the rifle, this time, held so naturally that it looked like an extension of his hand.

He surveyed the woods while his son took him by the arm and put his face up close to his father's. Larry was saying, "Is it true? Is it true what that guy said in there? Is it true what he said? Did you kill my mother?"

I could see the boy's distorted face just past the back of his father's head. I had no way of knowing if Gil Hosier replied or, if he did reply, what he said. But the boy's eyes grew huge and disbelieving.

Gil Hosier took one step backward then and almost lazily brought the side of the rifle butt alongside Larry's face. It was a deceptively powerful blow that knocked the boy several feet, where he dropped in absolute stillness. It was my only moment. I launched myself feet first from the roof, aiming at the back of Hosier's head.

He must have heard me coming. He had begun to turn when my feet made contact, so that I hit him full force between the neck and the shoulder. He rolled too fast for me to grapple with him and came to rest on top of the rifle, which he clutched to his belly. I did the only thing I could. I ran for the woods, hoping that a path would open for me. It didn't really matter for a while. For a while I *made* a pathway.

And as I ran, my mind was focused only on seeing the line of least resistance through the trees, zigzagging in any direction so long as that direction led upward. Upward meant *away* from the cabin. I felt that my feet were barely touching the ground. I was flying on adrenalin, nature's rocket fuel. If I tripped and fell on my knees or pitched forward at full length, catching myself only at the last moment on the heels of my palms, I felt nothing. I was up instantly again and flying—flying through the woods—like a terrified owl.

The timber had already begun to thin when I collapsed. The breath in my lungs was ignited gasoline that seared my flanks. I was heaving huge swimmer's breaths, my mouth distended like the bell of a trumpet. I knew I could not rest, and yet I had no breath to pump me higher.

When I was first truly able to catch my breath, I tried to regulate my breathing, to hold the air in my lungs so that every last drop of oxygen would get into my body. I was sobbing. I could feel the sobs and gulps of air bursting from my throat.

I rolled onto my back and stared up at the sky. How long could I rest like this? How long had I been gone? I had no idea of how much time had elapsed. I formed an image of Hosier loping easily and remorselessly behind me, the rifle growing like a tree limb from his hand.

And yet there was something wrong with the picture. Why should he run? Why should he exhaust himself, turn himself into a wreck like me? I had left a trail that a bulldozer couldn't have bettered, and he was an experienced stalker. He would do this *methodically*. I remembered the dismantled camera on the table in the cabin—each piece laid out carefully in a precise pattern. Hosier didn't hurry into things.

Using my final deep, resting breaths of air, I put together what I could. The rifle was generally accurate at seventy-five yards. (Did he have another? One with a scope? Somehow I doubted it.) Then my course was to stay at least a hundred yards ahead of him. He could stalk. Therefore my best course was to get out of the woods, where every twig was a signpost shouting, *"He went thataway!"* and get up, if possible, on rocky terrain, where tracks were harder to come by.

Also, I could not hear him. If he crept up behind me and shouted in my ear it would mean nothing to me, not until a bullet tore the top of my head off. Therefore, I had to get up above him, where I could *see* him, and he, please God, could not see me.

I got up and began to lope. The panic had ended, but with the end of panic came rationality, and the rationality terrified me. I did not know where I was or where I was going except that I was elevating, rising ridge by ridge up the side of the mountain. I hoped beyond hope that this was the entrance to the state park, where I could find picnickers, strollers, lovers, litterers—anybody at all who would be around me for protection or at least tell me how to find a road. On the other hand, it was a Wednesday, a weekday, so I could expect no weekend campers or leftover tourists. And it was two days after Labor Day, traditionally the cessation of visitors in these parts.

The trees had become stunted and twisted, and were spaced much farther apart so that there was no longer any problem in finding a path at all. My back felt naked, and I began to turn as I ran to survey the woods behind me. In this ragged terrain he could easily pop out of the timber and pick me off. I ran, revolving every now and then, and often when I revolved I fell, not onto the soil or pine needles that bedded the forest, but onto rock that tore the knees out of my pants and sheared the skin away from my palms.

At last I burst onto the rocky spine of the mountain that seemed to stretch forever to the north. The trees had ended, and now there was only rock, punctuated by small wind-tortured bushes that would not satisfactorily have hidden a fox, let alone a man. At about a hundred yards from where I stood, however, there was a long outcropping where a shaft of limestone had tossed up boulders when the mountain was born. It would give me rock-to-rock cover, anyway. I crouched down to gain breath for a burst of speed, and then dashed over to the boulder nearest me—a clay pigeon caught in the audition for the Olympics.

I crouched behind my rock, took a long, long look, and squared such tactics as I had in mind. He would have to come up pretty much the same way, I reckoned. As long as I stayed behind this line of rocks, I at least had a chance to reconnoiter. Where did the long spine lead? I hadn't the slightest idea, but it is an article of faith in this country that if you follow a straight path far enough you will come to a highway. I began a measured progress, crouching or falling behind a rock and then rising to dash to the next one. At each station I would pause to peer back and sweep the line of the horizon.

It meant that my flight wasn't as fast as it should have been, but on the other hand I didn't want to be a skeet target flitting along a line of rocks. The spine stretched interminably; my mouth turned to cotton. The sun was moving very gradually downward, and there was no water. I thought, very briefly, about Ben Gunn. There wasn't a soul or a sign of humanity anywhere.

Nor was there any sign of Hosier. I began to feel aggrieved, then foolish, and then a sense of eeriness dropped over me. Where was he? Where the hell *was* he? I wasn't making good time anymore. Supposing he'd just got back in his car and gone back to New York? Was I being hysterical? I thought it over behind a rock. No. When you looked at it, my every instinct said that he meant to kill me. He had been expecting me, and he wouldn't have talked like that unless he had expected me to be dead. Somewhere along the ragged edge of the woods below, Hosier was loping smoothly and smartly with a rifle he knew how to use very well growing out of his hand. What about the boy? Had Hosier killed him?

I spurted along from rock to rock, and with the sense of eeriness, fatigue, and thirst I became enraged. My flight-or-fight mechanism was beginning to sputter and short-circuit in my skull, and yet there was enough rationality spinning under the sweat on my forehead to tell me that no matter what the mechanism did, I had only the choice of flight. I had nothing to fight with.

I stayed for quite awhile behind one boulder, sensing another kind of panic, an aggressive panic that will make a baboon turn on a leopard. It is equally mindless, equally futile. I sat there, getting my breath and my brains back in order. I made up my mind that I would run until dark and then I would descend the other side of the mountain, because even in the dark you can tell up from down.

At the next boulder a gully opened below, part of a path that had ascended the other side. Where the gully came to a spearpoint of rock, a wrecked jeep balanced itself precariously on a long, slim boulder. The hood of the jeep had been rolled back like the top of a sardine can by an outcropping of limestone.

It was so totally unexpected, so anachronistic in this primeval moonscape, that my mind went blank. The machinery in my head started up with a roar. I stared at the wrecked jeep openmouthed. My brain spun and the old machinery clanked. What with the unreality and eeriness of my flight through the silent stones, my mind struggled to account for this sudden presence.

All right. I began to slide, hunkering, into the gully. *All right.* Whoever had been driving had had to be driving in the dark or at twilight. How else to miss the outcropping of rock that had sheared back the hood? Whoever had been driving had followed the gully, probably the remnants of a timber road, up to the summit. Time had betrayed him, and he'd found himself in the growing dark. The blow on the hood had skewed the jeep over so that it had bounded up on this sliver of rock, impaled, helpless. Had the driver been killed? Badly hurt? I approached the jeep and peered into the open seats. There wasn't a trace of blood. *All right.* He'd gotten out with a rueful laugh and made the trip back down the gully on foot.

I stared at the jeep as I might have stared at a dinosaur peering up over the ledge. The noise in my head began to howl. Hadn't I seen it? Of course I'd seen it. You think I hadn't seen Spencer Tracy crawl under the jeep during *Bad Day at Black Rock,* pump some gasoline into a little jar, put his tie in the jar for a wick (it was his tie, wasn't it?), and toss the jar so it fried Robert Ryan like your morning bacon? You bet I'd seen it.

The possibility of having a weapon overwhelmed me. It made me shaky for an instant, and I leaned on the jeep to put my thoughts together. One thing at a time, I told myself. How do you know that the driver, dazed (still smiling ruefully?), didn't leave something behind in the glove compartment—like a gun, for instance? Through the machinery a patient, leaden voice said, "Open the glove compartment." I opened it. The ends of a greasy towel fell out. As I began to extract the towel, two mason jars came to light (two Molotov cocktails, by God!). They were providentially filled with water, and the towel had been wrapped around them so they wouldn't smash in the hurly-burly. Well and good. I placed them lovingly on the seat, promising myself a long, long drink of water. There was a road map in there, a tire gauge, and the cheapest of plastic cameras. End of inventory.

My first intimation of disappointment came when I looked at the engine. The glass fuel strainer was empty, which meant that I'd have to extract any gas I got from the tank itself. Then a very real and sudden fear seized me. I stripped a branch from one of the bushes and opened the gas cap. The branch came back out of the tank as dry as when it went in. Whatever gas there had been was long since gone.

To get things to work for you the way Spencer Tracy did, you have to be a star. (You see him toss those guys all over the luncheonette?) I was not a star. I was a bum stranded on a mountaintop with an utterly useless jeep. My opponent was having all the laughs. Hell, he probably knew about the jeep.

The camera was lying next to the mason jars. I threw it with all my might up against a rock, where it burst open, spewing its dead film on the ground. Did that relieve my feelings? No. I opened one of the mason jars for a much-needed drink of water. Something, a faint smell, not much of one, warned me off. I lowered the jar and sniffed it again. Sharp—penetrating to the back of my head. I put a finger in and tasted the finger.

Suddenly I began to laugh. I could feel the laughter shaking in my chest. It was moonshine—white lightning—mule—you name it. It was homemade whiskey. And it explained a lot. My unknown driver had been bombed out of his mind.

I took a swig that turned into an arrow of fire going down my gullet. The blaze enveloped my guts and filled my chest with smoke. I began to cough—but happily. I held my jar and rested on the jeep, somewhat reorganized. When my system had cleared, I took another, more cautious, milder swig.

Hell, Hosier probably knew about the jeep! The thought rang back through the factory noise and galvanized me. Standing over the jeep with the jar in my hand, half crazy, half crocked, smiling to myself, I was the fattest target in the world. I glanced up, half expecting to see him grinning over the ledge at me. I made preparations to leave.

And yet—and yet— It was hard for me to pull myself away without any semblance of a weapon at all. I stepped back a few paces from the jeep and stared at it. There was something—*something*—and my mind strained at it.

Break things down to elements. I looked at the smashed camera—a bit of glass in the lens, some shards of Bakelite, and the dead film—dead film? *Nitrocellulose!* The film was nitrocellulose. My mind nagged at the edges of it. What could I do with it? Glycerine. Glycerine. Where? In the antifreeze in the radiator, that's where. It would be the last component of the fluid to evaporate, so if anything was left in the radiator, it would be the residue of glycerol. And to make the mixture sweet? Sulfuric acid—in the battery—again, concentrated by evaporation.

I took one more belt from the jar, the contents of which

themselves might have blown up City Hall, and set rapidly to work. I emptied both jars, however regretfully, onto the thirsty stones. I began with the frustrating task of tearing the film into smaller pieces, rubbing and splitting it on the sharp edges of the jeep's hood. It was far from satisfactory, but I put the pieces in the bottom of one of the jars.

Opening the petcock of the radiator was an agony of frustration. My fingers had been torn and splayed by the falls I'd taken, and it was only by mentally detaching them from my body that I was finally able to get the small handle of the petcock turned.

A thick, greenish liquid began to dribble out. I put the jar with the film in it under the petcock and went to work on the battery. It was, luckily, held in its brackets by wingnuts, which I managed to force. I drained the cells one by one into the other mason jar. It amounted to half a jar of battery acid. I went back to the petcock. The antifreeze had run its course, and there was an odd-looking mixture of the film and the green sludge filling perhaps a quarter of the mason jar. I capped both jars and put one in either coat pocket.

It wasn't until I'd begun to lope northward again, the jugs banging against my side, that I began to sense the futility of what I'd done. Perhaps I'd armed myself psychologically—any chance being better than none—but I sensed with a small spiral of despair that my weaponry was more the product of white lightning than of science.

The only things I remembered from my demolition training were that the chemical formula for nitroglycerine was $C_3H_5N_3O_9$—I'd long since forgotten the structural formula, if I had really ever remembered the long series at all—that the mixture was supposed to contain a little over eighteen percent nitrogen, and that (I recalled despairingly) it was to be mixed at ten degrees centigrade, about fifty Fahrenheit, or below if it was to work at all.

I loped on, the sweat pouring down my face and ribs, dealing with the suspicion that more had been blown out of my

212

head than eardrums. There was the possibility that a mountain stream might cool my jars to that temperature, if there was a mountain stream in this rock-bestrewn nightmare, which did not appear to be the case. Even with the right temperature, my mixture would have to approximate the correct proportions. It was blind man's bluff, a naughty game to play with nitroglycerine.

I saw the first sign of civilization in high white letters, *George and Mona 1967*. Good luck George and Mona, wherever you are. Other names began to appear, other dates, one weathered date of 1944. Well, we were approaching a lovers' leap. The surface was less level here, and I was conscious of ascending and descending small hollows in the spine of the mountain. Some of the hollows had caves or cave openings in them. Homes for panthers or bears at one time, I suppose. At last I knew I would have to rest again. I picked a spot above one of the hollows. The opening of a cave, the largest I'd seen, yawned beneath it.

Why not a cave? Why not hide in a cave until nightfall and sneak away? My mouth was on fire, thanks to the liquor as well as the afternoon sun that glared on me. I doubted that I could keep up any kind of a pace for much longer. Did I want to be discovered exhausted, unable to run, to fight, to protect myself? I eased myself down to the mouth of the cave and looked into the cool, cool dimness.

The mouth of the cave was a grin in the side of the defile. The lower lip jutted out to reveal the drop below, and then the limestone rose perhaps twenty feet up to where I had been standing. I moved to the corner of the grin and scrambled down the slope into the mouth itself. It was much larger than I'd suspected, and the tunnel with its high vaulted roof beckoned into a welcome darkness. On the floor of the tunnel, where the darkness began, something gleamed—gray and remote. I froze.

Chapter XXVIII

It was a dull gleam, like old worn silver, and motionless. I was conscious of trying, for the first time in many years, to strain to hear. There was, of course, only the dim roaring in my head.

Suddenly, clasping the jars in my pockets, I dropped to the cold limestone floor of the tunnel. There was no reverberation I could sense. I reached back to right the jars in my pockets. Nothing happened. I raised my head very carefully. The gleam had not moved.

As I approached it, the gleam opened to a long thread of silver. A pool of water? It did not reflect like water. It was not until I had crept all the way down and actually laid my hand upon the gleam that I realized that it was ice.

Ice that had frozen eons past—cold water, touched only briefly by the summer sun, that had never had a chance to thaw. The thread grew into a broader pathway of ice that stretched downward into the throat of the cave. I grabbed a stone and tried to chip some loose from the glacial surface. It was like striking steel. Nothing came loose. I would get no water here.

But I could get coolness, even cold, even, it struck me happily, my ten degrees C for mixing my happenstance grenade. I set the two mason jars on the ice and sat still to absorb the coolness. Would unforeseen events change the course of this man's career? I thought so. I planned ahead. In ten or fifteen minutes, my jars should be cool enough to mix. I would make my bomb, joining the contents of the two jars carefully. Then I would retreat a little farther into the cave, into the comforting dark, where I could look into the opening. Anyone coming in would be silhouetted against the light, or against the stars. If he had a gun growing out of his hand, I could sling the old grenade.

Perfect, huh? I hugged myself with happiness as the nitro chilled. I noted with pleasure that my breath was easing, even though my head still throbbed with the malediction of an afternoon hangover. I checked my watch. Had I been here five minutes? I thought so. I would give it another ten minutes to chill, and then I would pour the soup.

But in that ten minutes I grew chill with something more than the cave's insulation. My mind kept going over the plan like an irascible teacher. *Examine. Examine!*

I kept seeing myself crouched in the darkness. The silhouette appears with its gun, stepping confidently into the cave. It comes closer, grinning with success. It sees the gleam of my eyewhites. The rifle is raised. I sling the nitro.

And blow up the both of us. The cave is a perfect compression chamber.

Or try it this way. The silhouette appears with its gun at the mouth of the cave. It comes closer, grinning with success. The rifle is raised. I throw my nitro. *Nitro?* Nothing happens. He blows my brains out.

Or even better. I keep retreating down the cave to the point where he corners me like a Goddamned rat and clubs me to death. Or even while I'm fleeing down the throat of the cave, he fires a wild shot, but since I'm running in a kind of funnel, the ricochet gets me and tears me in half.

It began to appear that perhaps the cave was not the best of all possible worlds for Joe Binney.

Time was up. More than up. I'd been sunk in my disastrous reverie for more than fifteen minutes. I opened the jars and poured what I considered to be a judicious amount of battery acid over the film and glycerine. I put the cap back on the jar without looking. Whatever was happening in there was something I didn't want to see.

But nonetheless I had, I hoped, a live bomb, although on the other hand, I hoped it wasn't all *that* live. I held it in front of me like a grail as I made my way up the steep slope, rising perhaps fifteen feet from the floor of the cave to the corner of the grin. Then I assumed the high ground again behind boulders twenty feet above the lip of the cave.

There I rested, setting down my mason jar very carefully on a nice flat rock. Now, I thought. Now we get the pretty pictures. I envisioned myself dodging from rock to rock, falling on my ass but holding on, with never flagging presence of mind, to a mason jar full of nitroglycerine. *Boom.*

How's this one? I step out from behind a rock. What do you know? There's the man with the rifle. He doesn't shoot *me*. He shoots the mason jar. *Boom.*

It occurred to me that when I'd made my doomsday machine, I'd also painted myself into a corner. There was no way I was going to run around the rocky summit of the mountain with a jar full of nitroglycerine. The whole point of the enterprise—my being in these straitened circumstances, if I may use the phrase—was to stay *alive*, to keep someone else from killing me, not, not, assuredly, to kill myself.

So it came to me that these few boulders comprised my Alamo, not because I chose to stand and fight, but because there was no way I could run, no way I could surrender, and no place to which I could safely retreat in daylight. My rocks gave me reasonable protection from the sides, if Hosier should come along the same path I had taken. They would give me protection—indeed, they might even give me the chance to surprise him *mano a mano,* which would be a blessing for us both.

If he came up from below, I had a reasonable line of view peeping out from the curved space between the boulders. It remained only for me to keep my head swiveling around three quarters of the compass. If he had lost my scent, I needed only to wait for nightfall, when I could pick my way down.

But as I sat there, watching the sun gentle itself down the long curve of the evening, the sense of eeriness and desolation came back over me. I looked at my stupid jar. I was afraid to touch it, and yet I doubted its potency. True nitro is clear, or at worst a mild yellow. The liquid inside my blue mason jar appeared as a bilious green.

I thought about Hosier, possibly not even hunting, but possibly, too, drifting like a ghost up the mountainside. I thought about the boy with his jaw smashed. At every inch the sun sank lower, I felt a bit better. My head continued to swivel.

He appeared like a ghost; I mean almost literally. He had even found himself the leisure to change his clothes, so that he appeared all in white. He wore a white shirt, open several buttons from the top, and a pair of thin white cotton slacks. It looked almost as if he were clad in the pajama-type clothes worn by Mexican peasants.

A hunter with time to dress for a long stroll in the hot September sun is a hunter considerably self-assured. He materialized at the ledge coming up from the timber and headed directly for the cave. I couldn't decide if he'd seen me from a distance and now was closing in, or if he'd calculated which way I'd go and had simply taken a short cut, angling along a trail in the side of the mountain to this spot. By the cool look of him, I guessed that he hadn't traveled nearly the distance I had, which meant that he'd predicted correctly the route I'd take. The gun dangled as lightly as a swagger stick from his hand.

He arrived at the lip of the cave almost directly below me and stared down into the tunnel. He strolled over to the corner of the opening and knelt to examine the tracks I'd made in the loose gravelly ground going down to the cave. It took him quite a while to decide whether or not I'd remained in the cave and was hiding there, waiting for him in the darkness. At last he saw the heel marks leading in the other

217

direction and realized that I'd returned to the surface. He stood up and stroked his chin.

Hosier walked back to the center of the cave's lip and looked around the entire hemisphere surrounding it. Then he looked up. He smiled. He seemed to be staring directly into the small aperture I was looking from. He was smiling very broadly now.

He raised the rifle and aimed for the aperture. A thought overtook him, however. He lowered the rifle and turned around for another sweep of the horizon to make sure he had no witnesses.

I stood up and launched my bomb. The bottle exploded directly between his feet.

The bottle exploded—not its contents. It would have shattered exactly the same way if it had been filled with water or with white lightning, except that they wouldn't have spread the heavy sickening green stain on the inside of his cotton pants. He spun around and snapped off a shot. I could see the rock fly from in front of my little crevice. It would not have been bad shooting if carefully aimed. For a snap shot, it was horrifyingly accurate.

My mind was absolutely paralyzed with fright and indecision. I knew that I should remove my face from the opening, but I was afraid to lose sight of him for fear he would run up the slope of the hollow and shoot me from behind. My eyes, after all, are all I have.

I didn't know whether he could actually see the reflection of my eyes at that distance, but it was certain that he had me located. He raised his rifle for a careful aim this time, and I moved my face away.

A deadly hail of splintered stone flew from the opening. If I had been hit, it would have been hard to identify me. The hole was somewhat larger and had a mephitic smell to it when I put my face back at the bull's-eye. His face had an interested, calm smile on it now. I'd seen expressions like that after a successful day at the firing range. The smile vanished, and with dead seriousness he took another bead on the opening.

I felt hypnotized. I wanted to jerk back just before he fired, and I knew that, as a marksman, he would squeeze the trigger slowly—slowly. I tried to see his knuckles, which was foolish of me. But I did see him take a deep breath and hold it, which meant he was prepared to fire. I moved my face away from the peephole.

Some silences are more silent than others. For me, movement makes the time run fast or slow. I don't have any sounds to indicate that life or activity is continuing. I waited with my attention fixed on the opening.

Nothing happened. Nothing happened again—and again. Something had occurred down there. Either the gun had misfired or the clip had jammed. But nothing had happened up here. Maybe he had seen my face move away from the bull's-eye and was merely waiting for me to put it back. Should I oblige him? I calculated the odds. Could I get a quick look and jump back before he fired? He couldn't have held his breath this long. I decided to risk it.

I almost fractured my skull dashing my face up against the peephole, and for an instant I couldn't recognize what I was seeing. Hosier was doing some kind of an insane war dance, with his rifle held out at arm's length to balance himself as he gyrated on one foot, tearing his shoe and sock from the other with his free hand.

It took me a second to realize that the battery acid had soaked through his thin cotton pants and into his shoes. I didn't waste any time from there on. I grabbed a boulder with both hands and raised it above my head. I don't have any idea of what it weighed.

He saw me standing above him with the boulder on high, and put his rifle up, not pointing at me, but simply as a futile shield to ward off the huge rock coming down on him. It struck just next to him, but bounced up, hitting him on the hip. It spun him around on the lip of the cave, and his pivoting

219

leg slipped over the rim so that he toppled off the edge and onto the floor of the tunnel below.

Even if it had not been dangerous, I would not have had the strength to go down and get him. I sat and shook. And when the shaking stopped, exhaustion hit me as if I had been eviscerated. I sat behind my rocks clutching my knees. Indeed, if Hosier had survived, he could have come up then and bludgeoned me like a rabbit. I sat there holding my knees and rocking back and forth until the darkness fell. Then I stumbled to my feet and made my way down the other side of the mountain in the woods lighted only by moon and stars.

Chapter XXIX

They told me later they had found him in the morning far back in the cave—an ice cave. Apparently there are a number of caves like that up on the mountain. They are tourist attractions. I was one of the rare tourists who had never heard of one.

"You never saw the billboards?" one trooper asked me skeptically.

"I never look at billboards," I answered wearily.

A passing motorist had picked me up—brave man: After all, I was on my hands and knees at a road that paralleled the mountain. He took me to the troopers, where I explained what had happened, along with the approximate location of Hosier's cabin and relative location of the cave. They took me to a useless little hospital emergency room, from which I departed in an hour.

They said that both his legs had been broken, that his legs

had been crossed when he'd fallen the fifteen feet into the cave. Then he'd slipped down the tunnel floor on the slick river of ice. It seems that he'd kept trying to drag himself back up into the light, but was caught in the downward path of the ice and kept sliding, sliding back into the darkness below.

He'd frozen to death on the subterranean stream of ice— still clutching his rifle that was pointing upward toward the light. Later on, I saw some of the big glossies they made of the scene. He was staring up with that same quiet smile of confidence.

But on this morning I was ignorant of the fate of Gil Hosier and, in fact, did not even much care. I was in bed in my bedroom in my apartment, and there I proposed to recline until the clock wore out its circle. Presently, the bedside lamp flashed out a long series of rings. I hobbled to the phone in the front room. The little red light stuttered out, "R—U—O—K," and I said into the mouthpiece, "Yes, I'm O.K., Edna, but for Christ's sake don't call me again. My bones are on fire. I'll see you tomorrow afternoon."

I had stipulated the afternoon with Edna because I had other plans for the morning. I was preparing for my triumphal return, and as I lay in bed easing my wracked skeleton, I played the scene over and over in my mind. In my mind's eye, I saw City rush into my arms ("Thank God you're safe," etc.). The reason I was lying in bed and, alternately, in a tub of near-to-boiling water, was that if anyone had rushed into my arms at this point of the game, I would have screamed in agony and collapsed in a faint. It was not the response to City that I envisioned for myself.

The next morning rose on a better Joe Binney. I don't mean that I was a veritable springbok for alacrity, but neither did I move like a candidate for the mortuary. I bathed, shaved, and dressed very, very carefully, taking out a suit I had preserved for Sunday best since its purchase three years earlier. There are very few Sundays in my life, and even fewer that deserve the best.

By ten o'clock I was a presentable, nay, handsome,

engaging specimen of masculinity. I felt that my splendor was too much for the New York subway system and managed to attract the attention of a cabdriver for the trip up to the Groupe studios.

The receptionist was at her desk, but she barely looked up at me as I entered from the elevator doors. There was a book open before her on the tiny desk, but she didn't seem to be reading it—just staring at it. "Is Miss Bowers in?" I asked her. She replied with nothing more than a sullen nod. There was a very distinct change in the studio—a lack of vibrations. People had always been popping in and out of the door that separated the reception room from the studio proper, but on this morning there seemed to be an almost palpable sense of stillness. A paralysis had dropped over the place.

I expected to find City in the office that Ed Parti had inherited from Iris. The door to the office was open, but no one was there. I went back into the zigzag corridor that connected the recording rooms and wandered in a series of angles like a pathway in a maze. The last time I had been through this maze, there had been musicians, technicians, agents, and others hurrying with preoccupied speed from one room to another. Now not a single individual broke the short sightlines from one corner to another. I explored deeper and deeper, turning off one short alley to the next to peer in through the thick plate-glass, soundproof window that revealed each recording room. Nothing was there but untenanted microphones and uninhabited control boards. Silence is my norm, but this was a silence I could feel, a stillness, a kind of death.

I saw her at last in the big room at the end of the maze. Her back was turned to me, but it was a back I had memorized, from the crown of her hair to her delicate heels. She was seated on a stool at the far end of the room with a music stand holding a score in front of her. A large professional set of earphones was clamped over her hair, and her body moved to a rhythm in those earphones that was inaudible not only to me but to the entire world—music as personal and inaccessible as the machinery noises in my head or the tunes I could summon up in my audile memory. Her hands played imaginary instruments, and she would hit a switch in front of her every now and again, then make a mark on the score. Then she would punch the switch, and the movement in her shoulders would begin again. Her head would bob, and her hips would move, almost imperceptibly, on the high seat of the stool. I had never seen anyone quite so isolated from the world. I had never felt so isolated myself.

I was willing to stand there forever. I certainly knew enough not to interrupt. There is an inviolability about those rooms, like the privacy of one's own brain.

City punched the switch again and paused for a longer interval. She raised her head from the score to think things out and must have caught the distorted ghost of my image in a reflecting piece of metal. At any rate, she became aware that someone behind the glass was watching her, and her back stiffened. She turned around slowly on the stool and shaded her eyes to peer through the plate glass at the other end of the room from her. When she made out, at last, who it was, she stared impassively at me. Then she reached into her huge purse and pulled out her shades. She put them on as she walked to the door.

She did not throw herself into my arms and cry, *"Thank God, you're safe!"* She simply opened the door and stood facing me, the upper half of her face obscured and impenetrable. When she spoke, it was a single word that escaped from rigidly controlled lips: "Yes."

Because her eyes, even much of her cheeks, were hidden, I could not tell what she meant. I said, "What do you mean, yes?"

"I mean yes what is it you want." The lips had become a small tight slash.

"What do I want?" I repeated stupidly. "I want you."

"You want me for what? To ask me some more trick questions?"

"What kind of crazy bullshit is this?" I protested. "I didn't ask you any trick questions."

She had brought a pack of cigarettes along with the sunglasses. A tiny flat gold lighter was held in the cellophane of the pack. She took out a cigarette and lighted it. She leaned against the steel doorjamb with her arms folded up against her bosom and regarded me. "That's a nice suit you've got on," she commented. "Somebody must pay you well for what you do."

"City," I pleaded. "For Christ's sake tell me what's eating you."

"What's eating me," said City, "is having been turned into a cheap asshole by a small-time snoop."

"You've got everything wrong," I said. "Everything."

"Tell me something very simple," said City, "and never mind the bullshit. Why didn't you tell me Ed was a suspect?"

"It never even crossed my mind," I exploded. "Jesus Christ, City, don't you have any idea of how you come on? The only thing that mattered to me then about Ed Parti was what he meant to you. Besides," I added, aggrieved, "why do you think I came up to Groupe in the first place? I told you I wanted to see Ed."

"But just to talk to him," said City. "Not to smash his face open and wreck his life."

"Oh, boy!" My jaw clenched and my eyes rolled nearly to the back of my head. "What about him slapping *you* around?"

Her teeth showed in a grimace. "I could bite my tongue off for telling you that," she said, her lips snarling around the words. "I could bite it off for telling you anything."

"City—City—" I put my hands up pleadingly. "Let me explain something. I didn't just walk in here and beat him up. I'm not that kind of man, really I'm not. Didn't he tell you? He threw down on me."

"Threw down?"

"He put a gun on me, a rifle. What was I supposed to do?"

"Oh, yes," said City. "The famous rifle. The rifle you brought in to set him up with."

"It's a common procedure," I said. The words were being jerked out of me in gasps. My heart was thudding like a loose cannon in my chest. "You give the guy a chance to make his play. If he doesn't make it, he's probably O.K."

"And if he does, it's a trap," said City.

I felt my face close up. "Trapping is my business," I said. "All he had to do was put the rifle down. He freaked out and got clobbered."

"He got clobbered," she agreed, "but why? Why did you have to hit him?"

"Goddamn it, he had a gun on me!"

She took off the glasses, then, and the huge, dark-blue, luminescent eyes looked into mine. "With no real bullets in it," said City. She waited to watch my face freeze. "What a big laugh that must have been for you."

I flinched. "You don't know about these things," I muttered. "Things get started—a string of firecrackers. I did it automatically. Doing it automatically is what saves your life sometimes. There isn't always time to think things through."

"There's time now, though."

"Yes, there's time now."

"There's time for Ed, too," said City. "He's thinking things over, but from the other end."

I threw my hands up impatiently. "I hit him in the mouth," I stated. "Did it kill him?"

"Certainly not," said City. "But the wonderful people on Rikers Island tried to make up for your oversight."

This has always been the part I care for least. When you're done, you're done. Nobody wants to follow the caught quarry through the shadows of the system, not the cop, not the prosecutor, not the judge, not the jury. That is all supposed to remain in the shadows. At the close we all want that beneficent sign that rolls up in the movies: THE END. Only it isn't the end, and we know it.

225

"What happened?" I asked her.

She drew deeply on the cigarette. "The watch went first. The watch I gave him," she amplified. "They got that off him before he even knew what was happening. They had to take him to the dentist, an oral surgeon, actually, before he could even really talk or answer questions. Teeth were knocked out; some were broken off. His mouth was all slashed up inside.

"They booked him in with his face all swollen up like that, and they left him with just enough money and the right clothes to get mugged while he was in there. He got beat up all over again. Somebody got his jacket. They hit him and opened up all the sutures in his mouth again, and he was almost strangling in his own blood when the guards wandered by. Those men he was thrown in with—they were animals."

"The same animals he sold his drugs to," I objected.

"Ed's not really a violent man."

"He looked pretty violent staring down that rifle at me while he was coked up to the ears," I told her. "I'll give you that he's never been violent, but on the other hand, it's people like him who give violence a bad name. Everything is cool with them while they drift above the scene. Everything is supposed to happen in nice hotels, fancy apartments, discos, and chic restaurants. It's all a hoot until it gets down to the bedrock, and Rikers Island is the bedrock."

She stared at me without a glimmer of expression on what I could see of her face. "What I liked about you at first," said City, "was that there was absolutely no self-pity in you. You sort of shrugged off the whole thing about being deaf. I admired that. But now I see something else. You don't pity anybody else, either. There's no pity in you at all. Only rage."

"And Ed Parti," I countered, "I'm sure he's full of self-pity sitting around nursing his jaw, but did he have pity for anybody else? For the kid he turned on, Iris's boy? For all the kids he intended to turn on? For that silly band he had running around the country peddling drugs? For you? For me? For Iris?"

226

Her face drained of color. She began to say something, but clenched her jaw tight. "That's what I mean about giving violence a bad name," I went on. "The people who jumped him are at the bottom of the heap. They're violent because now its the only thing they've got left. When he found himself on the bottom of the heap, in the crunch, he grabbed up a rifle. He was going to kill me. That's as violent as you can get. He's no different from anybody else, either above him or below him."

Her shoulders sagged. She slumped against the doorframe and stared at her shoes. "City," I commanded, "look at me, please, please look at me."

She looked up, but not with an expression I wanted to see—anguish, despair, hopelessness. "I came here because I love you," I told her. Her face softened almost imperceptibly and without erasing the tragic imprint. "And I'll admit to you, for your own sake, that maybe I did hit him because he was the only thing I could see standing between you and me. Maybe, in a flash, I simply wanted to wipe him out of the picture. But I didn't just walk in here and kick him around. I'm not like that."

"It destroyed him," City told me sadly. "The whole thing has just destroyed him."

"Then he destroys pretty Goddamned easy."

Her face was much softer now, but still terribly sad. "Joe," she began, then reached up and touched my face. "Try to understand what I'm going to say. Ed will never put himself back together. Even now, out on bail, back at the apartment, where he knows that we're being watched for contacts, for everything, he wants me to go out and get him something— *anything,* he says—but *something* to help him stand it. And I won't do it. He was sleeping when I left, but I've got friends over there to see that he doesn't go out and try to make a buy or something just as stupid. You see how crazy and helpless he is?"

"And you still want him?" I asked her. "The Kleenex that

walks like a man? He's not your respons—"

She never let me finish the word. "He is my responsibility," she said. "I took him to bed because I wanted him. Before that he was simply a fine man with a fine job and a fine wife and kids. But I pulled him out to the drowning end of the pool."

"He's going to steal your life," I said bitterly. I felt like weeping.

"He even got beat up because of me," City said as if I hadn't spoken. "Only whores have men beat up over them."

"City," I said, "move out of there. Come on over to my apartment. I'll marry you in the morning. I'll fix the joint up. You can put in a stereo the size of a Mack truck. It makes no difference to me. You can turn the whole joint into a studio if you want to. I'll take care of you always. Come with me and be my wife."

It was a very sad smile, but it *was* a smile. Then she began to cry. "Do you know," she said, "that in all my life you're the first man who asked me to marry him and meant it? Oh—I've had offers. But somehow there was always a manager's contract on the other end of it. You're the first that meant it. I'll always love you for it."

"That sounds like a good-bye," I said.

She put her hands on my lips. "Not really," said City. "I have to stay with Ed now until he gets put back together, until he gets straight, exactly because I'm not a whore."

I tried to utter a protest, but she kept my lips sealed with her fingers. "I'll stay with Ed until he's straight," she said. "And then maybe I'll let you know."

She turned and went back into the recording room. The big door closed and sealed her off. She mounted the stool again, with her back turned to me, and clamped the earphones over her hair. She punched the switch, and in a few seconds she had begun to sway again to the silent music, infinitely remote, as distant as one of the galaxies so many light years away that we will never know if anyone existed there or not.

I stood and watched her for—how long? I don't remember. But until I couldn't bear it anymore.

I couldn't face going to the office. I went back to my apartment and dialed Edna. The little red light indicated how quickly she'd snatched up the phone. "I feel too bad to make it this afternoon," I told her. God knows it was the truth. "I'll see you in the morning."

There was a complimentary bottle of Old Granddad next to the empty cognac bottle. I opened that.

Chapter XXX

"Bring me the pledge. I'll sign it here and now."

I did not actually speak these words because, raising myself with a groan in bed, I was incapable of speech. But I knew, with every horrible dull throb in my forehead, that I had finished with liquor forever. At least for the foreseeable future—not that *that,* by any means, seemed to stretch far before me in terms of longevity.

I don't think I had ever drunk so much as I had in the last few days. I'd never had the occasion. I promised myself a monk's life of rigorous abstinence, diet, and strenuous exercise. If nothing else, it would keep my mind off City.

I took a long shower, washed my eyes with something that was supposed to get the red out, brushed my teeth, and gargled with an old-fashioned, ugly-tasting mouthwash that counteracted the stale coat of liquor inside my chops. My efforts at shaving were an exercise in the death of a thousand cuts. They left me a hideous patchwork of toilet paper that festooned my cheeks and chin.

I could not face the prospect of cooking breakfast for myself, so I went down to the local lunch counter. I spread the *New York Times* in front of me so I wouldn't have to look at the food. I read every word in the *New York Times*—over and over. The red got back in.

It was one o'clock in the afternoon before I got to the office. I held my hand up at Edna. "Don't ask me anything just yet," I begged her. "Just get me some coffee."

She watched me primly, dissatisfaction dripping from every pore, as I sifted through the piled-up mail, dropping coffee liberally on much of the correspondence. Finally I leaned back in the chair, as ready as I would ever be that day to embrace current events.

By the time I'd finished dictating, it was two-thirty.

"All right, now," I said, "let's take it to the end. Have you heard anything about the kid?"

"The troopers found him and brought him to the hospital," she said. "His jaw was broke. He couldn't tell them anything."

I wondered what the hell the kid had to say, anyway.

"You sure it wasn't him that shot Mr. Penton?" she asked me.

"Yeah, I'm sure," I answered. "He wasn't really familiar with the gun, either. He had the safety on, just like Ed Parti. He knew where it was, but if he'd been that familiar he'd have taken the safety off before he pointed it at me."

"He gets it all, now, huh?" Edna asked me.

"Yeah," I said. "Don't you think he deserves it?"

"I dunno." She scratched her head. "He's a drug addict and all. He'll probably just waste everything."

"Probably." I considered it. "On the other hand, he might get himself straightened out and fly right. It's hard to tell. What would you do if your father killed your mother and then tried to beat your brains out?"

She thought it over. "They should of let that woman alone," she said violently.

230

"Yes, they should have," I agreed.

She put her notepad on the desk. "When are you going to get that copy back so we can put it in the files?" she demanded.

"What copy?"

"The copy of the confession you showed them."

"That was no confession," I told her. "Are you nuts? That was the lease to the office." She examined this information while I looked at her. "Did you actually think that Probcziewski would give me a legal confession to fly around like a kite?"

"Don't mention that son of a bitch to me," said Edna.

"Oh," I said.

Her mouth straightened out until the lips disappeared. "Tell me the truth," she said.

"About what?"

"Did you know he was married and had three kids and a very nice house on Long Island?"

"No, I didn't," I told her honestly. "When did you find this out?"

"Afterward," said Edna.

Her notepad, with its curlicued history of the case, lay open on the desk. I stared at the page full of symbols I had seen for years but never bothered to understand. Had her passion for the big detective been jotted down somewhere in that thicket? Had the little pothooks marked my attention to her kneecaps?

My glance bounced off her kneecaps, traveled up to her eyes, and slid off into an embarrassed middle distance. "There's a difference between people like Probcziewski and me . . ." I began.

"I know," said Edna.

·I should have warned you."

She put her hand up. "You did warn me," she answered. "Who listens?"

"I didn't warn you enough," I added. "That lieutenant is

231

the kind of guy who accomplishes things. He'll be head of the department someday. If he gets enough night school under his belt, he might be the district attorney."

"You mean he's a winner," said Edna.

"That's right."

"What about you?" she asked. "Aren't you a winner?"

I looked at her and grimaced. "What do you think?"

"No," she said. "You're not a winner."

I fished through my messy pile of mail and pulled out a suspicious-looking envelope I had set aside. I opened it and found a check for three hundred and seventy-five dollars.

"Have you ever had lobster thermidor?" I asked Edna. She shook her head. "Will you give it a try if I take you to dinner?" She nodded her head. "If I smile, will you smile?" I asked her.

"You first," said Edna.